SEE NO EVIL

DAVID J. GATWARD

WEIRDSTONE PUBLISHING

See No Evil
by
David J. Gatward

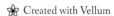 Created with Vellum

To LRB

Grimm: nickname for a dour and forbidding individual, from Old High German grim [meaning] 'stern', 'severe'. From a Germanic personal name, Grima, [meaning] 'mask'. (*www.ancestory.co.uk*)

PROLOGUE

When Brian Haygarth came to, he knew immediately that something was very, very wrong. The fact that he was 'coming to' in the first place should have been more than enough to have him worried, though. Whatever this was, how he was feeling right then, it was nothing like waking up after a good night's sleep or doing so with a bit of a hangover after a few too many beers the night before.

There had been no night before. Brian couldn't even remember the last time he'd had a drink, never mind a hangover; was it twenty years? It was at least that, probably longer. He'd been off the booze for so long now that drinking was little more than a distant memory.

Unlike the day he'd decided that enough was enough, because being drunk and in charge of a knackered, old chainsaw had nearly got him killed. He still woke up some nights to the god-awful sound of that blade snapping back at him to take off his head, and only good luck and maybe even the hand of God had kept him alive.

He could still recall enough of what a hangover was like, though, to know that this, whatever it was, certainly wasn't one. That thought should've been a comfort. It very much wasn't. Not least because he was tied to a tree.

At first, Brian hadn't realised he was tied to anything at all.

He'd come to—again, that was odd, he thought—and felt achy all over. Then, as he'd squeezed his eyes tight shut and tried to shake himself awake, the aches had turned into an orchestra of deep, throbbing agony and deadly stabs of pain.

Instinct had kicked in, called on him to check himself all over, to reach to where the pain was worst, which was everywhere, because a quick rub would help, he was sure. Except that reaching for anything right then was impossible, and as he made to move his hands, all he felt was panic.

Brian struggled against the ropes holding him fast, which were tied painfully tight around his ankles, waist, and neck. His arms were pulled behind him on the other side of the tree at his back and tied at the wrists. He couldn't even move his head: his mouth was free, but a thick, sticky tape wrapped around his forehead kept it firmly in place.

The only thing Brian could move were his eyes, and he was using those to full effect, darting them all over the place, trying to work out where he was, what was going on, his vision blurred because he wasn't wearing his glasses. The why of where he was would have to wait for a moment or two. *Best to panic about one thing at a time*, he thought. And he certainly had enough to be going on with there, that was for sure.

As far as Brian could tell, it was either early morning or early evening. He had no way to make sure, no watch to check even if his hands had been free, no way to see where the sun rested in the sky.

The tree he was tied to was one of many, and he could see no boundary to the woods around him, no field and fell beyond, just more trees blending into a smudged, blurry darkness thick as treacle. Faint light was coming to him from above, the grey sky visible through leafless branches, reaching up to touch it.

So, he was in a woodland, but where that woodland was, Brian hadn't the faintest idea. The trees were deciduous, a handsome mix of oak and ash, beech and chestnut, the air rich with the smell of earth, much like the ones on his own land. But trees were trees, and what they were was no clue at all as to *where* they were.

Under normal circumstances, he would've appreciated the trees a little more, breathed the air in deep, relished it. Now, though, the woodland around him served only to make him feel more alone.

Walking through the woods on his own land was one of the few things he really enjoyed, just so long as he didn't bump into any of those annoying hikers and ramblers, out trampling across his land like they bloody well owned it. Which they didn't, and which he took great joy in telling them whenever he could. Public footpaths were the bane of his life. He'd lost count of how many he'd managed to block off. It wasn't his fault; they shouldn't even be allowed there in the first place.

And so, to the why of it all, Brian thought. He needed to try and work out a reason for his current predicament and decide how to extricate himself from it, then find who was responsible and beat the living shit out of them.

Before he had a chance to do anything at all, to prepare himself in some way, the panic, which had already sent him cold, reached its cold fingers even deeper inside him, wrapped around his heart, and squeezed.

Brian did the only thing he could; he screamed.

The sound catapulted from him like it was an entity all on its own, a thing that had become conscious of its prison and needed to escape and was now free to scatter itself amongst the trees. On its way, it tore his throat to shreds, threatened to pull his stomach up and out of his mouth, and Brian tasted blood and bile.

Eventually, Brian's scream died, turning in a moment from the cry of a trapped animal to the rattling croak of something caught in barbed wire and unable to break free. He would've let his head flop forward had he been able to, but it was held fast, and any movement just tore at his hair. Then tears came, and there was nothing he could do to stop them as they raced down his face to fall to the leaf-bedecked ground at his feet.

The last thing Brian could remember was walking home from the pub. Just because he didn't drink didn't mean that he couldn't go to places where others did. And the food was good. He'd always been more of a fan of the atmosphere anyway, rather than the drinking, because drinking had been a solo occupation rather than a social event, and he'd never touched another drop since that terrifying day.

He'd taken a notebook with him to list all the jobs he had to do over the next few days, from sorting out a few fences and giving one of the tractors a service, to blocking up those sodding stiles that hikers kept using. He didn't give a stuff about their legal right to roam across his land; they needed to know that they weren't welcome and to bugger off. His sheep were his priority, and he'd dealt with enough dog shit, litter, and left-open gates to write a book about it all.

List done, Brian had eaten a tremendous meal of steak and kidney pie and chips, washed it all down with soda water, then headed home. Beyond that, he had nothing; his memory was a blank, which made no sense at all. How could his last memory not even be of arriving home, or heading to bed? What the hell had happened to him?

No, that wasn't the question, was it? *Who* had happened to him? That was it. He didn't care that the question didn't really make sense, because none of this made any sense; where he was, how he'd got here in the first place, why he was tied up, someone was responsible. But who? And more importantly, bloody well why? If it was a prank, he wasn't laughing, not least because he didn't know anyone who would think this was funny. But then again, why would anyone think this was amusing? And if it wasn't amusing, then—

Movement.

Brian's eyes caught it, followed it, saw a shadow drift between the trees in front of him. Or was he seeing things, his mind playing tricks on him, confused as it was, unable to grasp just what the hell was going on?

He narrowed his eyes, focused on the thing that had caught his attention, couldn't quite make it out, not just because his glasses were missing, but because of the tears and the sweat blurring his vision. There was something off about it though, he just wasn't sure what.

'Help!' Brian said, calling out to the shape.

The shape paused, stepped forward, and for a moment Brian felt as though a piece of the woodland had broken away from the rest of it to come in for a closer look.

'I don't know who's done this to me, or why,' Brian continued, 'but please, could you cut me down? I'm in agony, I can't move, and I need the loo.'

The shape took another step, said not a word, and Brian caught a flash of something in the faint blades of light cutting through the branches.

The silent response told Brian more than he wanted to know: whoever this was, they were responsible.

'Whatever this is, it isn't funny,' Brian said, impressing himself with his mastery of understatement. 'I'm not laughing, am I? Now, untie me!'

The shape, its edges blurry in the breeze, took another step.

'Look, please, just let me go, okay? Whoever you are, if I've done something to you, I can only apologise, though God knows what it is to result in this.'

No response.

'You can't do this,' Brian said, his voice rising, scraping the back of his throat. 'You can't!'

The quiet of the woodland was broken then by a bird call, then another, and another, only it didn't sound quite right to Brian. Such a call he would have expected to have come from above, from where the owners of the call, buzzards by the sound of it, would've been roosting. They buggers, too, he thought, taking his lambs, and he'd put a stop to that, too, hadn't he? Not his fault that he had to take drastic action. He had to make a living, so who was to blame, really? This call, though, had come from somewhere considerably closer.

The shadow darted forward and the bird call Brian had just heard burst into his left ear.

'What the hell?'

The call continued, drilling into Brian's head, then switched to his right ear, and this time something hard slapped into the side of his head, distorting the sound.

Brian's vision cleared just enough to see ... No, but that wasn't right, surely! He was seeing things, hallucinating because of the pain, the dehydration ... Then he remembered.

'You,' he said, realisation and horror fighting for attention inside his head. 'I've ... I've seen you before! I knew it! I bloody well knew it! No one believed me when I told them, not even the police! Walking around like ... like a ...' Then horror won. 'But you can't be real! You can't, it's not possible, *you're* not possible ...'

The volume of the bird calls increased. Brian pinched his eyes shut against the pain, sure at any moment his eardrum would burst. When he opened them again, the thing was still standing in front of him, and the sheer impossibility of it caused his mind to short-circuit.

At last, this shape, this thing standing in front of him, spoke.

'People have to understand, to know that it can't go on.'

'What?'

'I've tried. I've warned. But no one listens, no one cares.'

Brian went to reply, but the sound of the buzzards came again, then pain, as something sawed into the side of Brian's skull. The sound of it ratcheted through his head, reminding him of when he'd cooked himself a nice trout a few days ago, how his knife, though sharp, had still struggled to slice through the flesh, the bone.

Brian tried to scream, but it came out like a strangled miaow as the pain burned through him and he felt something wet and hot flow down the side of his face, his neck.

The figure in front of him was holding something up in front of his face.

'That's ... that's my ear! My bloody ear! You've cut off my ear! You bastard! My ear!'

Brian couldn't take in what was happening, what was now dangling in front of him, almost as though his mind refused to accept it as real.

'My ear! You cut it off! Put it back! I need it! Put it back!'

Brian went to say more, but then the sawing came again, switching to the right side of his head.

This time, Brian's yell was so primal, his whole body shook with it as he fought to pull free of his bonds, to yank himself away from what was happening to him, to run.

The sawing stopped. Brian stared at his ears as they were held up in front of him.

'You ... you bastard ...' Brian said, unable to hear his own words, the shredded remains of his ears filled with blood, making him deaf.

Through Brian's tears, the figure was a blurred mess, his own ears dangling in front of his eyes, blood dripping.

'Please,' said Brain. 'I don't know what you're talking about, who you are ... please ...'

The thing leaned in close, its voice a whisper.

'I'm vengeance,' it said.

Then Brian's voice was cut in two as, with no warning given, the figure stuffed something into his mouth, something bitter and foul, forced it in hard, giving him no choice but to swallow, because it was either that or choke. Then, as he tried to spit it out, the thing came at him in a frenzy, tearing into his flesh, shredding it. And the last thing Brian knew of life was pain.

ONE

Harry sat up in bed, realised immediately that doing so was a very bad idea, so lay back down again with a groan.

At the bottom of the bed, something warm and heavy stirred.

'Morning, Smudge,' Harry muttered, and the sound of his own voice was thick and distant, as though someone had snuck in overnight and stuffed cotton wool in his ears.

Smudge let out a long, slow huff of a breath, stood up to turn in a circle, before slumping down again onto the bed at Harry's feet.

Harry went to open his eyes, only to find that whoever it was who had been busy with the cotton wool had also glued his eyes shut.

Something was wrong, because in addition to his ears and eyes being out of action, he ached all over. With a heavy sigh, he reached up to rub his eyes, clearing away the sticky goo gluing them closed.

Laying there, in a cocoon of deep warmth, a thought Harry had little time for dared to rear its head. *Maybe I should take the day off?*

Harry couldn't recall the last time he'd been off work because of illness. Certainly not since arriving in the Dales. And before that? Nope, nothing. He'd missed work for other reasons, all of which had something to do with an injury of some kind collected in the line of duty like Scouting badges, but never illness.

With his eyes unstuck, Harry stared up into the darkness of the morning. He'd woken early thanks to a cough, and a moment of panic from not being able to breathe properly through his nose. His watch told him that six AM was still a snooze away, but even as he gave into it and closed his eyes, something at the back of his mind had him too awake to drift off. But what the hell was it?

Today was Wednesday, that much he knew, and he was fairly sure there was nothing special or important planned at work. Gordy was still around, thanks to Anna's move to her new parish in Somerset having been delayed a little. Matt was heading out with their new PCSO, Dave Calvert, to do some kind of community outreach thing, the details of which Harry had been told, but had immediately forgotten. Liz was running the office, Jadyn was over in Leyburn, and Jim was busy with something Harry just couldn't remember. There was rumour of a weather warning for later in the week, but there was also every chance that would turn out to be nothing more than a dusting of snow on the fell tops; no point worrying about that until something actually happened. So, what was it, then?

Harry yawned, rolled over onto his side, knocked an arm into the bedside table, and sent something fluttering to the floor.

Swearing under his breath, Harry reached out in the dark. He crawled his hand across the floor until he found whatever it was that he had just unseated, surprised to find his fingers close around a thin pile of papers.

Rolling onto his back, Harry reached up behind him and flicked on a small light clamped to the headboard just above his head. Bright light burned away the darkness, forcing Harry's eyes closed again, and sending a sharp pain to stab at the back of the inside of his skull. Smudge lifted her head, stared at Harry as though to express mild annoyance at the light, then rested it again on her front paws.

Opening his eyes, Harry found himself staring at a small collection of papers containing details of various houses for sale. He shuffled through them, momentarily baffled, his sleepy brain still sluggish.

Then he remembered.

'Bollocks ...'

Harry pushed himself up on his elbows and shuffled through the houses. There were five, each one booked in for a viewing at some point during the day. Everything had been arranged, and he would meet Grace at ten AM in Leyburn to have a coffee before heading off to the first one. So, even if he had wanted to take a day off sick, there would've been no point, because he already had the day off.

The houses were dotted up and down the Dale and he had no real preference for any of them. His own house had sold quickly, as had Grace's, so now all they had to do was find somewhere they were both happy with and keep their fingers crossed that everything would go smoothly. Harry had no doubt that it wouldn't because that was just the way of things, but at least they were moving ahead with their plan to get a place together.

When they'd told Arthur, Grace's dad, what they were doing, he had responded to the news by folding his arms, staring at Harry, and saying, 'And about bloody time, too, if you ask me.'

Harry had refrained from pointing out that they hadn't asked him at all, but it was good to know what they were doing had Arthur's support. Grace worried about her father, and Harry was very aware that whatever they decided, Arthur's needs would have to be considered, too. He had his own house and lived with an independence that bordered on the ferocious, but moving miles away from him was not an option. And that had meant a couple of lovely houses in Reeth, over in Swaledale, had been struck off the list straight away.

No bad thing, though, Harry thought, having no real desire to live in the same place where Police Constable Jadyn Okri had decided to park himself for a while. Though Harry wondered how long that would last, what with him and Jen getting more serious.

Steve, Jen's monitor lizard, still wasn't entirely sure about Jadyn being around so much, but Jadyn was trying his best to impress the creature. He'd even bought him a Christmas present, and Steve had been about as impressed with it as anyone could ever expect a monitor lizard to be when given a smaller, bright green, plushy version of himself.

An hour or so later, and after managing to struggle out of bed and stumble into the shower, Harry was down in the kitchen at the small table, Smudge in her bed by the radiator. He'd managed to find a collection of various medicines and throat tablets and painkillers in a drawer but had shied away from all but the paracetamol thanks to the best-before dates bordering on life-threatening. He'd managed some porridge, had another scan through the particulars of the houses, then checked the messages on his phone. There was only one.

See you later. Exciting! Grace x

Harry wanted to feel excited about the day ahead, but right then, all he felt was the call of his bed upstairs.

Maybe another coffee will help, he thought, so he reached across the table and poured himself another from the pot. Then, with plenty of time before he had to get into his vehicle and drive down the dale to meet up with Grace, Harry stood up, grabbed the coffee, and shuffled through his house to the lounge to slump down on his sofa.

Sensibly, he set an alarm on his phone, took a sip of the coffee, then a glug, before leaning back and closing his eyes. God, he felt rough, and as he drifted back off to sleep, he hoped that when he woke up again, he'd feel a whole lot better.

He didn't.

In fact, when he woke up, Harry was sure he felt worse, if that was at all possible.

'It's just a cold,' he said, leaning forward to push himself up onto his feet.

A few minutes later and wrapped up in enough layers to keep out an arctic frost, a purple and yellow bobble hat pulled down onto his head, Harry walked down the path in front of his house, ice crunching underfoot, then over the bridge that spanned Gayle Beck, Smudge at his side. The morning was bright, the sunlight harsh against the frost, which had spent the night coating the world in a crackled coating of ice. Following the beck to the small parking area by the ford, Harry tried to force himself to ignore how he was feeling, working to put an extra spring in his step, to breathe in the crisp air, but all that did was cause him to cough, which in turn made him trip up and nearly fall over a bewildered Smudge.

'Now then, Harry!'

Harry looked up, lifted a hand in greeting, but had no idea who it was that had just called his name, as he paused to watch them head off the way he had just come. Still, that was the Dales for you, he thought; everyone knew everyone else, and his face was certainly better known than others, not least because it was a difficult one to forget.

Once in his RAV, Harry drove into Hawes, stopping off to pop into the chemists and purchase an armful of cold remedies.

'You don't really look like you should be going anywhere other than back home to bed,' the woman at the checkout said.

'Not an option,' Harry replied, opening one of the bottles he'd purchased.

He read the instructions, shrugged, and took a hefty swig.

'On your head be it, then,' the woman said.

'On it?' said Harry. 'It's in it, and in just about everywhere else, too, I reckon. It's in my head, behind my eyes, and it's bunged my nose up something terrible.'

'Oh, you poor dear.'

Harry heard the faintest tone of sarcasm in the woman's voice, softened as it was by the genuine look of concern on her face. He then popped a throat sweet from a blister pack, nodded a farewell, and headed back outside.

The drive to Leyburn was slow, Harry leaning forward, hunched up over the steering wheel as he wiped away the fog on the windscreen. Outside, Wensleydale slipped by like a scene from the lid of a biscuit tin, the fells and fields a great, glittering swathe of frost, puddles like mirrors, rivers and streams bubbling beneath icy sheets and over waterfalls frozen into thin, white teeth. Harry's focus, though, was on the road ahead, and the scenery drifted past unobserved.

Arriving in Leyburn, Harry parked up in the marketplace, unable to recall much of the journey. He had arrived, though, which was a win, and whatever it was he had taken a slug of back at the chemists in Hawes had somehow managed to take the edge off how he was feeling.

Letting Smudge out of the rear of the vehicle, Harry noticed a shadow fall on them both.

'Nice hat.'

Harry turned to see Grace standing next to him. She was barely visible behind a thick scarf and bobble hat. He went to say something about what Grace was wearing herself, only to see her eyes widen as she stared at him.

'Bloody hell, Harry, you look like death!'

'Do I?' Harry said. 'That's an improvement on earlier, then.'

'Why didn't you call? We could've cancelled, or I could've viewed the houses on my own.'

Harry shook his head.

'I'll be fine,' he said. 'It's just a cold. Always worse in the morning, aren't they? And I've been to the chemist and bought a few things. I'm sure I'll be okay.'

'You don't look okay.'

'Nice scarf,' Harry said, keen to change the subject.

'It, like the hat, is a Dad special,' smiled Grace. 'He took up knitting a few years ago, does it sporadically. Can't knit anything other than scarves and hats, though.'

'What's he up to today if you're here with me?'

'He's already out with Tommy,' Grace said. 'Has been since the early hours, dealing with some rabbits. That lad's really taken to the work. He's a bloody good shot, too.'

Harry coughed, and the cough turned into a sneeze.

'And that's you being fine, is it?' Grace asked, then she nodded down at Smudge. 'And what do you think?' she asked.

Smudge wagged her tail.

'Coffee will do me good,' Harry said. 'And maybe some cake; give me a bit of energy.'

'And you're sure you're going to be okay?' Grace asked, checking once again.

'We're buying a house together, so we're going to view them together,' Harry said, finishing his sentence with a sneeze.

'It's almost as though your natural disposition is one that leans towards bull-headed stubbornness,' Grace said. 'But if you insist …' She pointed across from where Harry was parked to a small café. 'Coffee and cake, then?'

'Yes,' Harry said, and with another sneeze, followed Grace, Smudge trotting along beside him.

TWO

When Sam Dent first caught sight of the scarecrow as he entered the field, its arms stretched out as though to greet the chilly February morning with a cheery hello, he immediately wondered just how forgetful he was getting. Not only was he unable to recall erecting the thing, but also to think of even a single reason as to why he would have done so in the first place. This was a sheep farm. He didn't need a scarecrow. So why the hell was it there?

Parking up at the gate wasn't easy, thanks to the massive pile of rubbish that had been dumped there by some absolute arsehole over a week ago now. He had no idea who had done it, which was probably a good job, really, because he would be very happy to introduce their face to his fists. Diplomacy had never been a strong point.

Walking towards the dark silhouette, thumbstick in hand, Sam pulled out his phone to call his wife. By his side, Gyp was trotting along and sniffing the air. The dog was getting on now, his twelfth year nearly up, his age showing in the way his once pure black and white colouring was now peppered with flecks of snow, his face having grown grey. Yet he still wanted to be out as much as possible and had leapt into the passenger seat of Sam's vehicle with the ease of an animal ten years his junior.

'Where are you?' Debs asked, her voice sharp. 'I told you I needed to head into town myself. And what do you mean you've found a scarecrow?'

Sam could tell Debs was annoyed. But he wasn't about to tell her the real reason for his early morning trip out, that he'd forgotten it was Valentine's Day.

'I mean, that there's a scarecrow in the field,' Sam said, shaking his head at Debs referring to the small, picturesque village of Kettlewell as a town. His breath clouded in front of him, and each breath sucked in cold air. 'I just had to pop into Kettlewell for a few things, that's all.'

And those few things were a bunch of flowers and something fancy for breakfast. He'd managed to grab some fresh croissants and fruit juice, just enough to hopefully say *I love you*. The card, on the other hand, he wasn't so sure about, seeing as it wasn't a Valentine's card at all, but a cartoon picture of a Swaledale ewe standing in a field. He'd written, 'I love ...' just above it, with a big arrow pointing at the sheep. He hoped she'd understand what he was trying to say. Feelings weren't his strong point, especially expressing them.

'What? You're not making any sense,' Debs said. 'Why would being in town have you ending up at the field?'

Sam really couldn't be bothered to explain everything, because he knew that as soon as he was home, he would have to explain it all again. So, he did his best to keep the details brief.

'I went to town, I got what I needed, and I saw Aiden as I was on my way back.'

'Aiden? What's he got to do with it?'

'He told me about the scarecrow.'

'Why did he tell you about the scarecrow?'

'Because that lad who works for him had seen it, that's why,' said Sam, trying to stay calm in a veritable storm of questions. 'And I remembered then that you'd told me yesterday evening that you'd seen someone messing around in the field, so I went to have a look.'

Sam had meant to go have a look as soon as Debs had told him, but he'd had one of his funny turns and forgotten. Aiden had reminded him.

'Is it his?'

'What?'

'Is it Aiden's scarecrow?'

'Why would it be Aiden's scarecrow?' Sam asked, now regretting having called Debs in the first place.

'You never know with people,' Debs said, as though that was explanation enough. 'So, is that what I saw yesterday, then? Not someone messing around in the field, but a scarecrow?'

Sam decided to try and move the conversation along as quickly as he could.

'I'm walking towards it right now.'

'Which field?'

'The one with the rubbish in front of the gate.'

Sam heard the faint hiss of whispered swearing through clenched teeth.

'You're going to have to clean that lot up yourself,' Debs said. 'It'll start to stink if you don't.'

'Not my job, is it?' Sam said. 'I didn't put it there. Anyway, I'm not calling you about that, am I? I'm calling you about this scarecrow.'

'But we don't need a scarecrow,' said Debs. 'And yes, I'm afraid it is your job, because no bugger else is going to do it, are they? Haven't you learned that by now? No amount of campaigning and leafleting, and whatever else it is you and that little environmental group of yours get up to, is ever going to make a difference.'

The conversation was taking a turn Sam really didn't want to go down, not today.

'At least they're trying to do something,' he said. 'And it's not my group, I just follow them on Facebook! Anyway, you're not listening. I didn't call to talk about any of that. I called about this scarecrow ...'

'You're sure that's what it is?' Debs asked. 'A scarecrow in the field? And I am listening!'

'I'd hardly phone you about a scarecrow if there wasn't one, would I? Why would I make that up?'

'You called me about aliens once,' said Debs.

Sam pursed his lips and breathed through his nose for a couple of steps, the field beneath his feet crisp with a pale white frost, like icing sugar on a cake.

'It wasn't aliens,' he said, trying to remain calm. 'It was a UFO.'

'A UFO shaped like a—'

'I know what I saw,' said Sam, interrupting, remembering that eerie evening a year ago when, late one night while out in the fields, he'd seen something in the sky that to this day he just couldn't explain.

'Yes, but do you, though?' Debs asked.

'Yes.'

'Yes, but do you really?'

'Yes, I do, really!' Sam replied, growing increasingly exasperated. 'And it was this field, too, now that I think of it. Bit of a weird coincidence, isn't it?'

The silence from the other end of the line was so heavy, Sam was fairly sure he could hear it.

'You're saying there's a coincidence between you seeing a UFO shaped like a giant steak pie and a scarecrow in your field, is that it?'

'You weren't there, were you, Debs? No. You weren't. You didn't see it. I was.'

'Not a saucer, not a plate, but a pie,' said Debs, a faint giggle behind her words. 'Honestly, Love, sometimes ...' Sam was fairly sure he heard Debs roll her eyes. 'What was this other thing, then?'

'It doesn't matter,' said Sam. 'Really, it doesn't. This scarecrow, though ...'

The scarecrow was maybe twenty or thirty metres away now, and for the first time since spotting it, Sam's confusion and bemusement at its appearance curled at the edges just enough to make him pause.

'What the hell are you doing here?' he muttered to himself, went to take another step, then paused.

The stillness of the cold morning, which only a few minutes ago had seemed so peaceful, suddenly grew teeth, and an icy squall spun into him, causing him to stumble back a little. Unsteady on his feet for a moment, Sam was thankful for the thumbstick, which stopped him from toppling over, but only just. Wooziness spilled through him, and he closed his eyes to try and squeeze away the nausea that washed over him in waves.

'Sam, Love? You still there?'

'Yes,' Sam replied. 'Just a funny turn, that's all. Probably a migraine coming on.'

'Another one?'

'It's nothing.'

'If I have to drag you to the doctors again about that, then I will,' Debs said. 'Even if it means hogtying you and carrying you there in a front loader.'

'You mean you wouldn't just throw me over your shoulder, then?' Sam replied with a laugh.

Debs had hit her fifties with the realisation that, like himself, she'd put on a few pounds. Sam had helped her turn an old outbuilding into a makeshift gym, with the full intention to use it as well. But whereas he had allowed life to get in the way, Deb's had soon become addicted to exercise. The problem for Sam was that he found it almost impossible to do exercise for the point of exercise. And he was fairly sure working on the farm kept him in decent shape. Ish.

Part of Sam also wondered if that UFO had been partly that woozy feeling before a migraine. Sometimes, when his vision went, the world would swim, and he'd see things. But he was sure it had been real, as real as this bloody scarecrow, and he'd put money on it, too, if he had any.

Sam forced himself to stand tall, saw Gyp sitting on the grass and staring up at him, head cocked a little, concern in the old dog's eyes.

'It's alright, lad, I'm fine,' he said, and reached down to scratch the dog's head.

Gyp wagged his tail, and Sam took that as a signal to walk on.

Around them, the deep greens of the fells glimmered under the glare of a sun still low on the horizon. The day was already bright, barely a cloud in the sky, and Sam breathed deep the sweet air with the urgency of a parched man given a cup of water. He could taste ice in that breath, wondered if snow was coming, hoped it wasn't.

Gyp stopped.

'Come on, lad,' Sam said, walking on. 'Sooner we're done here, the sooner we can—'

Gyp growled.

Sam looked back to see the animal staring past him, snout low, the hairs on his back raised. And that was odd, he thought, because of all the dogs he had ever owned, and he'd had a few over the years that was for sure, Gyp had always been the calmest. Never easily riled, barely even a bark, the dog had been good-natured from the off. What the hell was wrong?

Sam looked to where Gyp was staring and saw that the dog's eyes were fixed firmly on the scarecrow. He laughed.

'You do know I'm still here?' Debs said, her voice catching Sam by surprise.

'Yes,' he said, the lie not entirely convincing.

'You're getting worse, you know that, don't you?' Debs said.

'I'm not getting worse. I'm just getting old,' said Sam.

'Fifty-three isn't old,' said Debs. 'And what was so funny?'

'Gyp,' Sam explained. 'He's taken a disliking to this here scarecrow. Can't say I blame him; ugly bugger it is. You should see him! He's eyeballing it something terrible.'

Debs laughed.

'Daft animal,' she said, then added, 'Reckon he's going odd in his old age, like someone else I know.'

By now, Sam was only a few paces away from the scarecrow. Gyp still hadn't moved. What the hell was wrong with him? Warranted, this odd figure dressed in ragged, grubby brown corduroys and a long, waxed jacket just appearing out of the blue was strange, but he had no doubt there was an explanation. And then, in that moment, he knew what it was.

'George ...' Sam said, the name hissing out between gritted teeth.

'What was that now?' said Debs.

'This,' said Sam. 'The scarecrow, it'll be George, won't it? He'll have done this, you mark my words.'

'George put a scarecrow in your field?'

'Yes.'

'Why?'

'Because he's a bastard, that's why.'

Debs laughed.

'Don't be ridiculous! Why would he do that?'

'I've already said why,' said Sam. 'He doesn't need any other reason.'

Once again, Sam was fairly sure he heard Debs roll her eyes, but this time, and for good measure, threw in a despairing shake of her head as well.

'You've still not made up, then?'

Sam was astonished that Debs would even ask.

'Made up? Of course, we've not bloody well made up! Why would we? Why would I even give him the time of day?'

'You're acting like children.'

'He started it.'

'I rest my case.'

'But he did!' said Sam. 'And you can't say that he didn't.'

'I can say that I don't care,' said Debs. 'I can say that this has been going on for five years now, and that if I could knock your thick heads together, I would! To think two grown men, both nearing sixty years old, could bicker and squabble over something so utterly ridiculous!'

'It is not ridiculous,' said Sam, now standing in front of the scarecrow. Close up, he noticed that it seemed more substantial than he'd initially expected. The sturdy piece of wood rammed into the ground between the scarecrow's legs was buried deep, like a fence post.

'You know, I bet you can't even remember why you fell out in the first place,' Debs said.

'He bought that tup I wanted,' Sam said, the memory so clear that for a moment he almost felt like he was back at the auction mart in Hawes. And there, on the other side of the ring, was George. Grinning.

'What, and you think that five years on from that, he's decided that the best thing to do with his time is to sneak into one of our fields and plant a scarecrow, is that it? Why, Sam? Why would you even think that? What reason could George possibly have to do it? No, don't answer, because there isn't one, is there? We farm sheep, remember? Sheep! We don't need a scarecrow, so it's not even funny! Weird, yes, but funny? No. And George is many things, but weird and funny aren't the adjectives which spring immediately to mind, now are they?'

Sam was walking around the scarecrow, rubbing his chin as he tried to work out George reasons for putting it there in the first place, the thumbstick now tucked under his arm. Gyp still hadn't moved, still eyeballing the scarecrow, snarling.

George certainly spent a bit of time on it, Sam thought, and he was almost impressed. In addition to the brown corduroys and long jacket, the scarecrow was wearing knitted gloves, Wellington boots, and a wide-brimmed hat, its head facing forward as though held in place somehow. The thing certainly hadn't been thrown together in a hurry. Indeed, if it wasn't for the fact that its arms were outstretched, he found himself half wondering that if he turned his back, it wouldn't just walk off to find the nearest pub.

'Fun though this is, my love, I'd best get to work,' said Debs.

'You and the twins out dealing death again?'

'Rats need clearing out, and terriers are the best there is at it,' Debs replied, and Sam smiled at the thought of the love of his life's passion for her own business, that being pest control. 'What are you going to do? You could bring it home for the veg plot if you want; might keep those pigeons away once we have a few things growing again. With these funny turns you keep having, I'll not be having you out with the shotgun taking potshots.'

Sam went to reply, but then he noticed something; the glove on the scarecrow's left hand hadn't been pulled on fully.

'Sam?'

He leaned in for a closer look, narrowing his eyes, reaching out to touch where the arm of the scarecrow was strangely bare.

'Sam, if you're ignoring me ...'

Sam's fingers touched the scarecrow, and he snatched his hand away like he'd just been thumped with an electric shock.

'I'm serious, Sam ...'

Sam shook his head, refusing to believe what that simple touch had just told him. Because it couldn't be true, made no sense, was impossible.

He reached out again, only this time, instead of using his hand, he brought up his thumbstick. The ferrule touched the brim of the hat on the scarecrow's head and Sam used it to gently lever it up just enough so he could see what lay beneath.

Gyp's growl turned into a bark. But Sam's eyes were on something else.

Sam forced himself to look, even though it was the last thing he wanted to do because every part of his being was telling him to just run, to get the hell away.

'Debs ...'

'What?'

'It's not a scarecrow,' said Sam.

THREE

Police Constable Jadyn Okri was out on a foot patrol in Leyburn and was rather wishing he'd worn warmer socks. The thought wasn't quite the high-pressure problem he'd envisaged his now highly trained and experienced police mind would spend its time pondering. Crime lords and trafficking gangs and cold-eyed killers, yes, but socks? Not so much. Right now, though, it was all he could think about. His feet were freezing, and no amount of walking around the streets was helping.

'You're providing a visible presence to reassure and deter crime, just you remember that,' Matt had reminded him at the office that morning, as he'd waved him off. 'But if you do get a chance to pop into that little bakery for me, like, that'd be great.'

'But I thought Cockett's provided for your every need?' Jadyn had asked.

'It does, in all but one area, that being the provision of a pork pie with a slice of black pudding on it. And all the better when you get them warm.'

Jadyn had already bought the requested pork pie, and at the same time given into temptation and bought one for himself, and on finding the pies to be warm, snaffled his almost immediately. Though delicious, the pie had made no difference at all to his feet.

Leyburn was already busy, and despite the cold, Jadyn was enjoying his walk around the place. He'd heard plenty while in training about the importance of building a good relationship with the local community. A few of those he had been training alongside had wondered how they were supposed to ever find the time, what with everything else a police officer had to do.

Working with the team in Hawes, however, had shown him not only that it wasn't just a case of finding, but making, the time to do it, but also that it was a hugely important part of the role. And it wasn't all about intelligence gathering either, though there was a fair bit of that to what he was doing. Building trust between the community and the police was, as Harry, Gordy, and Matt had drilled into him, an integral part of the role, and if that meant helping catch sheep, popping into pubs and other local businesses to chat to the staff, even visiting bakeries, then that's what you did.

At first, Jadyn had felt hugely self-conscious about being out and about just talking to people. And after what had happened to him there in those first few months in Wensleydale, Leyburn could, if he had allowed it to, be a place he'd rather not be in at all. Getting snatched into a van by a bunch of masked, murderous thugs was enough to put anyone off a place, but Jadyn had refused to allow that experience to win.

With the counselling he'd received, and the support not just from the team but the local community, too, he'd soon settled into seeing the place for what it was, a hard-working market town populated, like the rest of the Dales, by people who had made him feel welcome.

His feet were still cold, though, and after popping into the little bookshop in the marketplace, he had decided that enough was enough.

A few minutes later, Jadyn was standing inside The Walking Shop, and considering the reason for his visit, it couldn't have been better named. His problem now, however, was choosing the actual socks he wanted.

'So, what kind of walking do you do, then?'

The question had come from the member of staff who had approached him with a helpful smile within moments of setting foot inside the door.

Jadyn was fairly sure that, 'The kind that involves my legs and feet' wasn't the answer.

'I just want something a bit warmer than what I'm wearing right now,' he said, and lifted a leg of his trousers to show one of his socks.

The man dropped to his heels.

'You can't walk in these!'

'I can't?' Jadyn said, noting the shock in the man's voice, and immediately concerned that he was somehow damaging his feet irreparably. 'Why not?'

'They're just supermarket socks,' the man said. 'There's no cushioning, no wicking of moisture. Worst of all, though ...'

'Worst of all, what?' Jadyn asked, already baffled by the mention of cushioning and wicking.

'They've got tiny dinosaurs on them.'

Jadyn laughed at that.

'They're not dinosaurs, they're Steves,' he said.

The man stared up at him, confusion in his eyes.

'Steves?'

Jadyn attempted to explain.

'My girlfriend, she's got this massive lizard, and it's called Steve, and ...' From the look he was getting from the shop owner, Jadyn immediately wished he'd just kept his mouth shut, but he continued anyway. 'He's huge, like this big'—he stretched his arms out wide to try and get across just how big Steve was—'and he doesn't really like me, or didn't, but now kind of tolerates me, and that's progress, so these were my Christmas present.'

'From your girlfriend?'

'No, from Steve.'

'The lizard.'

'Yes. He sometimes even lets me sit next to him on the sofa.'

'Steve sits on the sofa.'

'Not so much sits,' said Jadyn. 'Sort of lies there taking up the whole thing. His favourite programme is Red Dwarf.'

That last detail Jadyn knew he should've kept to himself because the confusion in the man's eyes was now starting to edge very quickly towards fear.

'Anyway, back to the socks,' the man said, standing up to guide Jadyn over to a rather overwhelming display of them on the wall. 'Any take your fancy?'

No, Jadyn thought, *they don't, because they're all just socks, aren't they, and I've never got excited about socks.*

'Those,' he said, pointing at a random pair with red and blue stripes.

'They're more suited to serious mountaineering,' the man said.

'They look warm, though.'

'They're all warm, especially when compared to what you're wearing right now. But then, I'm not sure what wouldn't be.'

'You don't like my socks.'

'I like them,' the man said, 'just not for walking around when it's minus two.'

A few minutes later, and with new socks not just bought but pulled on, Jadyn was walking around Leyburn again with the toastiest of feet, trying to ignore just how much they'd cost him. He was just thinking about Jen, but more so Steve, and wondering if he should pop into the pet shop over the other side of the road to buy the grumpy lizard a snack, when his phone buzzed.

'Liz?'

'You busy?'

Jadyn decided to not say what he'd just spent the past twenty minutes doing and said, 'No, why?'

'Got a call in from a Mr Howes, asking if we can have someone over to help him deal with a situation.'

'That's a bit vague,' said Jadyn.

'I didn't quite understand what he was saying myself,' said Liz. 'He was quite irate, mentioned something about fish and the river and pollution. I could hardly get a word in edgeways.'

'Fish?' Jadyn said.

Liz gave him the address.

'He said something about vandalism and rude signs—he was very keen to tell me just how rude, as well—and I'm fairly sure that he used the word *yeti*, though it might have been jetty, seeing as he's down by the river.'

'That's more likely, I think,' said Jadyn.

'He's waiting for you,' said Liz. 'Can you head over now?'

'Well, there's nothing else pressing. Let him know I'm on my way.'

Call over and laughing to himself about what Liz thought she'd heard this Mr Howes say, Jadyn was about to head back to his vehicle when a shout further up the street hooked his attention, and he was nearly knocked off his feet as a group of maybe half a dozen people dressed in jeans and hoodies raced along the pavement.

He turned to see a man standing on the other side of the road, outside the old Leyburn police station, and pointing directly at him. Behind him, two large doors stood open in an archway.

'Why didn't you stop them?' the man shouted.

'What? Who?'

'Those buggers who nearly ran you over, that's who!'

Jadyn looked back to where the group had gone and saw feet disappear around a corner.

'Well, don't just stand there, you muppet!' the man yelled, waving something in the air that looked like a rolled-up newspaper. 'Get after them!'

Jadyn was fairly sure he needed a reason to chase after someone beyond just '*get them*' and being called a muppet.

'What did they do?' he called back.

'They were trespassing!' the man shouted, pointing now at the large building behind him. He went to say something else, but a truck rumbled past, not only blocking his route but drowning him out.

The truck rolled on, and the man dashed over to a crescendo of beeping car horns as he dodged two cars going in opposite directions.

'That was dangerous,' Jadyn said. 'You could've caused an accident.'

'And if you don't help me chase after them, I'll be causing another one right here, I can promise you that!'

He prodded Jadyn in the chest with what he had in his hand, and he could see that it wasn't a newspaper at all, but what looked like sheets of paper scrunched up in a roll.

Jadyn decided to let the not exactly thinly veiled threat pass for now.

'Wait here,' he said.

'No,' the man replied, turning as he spoke. 'I'll be over there in the old station, checking to see what they've actually been up to. You'd think they'd have something better to do, wouldn't you?'

Jadyn turned on his heel and sprinted down the high street towards the marketplace and took a sharp right, his feet slipping on ice just enough to make his heart leap into his throat.

Some way ahead of him, he saw the group, still running, but disappearing into the shadows at the end of a narrow lane leading out of the top end of the marketplace. Beyond that lay the Leyburn playing field, a playground, and then open countryside. Jadyn didn't fancy his chances of catching them, but he decided to give it a go regardless.

At the end of the lane, Jadyn sprinted into the playing field, the empty goals netless, the grass crisp with frost, and crisscrossed with the footprints of bird and beast.

A shout and a laugh caught his attention from the far corner of the field. He looked over to see the group waving at him.

Jadyn knew he had no chance of catching them; they were too far away now for him to close the distance, but if he got close enough, he might be able to get a description. And there was always the off chance that one of them would trip over and he would be able to grab them and ask a few questions.

Heart thumping, he gave the chase one last go, his legs

pumping hard as he charged across the playing field. The group continued to wave, goading him on, challenging him to try and catch them. Then, as Jadyn sped across the centre point of the field, they turned tail and bolted into the trees.

By the time Jadyn arrived where the group had been, his lungs in his mouth, his heart racing, the only sign that they had been there at all was the collection of footprints smudged into the frosty mud. Then he spotted something else in a puddle of frost-covered, gloopy mud. It was a folded piece of paper.

Maybe it had been dropped by one of the group, he thought, and picked it up. Jadyn stuffed it into a pocket and made his way back across the field and into the marketplace, happy to notice that his feet were still warm. He was still wincing a little about the cost as he crossed the road to head over to the old police station and speak to the man who had shouted to him and directed him after the group.

Walking through the archway and into the building, Jadyn was soon in a rough courtyard, the surface broken by scrub and weed. In one corner stood a brick building that looked as sad and dejected as the rest of the property. Jadyn could see that at some point in its past, it had been quite a place, but time had done its best to give it a depressed feel, as though all it really wanted to do was shuffle off into a dark corner and sulk.

'Did you catch them?'

Jadyn turned at the voice to see the man approaching from an open door at the back of the building.

He shook his head.

'Too much of a head start,' he said. 'Lost them over the playing field.'

The man gave a shrug.

'There's no damage,' he said. 'Not as you'd be able to tell anyway, seeing as the place is a mess. To be honest, they just gave me such a fright when I found them that I just gave chase. And I'm sorry I said what I said. Heat of the moment, and all that. I'm Tom, by the way,' he added. 'Thomas Rowe.'

Jadyn introduced himself, then asked, 'And you own this? It's a bit more impressive than what we use over in Hawes.'

'Fancy a look around?' Tom asked. 'There's even an old cell.'

'Seriously? We have to go to Harrogate if we want to hold someone,' said Jadyn, then his mind switched back to the reason he was there in the first place. 'Any idea what they were up to?'

The man shook his head.

'Not a clue,' he said. 'Found these, though.'

He held out the roll of papers Jadyn had seen him with earlier.

Jadyn took them and as he started to unroll them, a call came through on his radio.

'I'll be inside,' Tom said, and with a nod, left Jadyn to answer the call.

Liz was on the other end.

'Sorry, there's been a bit of a delay,' Jadyn said, but before he could say what had happened, Liz cut him off.

'We've had a call in from over near Kettlewell,' she said. 'A farmer's found a body in his field. His name is Sam Dent. If you head over, I'll have backup sent ASAP.'

Jadyn's world stopped, and no matter how warm his feet had been a few moments ago, his whole body was now cold.

'I'll get over there,' he said. 'Any other details? And what about Mr Howes and the yeti?'

'I'll call Mr Howes and explain. With regards to what you're heading over to, Mr Dent said that the body looks like a scarecrow.'

Jadyn wasn't sure he'd heard correctly.

'Can you say that again?'

'He found it this morning in his field,' Liz said. 'He thought it was a scarecrow, but on having a closer look, discovered that it very much wasn't.'

'This isn't a prank call, is it? Or something else you've misheard?'

'He sounded more than a little traumatized by what he's found,' said Liz. 'I've called for an ambulance.'

'Definitely not a prank call, then.'

'No,' said Liz, 'but the ambulance won't be sent until I hear back from you that you're on-site and are able to confirm what's been reported.'

Liz gave Jadyn the address and the details of the man who had found the body.

'You've two routes you can take,' she then explained, 'but if I were you, I'd go via West Burton. It's longer, but the roads are better. If you head over through Gammersgill, you'll spend half your time reversing to find a passing place to let someone through.'

'Anything else I need to know?' Jadyn asked.

Liz said, 'Nothing more to add to the scarecrow issue other than Mr Dent was very keen to point out that being a sheep farmer, he doesn't need one.'

'Not sure how that's relevant.'

'Same,' said Liz, then her serious tone broke just a little. 'Oh, and just so you know, he did mention something about UFOs, but by that point, I think he was just rambling.'

'UFOs? In the Dales? And you're absolutely sure this isn't a prank?'

'Maybe they're here for the cheese,' said Liz, and Jadyn was sure he heard her shrug. 'Anyway, head over and see what's what. I'll update the rest of the team. Call in when you know more.'

Call over, Jadyn ducked inside the old police station to let Tom know that he was heading off, and that if he had any further problems with trespassers, to give him a call. The station was quite a mess, and ducking his head around the door of the old cell was enough to tell him that it was a place he didn't want to be. He also spotted a hefty-looking gun cabinet inside, which struck him as odd.

With no sign of Tom downstairs, he headed to the upper floor, where he discovered that some of the rooms had been given over to living quarters. He guessed that, at some point, whoever had been in charge would have lived there, too, a thought that made him shudder, because in that situation, there would never be a moment where your life wasn't impacted by the job. He also noticed a faint but distinctive aroma in the air. It was sweet, sickly, a smell he recognised and left no doubt about what the group he'd chased had been up to. He'd never touched cannabis himself, never smoked it, never even tried it in a brownie, but knew plenty who had, and the stink of the stuff was something he had never liked.

Unable to find Tom, Jadyn assumed he had left while he'd been on the call with Liz, so walked back outside, through the archway, and on towards his car. A few minutes later, he was heading off towards Kettlewell, wondering what, exactly, he was going to find, the roll of papers Tom had given him lying forgotten on the back seat.

FOUR

Jadyn realised too late that rather than following Liz's instructions to go via West Burton, he had instead blindly followed the satnav. Turning around would only add to the delay, so he carried on, vowing not to tell Liz.

The road was snake-thin, the bottom of every shadow-filled dip booby-trapped with icy puddles. There seemed to be no rhyme or reason as to how the road had been laid out, why it needed so many humps and bumps and dips. Jadyn guessed that the lane was, like so many of the older thoroughfares in the Dales, ancient beyond the memory of the hills, each bump and sharp bend an echo of when it had been a rutted track travelled by carts, its path dictated by ancient trees and the undulating lay of the land.

After the sixth vehicle he had reversed to let through, Jadyn stopped counting, only to find himself behind a tractor with and trailer winding its sleepy way through the dale. It was only when they came to a section of the road that sat on open moorland that Jadyn was finally able to get past, and the farmer lifted a friendly wave as he pulled over onto the tufted grass.

The bleakness of the route gave Jadyn an odd sense of being thrust back in time, and he half wondered if he wouldn't soon see a drover herding sheep over the fells, or whether the road in front of him would become a track worn into the hills by foot and hoof and wheel, rather than pinned so neatly in place with Tarmac.

Eventually, the road started to give way to another view, opening out to hills far off, most still slumbering beneath thick cloud hugging their sides. Drystone walls once again sprung up to either side of the road, which still grew no wider, pulling him past a farmyard on his left, where sheep tussled with each other as they munched on hay brought to them on the back of a quad bike by the farmer. Then on, around a hairpin bend, to see a river opening out below, before Kettlewell welcomed him.

With no time to stop for a wander around the village, Jadyn took a lane leading out again and eventually came to his destination, parking up behind a pickup truck that had once been yellow, but age and a rough life outside had turned it to a dirty cream.

A man climbed out of the truck and came over to Jadyn's vehicle before he'd even had time to unclip his seatbelt. He rapped a knuckle on the window, gave a nod.

'You'll be the policeman, then,' he said, his voice muffled a little by Jadyn's still-closed door.

Jadyn mouthed a yes, sent his seatbelt zipping up into its reel, then opened his door and climbed out.

A sharp wind caught him as he left the warm cocoon of his car and he shivered.

'Police Constable Okri,' said Jadyn. 'Mr Dent?'

The man looked Jadyn up and down.

'Did you put all that on to come out here, then?'

'Put all what on?' Jadyn asked.

'The uniform,' said Mr Dent, pointing at the constable. 'It's very smart, but doesn't look all that warm. You have a coat, don't you? It's a bit nippy out, like. Worse than yesterday, I reckon. Hard to shift the cold when it gets like this. It seeps into the soil and if there's no sun, then it's proper brass monkey weather.'

Jadyn saw that Mr Dent was dressed in the usual uniform of a Dales' farmer; Wellington boots, hard-wearing trousers dotted with mismatched patches, and a waxed jacket that had seen better days, but which he had no doubt would still see the man through a few more winters. On his head was a knitted black skull cap. He wasn't wearing gloves, and seeing the man's huge, bare hands only made Jadyn feel the cold all the more.

Jadyn reached into the back of his vehicle, grabbed his coat, then shutting the driver's door behind him, blew on his own hands before thrusting them into his pockets.

'You're Mr Dent, yes?' he said, noting that the man hadn't as yet confirmed his identity.

The man gave a nod.

'That's me,' he said. 'Call me Sam, though, otherwise you'll make it sound like I'm in trouble myself, and I'm not. Because what I found in that field, it's nowt to do with me, that's for sure.'

'And when did you find the body?'

'That was earlier this morning,' Sam said. 'Friend of mine spotted it and told me. No idea how it got there, or when, really. Not been along here for a few days myself.'

Jadyn took down the name and number of the person who had told Sam about the scarecrow.

'Probably best if you just show me where to go and I'll have a look,' he said. 'Then you can wait in the warmth of your truck.'

Sam laughed at that.

'Warmth? In that thing? You're having a laugh. Heater broke years ago. Never bothered fixing it. I carry an old sleeping bag around with me, though, and a few odds and sods, just in case I get caught out in the snow or something.'

'That's actually very sensible,' said Jadyn.

'I'm a sensible man, though my wife would say I'm just paranoid,' Sam said, then pointed up the lane. 'The scarecrow's up there. The field's on your right. Can't miss it, thanks to the massive pile of rubbish you'll find in front of the gate. That needs sorting out as well, you know. Don't see why it should be my responsibility, do you? I didn't put it there, did I? Have you ever seen a UFO?'

Jadyn had been about to head off in the direction Sam had

pointed, but the strange question caught him off guard. He remembered Liz mentioning UFOs during the call, but hadn't expected to be talking about them at all, never mind so early in the proceedings.

'A UFO? I don't think so, no,' said Jadyn. 'And my guess is I'd remember if I did.'

Sam said, 'You see, I'm half wondering if it's something like that, myself. You hear of those cattle mutilations, don't you? This could be like that, couldn't it?'

'I'm not sure I follow,' said Jadyn.

'Well, you'll see in a minute how odd it is, him being all stuck there like a scarecrow. So, what if it was a UFO that did it? Well, not the UFO itself, but the folk driving it or flying it or whatever? Can't rule these things out, can you?'

Jadyn wasn't sure what to say.

'Perhaps it's best if I go and have a look myself,' he said at last, stepping away from Sam.

'I'm just saying,' said Sam, calling after. 'It's where I saw the UFO, so who's to say they've not come back and done this? Maybe it's a message or something, like a crop circle.'

Jadyn kept walking; Sam stepped in beside him, still talking.

'Trouble with crop circles is they're mostly folk having a bit of a laugh, aren't they? A bit of bailer twine, a short plank of wood, a length of rope, and a couple of folk can't half create an amazing pattern in a field.'

'Can't say that I know much about them,' said Jadyn.

'I don't either,' said Sam. 'Fascinating though, isn't it?'

Sam continued to talk, covering not just crop circles and aliens, but lizard people, the Illuminati, even Earth being hollow.

A couple of minutes later, Jadyn saw the pile of rubbish, and following Sam, clambered over it and into the field directly behind.

Sam was right, he thought, *something really did need to be done about the rubbish, but right now, it wasn't a priority.* What was, was the figure standing still as stone in the middle of the field.

'There he is,' said Sam, pointing across the field.

Jadyn paused, taking a moment to gather himself. He was first on the scene, so it was important he did this right, didn't miss anything, because if he did, Harry would certainly point it out. Not in a mean way, but certainly in a next-time-do-better way, he was sure.

This is a lonely place, he thought. The village of Kettlewell may have only been a few minutes away down the lane, yet where they were had an eerie quietness that gave him more than just a shiver from the cold. *It's that ancientness of the fells again,* he thought, like he'd experienced on the drive over, only now it felt like he was being watched.

The field was entered from the lane by the gate, and two further gates led off into adjoining fields, all of them bordered with dry stone walls. Ice was still on the ground, the grass of the field a swathe of white crystal bright under the sun.

The only tracks Jadyn could see were a single set of footprints leading from the gate to the figure and back, which he assumed belonged to Sam.

'Away, then,' Sam said, and started to walk away.

'Mr Dent,' Jadyn said, calling the farmer back, 'I'll be fine on my own, thank you.'

'You sure about that?' Sam said. 'It's a hell of a sight, make no mistake about that.'

'I'm sure,' said Jadyn. 'But this is a police matter now, so probably best that you make your way back to your vehicle. If and when I need further assistance, I'll let you know.'

'I'm not needed, then?'

'We will need to take a statement from you,' said Jadyn. 'But until then, if you could wait in your vehicle?'

Sam jumped back over the gate.

'I can nip into town for something to eat, if you fancy?' he asked, looking back at Jadyn, and leaning on the gate. He tapped his stomach. 'Getting a bit peckish myself, like. What do you want?'

Jadyn worked hard to not smile.

'I think it would be best if you just waited for now,' he said.

'If you insist.'

'I do.'

Jadyn made his way over to the figure. Approaching it alone, he was struck by the oddness of what he was seeing. The fields were empty, the sheep gathered in for lambing season, which was just around the corner. And yet, standing alone in the middle of this world, asleep beneath a cold bright sky, was something that looked, for all intents and purposes, like a scarecrow.

A good twenty metres from the body, the oddness of what he was staring at brought Jadyn to a dead stop. *It isn't that it's trussed up like a scarecrow that made it odd,* Jadyn thought, *but the loneliness of it.* There were no crops for it to watch over, no birds to scare. Instead, it was simply standing there, staring at him across a field chilled by the long arm of winter. He had to force himself forward, to close the distance so that he could decide on what to do next, while remaining aware that this was a crime scene.

Jadyn circled the body once, twice, staying far enough away to hopefully not disturb any evidence. Not that he could see what evidence there would be; the ground was hard, no footprints would be found. Perhaps Sam was right after all, and this was all down to aliens.

The ridiculousness of that thought gave Jadyn enough courage to edge closer. The figure was wearing a long jacket, and a hat was pulled down on their head. From what Jadyn could see, it was held in place by a stake hammered into the ground, arms outstretched on a transverse bar, its face staring straight out, over towards the gate.

Beneath the brim of the wide hat, Jadyn saw skin pale as milk. At first, he thought he was staring at a mask, the kind left over from Halloween; a ghostly face torn apart by deep wounds, flesh hanging off in thick strips, everything made all the more horrific with fake blood congealed around the eyes. The effect was very realistic, and Jadyn was close to thinking this whole thing was some kind of prank, when the body moved.

Jadyn jumped back, stumbled, ended up on his back, his heart racing hard enough to break out of his chest.

For a moment, he didn't move, wondering if he was seeing things.

Slowly, carefully, he sat forward, then pushed himself up onto his feet. He approached the body once again, this time to check for a pulse, found nothing. Then a reeking stench enveloped him, slipped into his nose, his mouth, and he gagged on the gasses escaping from the body.

Retching, and yet somehow managing to stop himself from throwing up, Jadyn leaned his hands on his knees, then reached into a pocket and pulled out a small tub of vapour rub. He dabbed it under his nose. It didn't quite get rid of the stink of death that had just come to him, but it provided at least some barrier. He straightened, aware now that this was no prank, that it wasn't a mask covered in fake blood, but something else entirely, and called Liz.

'You're on site?' Liz asked.

'Arrived about twenty minutes ago,' said Jadyn.

'I'll get the ambulance on its way, then,' Liz said. 'Gordy and Jen are heading out to you now, too.'

Jadyn was unable to pull his eyes away from what he had discovered.

'Liz? We need Harry,' he said.

'He's on leave today,' Liz replied. 'And we both know how rare that is, don't we? Viewing houses with Grace, remember? I can't go interrupting that, can I? We can handle this.'

'We need to tell him, and now,' said Jadyn, at last able to take himself away from the body and head back to his car for some cordon tape. 'Because as soon as he hears about this, he'll want to be here anyway. Trust me.'

Liz was quiet for a moment, then said, 'Trust you? Why? What's wrong?'

Jadyn breathed in deep the cold, wintery air as it scratched and clawed its icy way down the fells towards him. He turned around to have one last look over at the body before climbing over the gate and out of the field.

'Whoever this is that I'm looking at,' he said, 'they haven't got any eyes ...'

FIVE

Harry was trying to give the estate agent the impression he was listening when really all he wanted to do was go home, lie down in a quiet room, and go to sleep. He knew he was never great at being ill, so he was pushing through as best he could, but he was already getting the impression, from both Grace and the estate agent, that his enthusiasm was obviously lacking. Even Smudge was looking at him like he was behaving strangely.

The cold of the morning wasn't helping any either. Usually, he would appreciate it, be amazed by the magic the frost created by painting the Dales with crystals. Today, though, he just wasn't interested.

The estate agent, a woman dressed in a smart blue suit and called Madeline Trent, a name which had taken Harry quite by surprise, had shown them around three properties so far, one of which hadn't even been on their plan. It had supposedly just come on the market and was a bargain. Harry had decided very quickly that he and Madeline had very different ideas as to what that word meant, but then Harry had soon realised that whatever Madeline was saying, he was clearly interpreting differently to how she intended.

Madeline had described that particular property as, 'tucked away and with huge potential,' but to Harry it had been run down to the point of maybe being better off if it was introduced to a bull-dozer, and so remote he was almost surprised to read on the particulars that it had electricity, never mind running water.

The other two properties had also been effused over by the very enthusiastic Madeline, with both being in enviable locations and recently updated throughout. Of those two, Madeline had gone to great lengths to tell Harry and Grace that one had been individually styled and that the interior really had to be seen to be appreciated.

As soon as she had opened the front door, Harry had decided that he would have been more than happy with not seeing it at all, so garish were the colours used throughout by the current owner that he was surprised they hadn't been required to wear protective eyewear.

With one more property to view, and another that Madeline was very keen she take them to, Harry needed a break.

'Trust me, it's not that I'm not enjoying myself,' he said to Grace, as they headed to the next property. 'It's worth it just to experience Madeline's sales pitches.'

Grace laughed.

'She certainly gets full marks for effort.'

'I could just do with a few minutes not being asked to consider how much potential yet another property has. Because I don't care about potential! I just want a place we both like that we can move into. Not too much to ask, is it?'

'Not a fan of DIY, then?' Grace smirked, clearly knowing the answer. 'No urge to spend your evenings and weekends ripping out walls and laying floors?'

Harry shook his head.

'I hate DIY. Why the hell would I ever consider putting a bath-room or a kitchen in myself when there are plenty of people out there who do it as their job? Makes no sense. Can you imagine if everyone took the DIY approach to other areas of life? In fact, it's something the police actively discourage. If there's one thing we say consistently, it's to leave it to us.'

'You're comparing putting up a shelf to solving a murder, is that it?'

'Not quite, no, but you get my point.'

'I do,' Grace said, 'but if we take a break now, it'll only prolong the pain, won't it? And you never know, we might even like one of the next two houses.'

Harry stopped mid-stride, not because he wanted to, but because the sneeze that exploded from him was almost strong enough to knock him off his feet.

'Bloody hell, Harry!' Grace said, staring at him.

'Yeah, my eyes nearly came out with that one,' Harry said, rubbing them to make sure they were still there.

'Maybe you're right,' said Grace. 'Maybe we should call it a day.'

Harry shook his head.

'No, I think you're right; better to press on and get it done. Like you said, one of the next two might be just what we're looking for. And this is a big deal for us both, isn't it, buying a house together? I'm not one for delaying things once I've set on a path to getting things done.'

Grace stared at Harry for a second or two.

'Only if you're sure.'

'I wouldn't say it if I wasn't sure,' Harry said, and to give Grace no chance to reply, he set off walking again, only to stop a few paces later when his phone buzzed.

Pulling the phone out of his pocket, he saw the number on-screen and immediately felt even more tired.

'Something wrong?' Grace asked.

'It's the office,' Harry said, and watched a frown crease Grace's brow.

'But you booked today off.'

'I know.'

'Why would they be calling you?'

'That's what worries me,' Harry replied, and answered.

The conversation was short, and when Harry finished it, he caught the concern on his face reflected in the look Grace was giving him.

'It's bad, isn't it?' she said.

'Very,' Harry replied. 'I'll spare you the details, but a body's been found in a field over Kettlewell way.'

'Farming accident?' Grace asked. 'A hiker? The number of people I see heading out into the hills ill-equipped, I'm stunned we don't find the Dales littered with bodies.'

'No ID,' said Harry. 'Farmer found the body this morning. Thought it was a scarecrow. Turns out, it very much wasn't.'

'A scarecrow?'

'That's what the message said, yes.'

Ahead, Madeline had stopped, clearly having noticed that Harry and Grace were no longer on her heels.

'Everything okay?' she called, trotting back towards them.

'You'd best get going then,' Grace said. 'Really, I should be saying you're in no fit state, but it's not like you're going to listen to me, is it?'

'Not really, no,' said Harry, as Madeline came to stand in front of them. He looked at her, almost blinked at the shininess of her smile. 'Afraid I have to go.'

'Really? Why?' Madeline asked. 'But this next property, I promise you just won't want to miss it.'

'I'll take that risk,' said Harry. 'Grace is still coming along, though, so I'll be there in spirit.'

'It's not the same as experiencing a place for yourself though,' said Madeline. 'If you want to know a house, decide if it's right, you really do need to walk its halls.'

Harry nearly laughed out loud at that last bit; walk its halls! As though any of the properties they'd viewed thus far had been large enough to contain a hall bigger than a cupboard!

'What about Smudge?' Grace asked.

Harry glanced down at his dog, who stared up at him with doe eyes, then leaned into him a little.

'I'll take her,' he said, scratching Smudge's head.

'You soft bugger,' Grace smiled.

Harry leant over to kiss Grace, then thought better of it.

'No, I don't want to be giving you whatever it is that I've got,' he said. 'I'll call you in a while, let you know what's what.'

'And I'll message you about the houses,' said Grace. 'But if I like one of them, I'll just buy it, shall I?'

'I guess,' said Harry. 'Why waste time?'

'Exactly.'

With a quick goodbye to Madeline, Harry took Smudge's lead and strode off back towards where he had parked the RAV. Then his stride started to feel painful, his energy vanished with the exertion, and he slowed to a gentle stroll, albeit one with enough purpose to have people move out of his way.

Once in his vehicle, with Smudge strapped in behind, and having survived another monstrous sneeze, Harry eased out into traffic and made his way towards Kettlewell.

The journey was uneventful, and when Harry arrived at the destination Liz had given him, he could remember little if any of it, bar rolling through West Burton and as he always did when he went through it, being astonished by just how beautiful the place was.

Spotting Jadyn's vehicle, Harry parked up behind it, then climbed out to be greeted by the young constable and the man he assumed was the one who had found the body.

'Constable Okri,' Harry said, locking his RAV, and feeling a little envious of Smudge asleep on the back seat.

'Sorry, Boss,' Jadyn said.

'Unless you're responsible for what you're about to show me, then there's nothing to apologise for, is there?' Harry said, then looked over at the man. 'I'm DCI Grimm.'

'Sam Dent,' said Sam. 'I still think it's UFOs, you know?'

Harry narrowed his eyes at that, but decided to ignore it, and asked, 'You found the body, then, correct?'

'Aiden told me about it,' said Sam.

'Aiden?'

'He's a gardener,' Sam explained. 'Bloody good one, too, if that's what you're into. I'm not. Well, not fancy stuff. A few potatoes, that kind of thing, but nowt else. Not the time to be messing around with flowers and pots and hanging baskets, have I?'

'No, I suppose not,' said Harry, already losing track of what they were talking about.

'I was obviously keen to have a look myself, so here I am, and there it is. And I don't need one, do I? So, why would it be there? I'm a sheep farmer, aren't I? Not much need for a scarecrow.'

Whatever Sam was saying was clearly a few steps ahead of where Harry was in his understanding of what had gone on.

'Is there not?' Harry asked, genuinely wondering why.

'Of course there isn't!' said Sam. 'Sheep farms don't have scarecrows, do they? What's to scare? Buzzards and crows can be a pest with the lambs, like, but a scarecrow would do bugger all.' He looked thoughtful for a moment. 'Maybe I should give it a try, though? What do you think?'

Harry decided the best course of action was to give no opinion at all, so turned his attention to Jadyn.

'Gordy's on her way,' said the constable. 'And so is Jen. Ambulance will be here at some point as well.'

'What about Matt?' Harry asked. 'Isn't he with Dave?'

'They were meeting with the church council, I think, over in Middleham, but then got a call out to attend to something over in Swaledale,' Jadyn answered.

'What kind of something?'

'Matt mentioned a ukulele player causing a disturbance, but he'll be over when he's done.'

'Did you just say, ukulele player?' Harry asked.

'I did,' said Jadyn.

'Thought so,' said Harry, but decided it was best for everyone he left it at that. Scarecrows, UFOs, and now ukuleles? *I really should've just stayed in bed,* he thought. 'So, where is it, then, this scarecrow?' he asked.

'This way,' said Jadyn, and led Harry along the lane.

SIX

Detective Inspector Gordanian Haig arrived at the location given to her by Liz and was in no mood for any nonsense. She'd had enough of that already this morning. Having always prided herself on her calm demeanour and self-restraint, her ability to stand back and assess things first, before acting, her patience was now so thin she could use it as a reed for a clarinet. And Gordy didn't play the clarinet, or any instrument for that matter. Certain things, however, would take her from kitten to hell cat in a heartbeat. And nonsense, in all its forms, was top of the list.

First, she'd had to arrange for a new removal company to step in where another had let both her and Anna down, citing reasons which had included, quite inexplicably, an exploding microwave. They were moving from the Dales to Somerset, and she was not about to have the whole thing sabotaged by dangerous home appliances.

She had then found herself dealing with an altercation at a service station between a motorbike owner and someone towing a caravan, the argument itself over why the motorbike owner had taken so long in the shop just to choose a chocolate bar.

And finally, to top it all off, a helicopter had landed in a field without permission to do so, all because the pilot and his wife thought it looked like a lovely spot for a picnic. And in this weather, too! They'd been on their way to Simonstone Hall, a beautiful hotel just a mile or so outside Hawes, and had got a bit peckish, apparently.

Gordy had found them sitting out on a blanket in the middle of a field still white with frost, wrapped up in very expensive down jackets, drinking champagne and nibbling on cheese straws, the hamper beside them small, but certainly well stocked with tasty morsels.

She had expected to be dealing with an irate farmer, too, especially as the report she'd received about the call was that the language he'd used had been mainly swearing, most of it yelled down the phone. However, what she'd walked in on was the farmer and his dog joining in with a glass of champagne.

'We're all sorted now,' the farmer had said when Gordy had turned up after marching across the field to send the pilot and his wife on their way. 'Nowt but a bit of a misunderstanding, that's all.'

The pilot's wife had then offered Gordy a glass of champagne and the glossiest smile this side of a magazine cover.

'It's non-alcoholic,' she'd said, lips so shiny Gordy had wondered if they were made of latex and could be peeled off should the need arise. 'Hugo has never touched a drop when flying.'

Gordy had declined, encouraged the couple to move along, then stood back and watched as they had, after clearing everything away, lifted off to finish their journey at the top end of the dale.

'First time I've ever had caviar,' the farmer had said as the helicopter had floated off into the blue. 'Can't see what all the fuss is about.'

And now, here she was, over in Wharfedale, once again stunned by the beauty of the Dales, and yet finding that darkness and evil liked to stain it regardless.

At the back of her mind, there was also a wee bit of concern for Anna. She'd seemed a bit off for a few days now, not quite herself, like she was coming down with something. She'd been suffering from headaches, which she would get occasionally because of stress, but this was different. Then her temperature had gone up a little, and she'd seemed increasingly under the weather.

A cold, most likely, they'd both thought, especially considering the time of year and that colds and flu were doing the rounds. She hoped it wasn't anything worse, not just because she cared, but because Anna had a habit of just soldiering on regardless.

She had no doubt that there were vicars who worked only one day a week, but Anna? Her view of a day off was to spend it visiting people, opening a village fete, attending an emergency call at the local care home, and any of the other dozens of tasks she could list as part of her job. And Gordy couldn't help loving her all the more for it.

Leaving her vehicle and pushing all thoughts of Anna to the back of her mind, Gordy walked along the lane, surprised and then annoyed to be striding past Harry's vehicle, spotting Smudge fast asleep on her back on the back seat.

No decorum that dog, she thought, continuing on her way, noticing a waft of heat coming off the bonnet as she did so; Harry obviously hadn't been here too long himself, and that made her think he'd come here in a rush. She also knew that he was supposed to be on leave today, something about looking at houses with Grace. He was as bad as Anna. Persuading him to take leave at all was a constant issue.

So, just what the hell was he doing here, then? Well, whatever it was, she'd be having words. Though she respected the man enormously, and had warmed immediately to his gruff, no-nonsense way of approaching everything from an investigation to managing the eclectic team they were part of, sometimes she wanted to give him an almighty slap, just to see the look on his face. She knew it wasn't that he didn't trust the rest of them to do their jobs, more that he simply couldn't help himself. Again, much like Anna. But that was no excuse. And today, Gordy was very much not in the mood for excuses.

Walking on past Jadyn's vehicle, then an old pickup truck she guessed belonged to the farmer who had discovered the body, Gordy decided to try and ignore her annoyance at Harry's appearance for now, though she could feel her nostrils flaring a little at the thought of it. She was soon at the entrance to the field, her eyes drawn to the pile of rubbish blocking her way.

Gordy stopped, stared at the dead plants and broken pots scattered about the heap, and ground her teeth at the sight of it, constantly stunned by the stupidity of people. She had never been able to understand the carelessness and wanton vandalism of some, why they saw no problem at all in ruining a place with their revolting mess. What the hell was wrong with them? What kind of thought process was it that went from having the rubbish in the first place, to then thinking that the best thing to do was to just dump it, and to hell with the consequences?

Her nostrils flared again, and she could hear herself sucking in sharp, annoyed breaths through her nose.

No, she thought, *that was a problem for another day, perhaps another member of the team.* She turned her back on the rubbish, did her best to ignore the quite astonishingly pungent smell of it, and clambered over it to get to the gate, which was pulled open and attached to the wall by way of a length of orange bailer twine looped over an ancient, rusting hook pinned into a large stone in the wall.

With her hands stuffed in her pockets against the cold, Gordy made her way across the field to where she could see four figures. Three of them turned to watch her approach, the fourth remained still, their arms outstretched almost like they were trying and failing to shoo the others away.

Gordy lifted a hand in greeting.

'Morning,' she said, coming to stand with Harry and Jadyn. She looked at the man standing with them and added, 'Detective Inspector Haig.'

'You're Scottish,' the man said.

Gordy's eyes went wide.

'I am? Dear God, man, when did that happen?' She then

looked at Harry, who, she noticed, looked even less happy than usual, his eyes red, the usual scowl on his face turned up to ten, though the scarring always made it hard to tell if he meant it or not. 'Why did you never tell me? How long have you known?'

'I'll be honest, I thought you were already fully aware,' Harry said, his voice crackling with phlegm. 'Sorry if it comes as such a surprise.'

'Your accent,' Jadyn added with a whisper, as Harry sneezed. 'That gives it away.'

'I have an accent?'

Jadyn nodded.

'Crivvens!' Gordy said, placing her hands on her hips, and really laying her Highland accent on thick. 'And I might even add a, "help ma' Boab!"'

Three pairs of eyes stared back at Gordy with varying degrees of surprise.

'Who's Bob?' the man asked. 'And why do we need to help him?'

Gordy sighed and quickly removed herself from the caricature of being Scottish she had just drawn.

'You must be Mr Dent?'

'I am, but less of the Mr, just call me Sam,' the man said, then jabbed a thumb behind him. 'Now, back to this Bob fellow you've just mentioned. Is that him, then? You already know who it is? That's some speedy police work.'

Gordy looked over Sam's shoulder to the body, which was standing inside a circle of cordon tape about fifteen metres across. She decided against answering his questions, fairly sure he would have never read, never mind heard of, Oor Wullie or The Broons.

'What've we got, then?' she asked.

'Not a clue,' Harry said. 'I've only just arrived myself. I was about to pop over for a closer look when we heard you arrive, thought I'd wait, share the joy.'

'You're so thoughtful.'

'No, I'm not.'

'No, you're right there, you're not,' Gordy agreed. 'Aren't you supposed to be on leave today?'

'I am,' Harry said, wiping his nose with his sleeve, then giving a large, moist sniff.

Gordy waited for Harry to say more. When nothing was forthcoming, she said, 'Leave is not another word for being at work. You do know that, don't you?'

'Liz called me,' Harry said.

'I asked her to,' Jadyn added. 'When I saw what this was, I knew he'd want to be here.'

Harry glanced at Jadyn.

'He? I'm standing right next to you,' he said.

'There's a vast, cavernous expanse between want and need,' Gordy said, her eyes still on Harry. 'What did Grace say? You're supposed to be spending the day with her, correct?'

'I am,' Harry said. 'And she was fine with it. She understood.'

'Did you give her any choice in the matter?' Gordy held up a hand as Harry went to speak. 'No, don't answer. You're as bad as Anna, you know that, don't you? Workaholics. It'll be the death of you!' She paused, took a breath to calm down. 'Shall we get on?'

Harry handed Gordy disposable covers for her shoes and a pair of rubber gloves, then lifted the cordon tape to allow her through.

'I'll stay where I am, if that's all the same with you,' Jadyn said.

'It isn't,' Harry said. 'Now we've Gordy here, get yourself over to the gate as Scene Guard. You've something in your car you can use to record everyone arriving and leaving?'

'I have,' Jadyn answered.

Harry turned his eyes on Sam.

'Having already asked you to leave three times, if I have to ask again, I'll be having Constable Okri here arrest you. Is that understood?'

'Arrest me? But I only came over because I thought I could be useful. The police are understaffed, aren't they? Just offering a helping hand, that's all.'

Harry said nothing more, and Gordy joined in with the stern stare he was giving Sam.

'This way, please,' Jadyn said, and at last, Sam turned and headed off back towards the gate, Jadyn following.

Harry was still holding the cordon tape in the air.

'After you,' he said.

Gordy ducked under the tape.

'Jadyn seemed keen to be anywhere but here,' she said, as they walked over to the body.

'Had a bit of a fright,' Harry explained.

'Well, you do look rough,' Gordy said, and Harry's answer was a hacking cough which doubled him over. 'Now, I know I'm only a Detective Inspector, but evidence so far suggests to me you're ill.'

'I'm fine,' Harry said.

'You're a terrible liar.'

'Anyway, it wasn't me that scared him. It was the body,' Harry said, and Gordy could tell he was ignoring what she had just said. 'You know how when bodies decompose, they fill up with gas, and then that gas needs to escape? Let's just say that he was a little too close for comfort when a cloud made a break for it and he took it full in the face.'

Gordy tried to not laugh, gave up, and roared.

'Poor lad,' she said, welcoming the warmth of the moment, smiling.

'His description of what happened was pretty detailed,' Harry said, holding out a small tub of vapour rub. 'You'll need this.'

Gordy dabbed a good load under her nose.

'The body's been here a while then?' she asked, though it was more a statement of fact; if the body had decomposed enough to expel enough gas to turn Jadyn's stomach, then she doubted it was fresh.

'No idea how long though,' said Harry. 'Scene of Crime team is on their way, so we can leave that to Rebecca. It's definitely ripe, though.'

'District Surgeon?'

Harry gave a nod.

'Margaret will probably be here before they are,' he said. 'Not that she'll be able to tell us anything we don't already know.'

'Those boxes always need ticking,' said Gordy. 'What do we know so far?'

'Not much,' said Harry. 'Male, probably in his forties, though that's hard to tell, what with everything that's been done to the poor bastard.'

'You're right, that's not much.'

'His eyes are gone,' Harry added. 'And his face looks like it's been torn apart somehow.'

'Could be birds took them,' Gordy suggested. 'Crows, buzzard, a kestrel, or something.'

'Perhaps,' said Harry, and Gordy heard the tone that told her it very much wasn't birds.

'His eyes, though,' she said. 'Why would someone take his eyes?'

'Souvenirs would be my first guess,' Harry said. 'I've seen worse taken from a body.'

'We both have,' said Gordy.

'Maybe worse is the wrong word,' Harry added. 'It's all worse, isn't it? There's nowt I can think of that's worse than having someone do something like this to you, then take a keepsake home to remind them of the event.'

'Unless they were conscious at the time,' said Gordy, working hard to not smile at that infiltration of the Dales into Harry's sentence. 'And how do you mean, torn apart?'

'The skin's not just cut, it's been ripped away from the face,' Harry explained. 'Jadyn thought it was a Halloween mask when he first saw it.'

As they closed in on the body, Harry sneezed. The sneeze then turned into another cough, and Gordy watched as he buried his face in his hands, his shoulders racked with the force of it.

'If you don't mind me saying so, you sound absolutely bloody awful,' said Gordy.

'I do mind.'

'And yet I still said it anyway.'

'It's just a cold, that's all,' said Harry, continuing on his way. 'I'll be fine.'

'You don't sound fine.'

'Well, I am, so stop asking.'

Gordy walked no further, waited for Harry to realise she wasn't at his side, and gave the DCI a hard stare, the kind she knew that even Paddington Bear would be proud of.

'I've had one of those days already, Harry,' she said, folding her arms. 'One of those days where, to be frank, right now I'm just not in the mood to take any nonsense. Not even from you.'

Gordy watched her words bounce off Harry, but her tone had sunk in a little, so that was something.

'There's no nonsense here,' Harry said. 'Just a job to do.'

'On your day off.'

'This is important.'

'And so is buying a house with Grace and not being halfway into the grave yourself by the sounds of it.'

Harry sneezed.

'Enough of the drama, can we just get on?' he asked, and took a step closer to the body.

Gordy didn't move.

Harry stopped and turned around to face her once more, wiping his nose on his sleeve as he did so. He went to speak, but Gordy got in there first.

'Right now,' she said, 'I'm trying to decide whether kicking a superior officer up his royally stubborn arse is the only thing that'll have him listen to what I'm saying. Because you're going no further, Harry. Not one more bloody step.'

Gordy watched as Harry exhaled hard out of his nostrils, an angry bull not best pleased with being challenged. But she could tell that he was fading, even as he stood in front of her and did his best to puff out his chest.

'I'm fine,' Harry said. 'And Grace is fine, too. She understands what it's like being with a police officer.'

'I don't care if she sent you over here herself while playing a fanfare on a bloody kazoo!' Gordy replied. 'You're to get yourself home right now. And there'll be no arguing, either, so don't even try. Get home, have a hot toddy, rest. You're the second person today I've given those exact instructions. And I'm not a fan of repeating myself.'

Gordy almost laughed then as her words caused a faint look of shock to ripple across Harry's face at being talked to like that.

'You seem to be confused by our roles here,' he said. 'I'm the SIO on this.'

'Are you bollocks, like!' said Gordy, alarming herself a little, not just with what she'd just said, but how she'd said it.

Harry's eyes widened even further.

'Detective Inspector,' Harry began, but Gordy was having none of it. Not today.

'Don't Detective Inspector me,' she said. 'I've had one of those mornings, one bubbling over with nonsense and idiocy and ignored illness, and I'm having no more of it. You're to go home immediately. Call Grace, tell her that's what you're doing, then get yourself to bed.'

'You can't order me around.'

'I just did.'

Gordy watched Harry's shoulders sag.

'You're not going to stop until I bugger off, are you?'

'No,' Gordy said. 'I can match you with stubbornness any day of the week, believe you me.'

A faint smile broke across Harry's face, and he looked over again at the body.

'You know, now that I think about it, I reckon you can handle this after all,' he said. 'You don't need me. Probably best I head home, take the day off.'

'Agreed.'

'I'll be leaving it in your capable hands, then, Detective Inspector Haig.'

'Wise decision.'

'All of my decisions are wise,' said Harry. 'And a hot toddy will help, you think?'

'A good slug of single malt, lots of lemon juice, lots of honey, and some boiling water. Can't beat it.'

'Ingredients I'm surprised to say I actually have in the house,' said Harry.

'Then, at risk of repeating myself, do bugger off,' said Gordy.

Harry headed back to the cordon tape, lifted it over his head, and stepped outside of the crime scene.

'Have fun,' he called back to Gordy without turning around. He lifted a hand in farewell, only to cut himself off with another cough.

'I doubt that,' Gordy muttered, pulled on a pair of disposable rubber gloves, and made her way across the last few metres between her and the body.

SEVEN

As golden hours went, Gordy knew that for what she was now investigating, hers was long gone. She had always thought the term itself to be a little misleading. The principle was that there was a short period of time after an offence had taken place when the police had the best opportunities for collecting forensic evidence, to hopefully lead to a quick arrest. It was never an hour, for sure, but even if she stretched it to a few hours, perhaps even a full twenty-four, Gordy had a sense that whatever she or the forensics team was going to find here was going to be scant at best, and most likely non-existent.

The sickly smell of the body reached Gordy sooner than she expected and she was thankful for the dab of vapour rub under her nose Harry had given her. But still, the stench worked its evil spell. It pushed its way into her nostrils and down into the back of her throat, thin tendrils of putrefaction burrowing deep.

Careful as she was to not breathe through her mouth, Gordy could still taste it, and only years in the police gave her the strength to ignore the urge to gag.

The familiarity of it is the worst, really, she thought, noticing how subtle notes in the aroma could remind her of meals she'd left in the fridge too long, odd forgotten Tupperware filled with mystery meats found lurking at the back behind yoghurt and vegetables and cheese. The problems Gordy had encountered so far that day crumbled to nothing as death now called her forward.

The crime scene itself was as shocking as it was barren. Yes, there was a body, and she could see the violence that had been carried out on it, but that was about it. It was tied to a post in a field, its arms outstretched, and there was nothing around that she could see right then, which would suggest the reason for it being there in the first place, or how it had even got there.

The field was empty, no animals were grazing, the boundary of walls a grey-white as though built of huge, ancient teeth. As far as she could see, there were no drag marks in the grass between where it stood and the gate. This suggested to Gordy that it had taken place in the field itself, rather than elsewhere, and then the body moved here postmortem.

Gordy looked about the field, mainly to give her eyes a break from staring at the awful vision in front of her. Had this person, whoever it was, been brought here by their killer? Was it under duress, or had they known them? Was there more than one perpetrator involved? What the hell kind of circumstances could lead to something like this in the first place?

She imagined how the field would be in the dark hours, with no light from nearby houses, and only the stars to light the way. The nights had been thick with cloud the past few days and under such cover, terrible deeds could be committed without the risk of witnesses.

Rubbing her eyes, Gordy focused again on the body. She circled it widely, seeing if she could spot anything out of the ordinary, beyond that of a body trussed up like a scarecrow, and without any eyes.

With nothing jumping out at her, Gordy closed in on the body, the smell of it growing ever stronger as the wind whipped at her coat, a cold blast pushing down her neck, causing her to shiver. She stood in front of it and stared.

The body was upright, its feet touching the ground, knees bent a little, the head pulled back with tape around its forehead and attached to the main post. Getting the body into that position would've taken a good amount of strength, but that was assuming the victim had already been dead or unconscious.

If the victim had still been conscious when it was done, however, some serious persuasion would've been needed. She'd seen just how effective threats could be at forcing people to do the seemingly perverse and deadly—a family at gunpoint, a loved one thrown in the boot of a car, and worse.

Gordy saw that the body was tied to the post by a thick rope wrapped around the waist and under the shoulders. Another thinner post was attached to the larger one somehow, though the means of attachment was hidden, the thin post threaded through the sleeves of the victim's jacket. Around the victim's arms, more rope had been tied.

The whole, gore-laden tableau was almost religious. The body hung up as though crucified, with the top of the main post extending just above the victim's head, giving it the impression of a makeshift cross.

Was that what this was? A killing done in the name of whatever God or entity the one responsible believed in? She had experienced something like that before, the case years ago now, but it still haunted her. But how could it not? Children had been involved, their parents, and the madness of it all, the brutal slayings and the wide-eyed, fanatical belief of the killers ... *No,* she thought, *now was not the time to be haunted by those particular ghosts.*

Gordy forced herself to look at the shattered remains of the man's face, though at first it was hard to make out any detail beyond the absolute demolition of his features.

The eye sockets were black and hollow, the eyelids crusted open with dried blood. The mouth was open and she could see that a number of teeth were missing, others hanging on by the root. She noticed, too, that the tape holding the head back was also ripped, the gashes revealing deep wounds beneath. If the victim had been conscious at the time... Well, it didn't bear thinking about, yet she did anyway, unable not to, her mind filling with a cataclysmic blast of imagined horrors.

Managing to close the hellish vision down, Gordy was about to lean in for a closer look when a shout caught her attention. She turned around to see a small, stout figure marching towards her, a hand held aloft in a wave. It was the District Surgeon, Margaret Shaw.

Gordy returned the wave, welcoming the distraction, and stepped back from the body to wait for the new arrival, moving herself out beyond the cordon tape.

'Detective Inspector Haig,' Margaret said, as she came to stand in front of Gordy. She was dressed in a waxed jacket that looked like it should've been committed to the bin years ago, a woolly hat full of badly repaired holes, and denim trousers and green Wellington boots, both of which were covered in numerous patch repairs, like a barely controlled rash. 'No DCI Grimm? I was under the impression he was here.'

'Oh, he was,' Gordy said. 'And now he's not.'

Margaret frowned.

'I'm sensing there's a lot more behind what you've just said than you're letting on.'

'I sent him home.'

'Are we talking about the same person here?' Margaret asked, a laugh curling her words as much as the corners of her mouth. 'Male, face like a road accident, and about as stubborn as a lid of Marmite?'

Gordy chuckled.

'That's a very specific reference.'

'Ruined my breakfast this morning,' Margaret said. 'Couldn't twist the bugger off at all. Pouring boiling water on it didn't help either. Had to make do with jam.'

'Not quite the same.'

'I don't even know what kind of jam it was,' Margaret said.

'Label was faded, and it didn't help that I can't read my own writing.'

'So, it was your jam, then? You make your own?'

'Which should've been warning enough, don't you think? At a guess, it was damson. Could've been blackberry. Hard to tell, really. The overall flavour, though, was definitely ... jammy.' She looked past Gordy to the body. 'Which is a good way to describe the smell coming off our friend here, don't you think?'

'Jammy?' said Gordy, unable to hide her disgust or her agreement. 'Think I'll remember that one.'

Margaret was quiet for a moment and Gordy watched the woman stare at the body, brow furrowed as though deep in thought.

'Well,' she said at last, 'I'm confident in my assessment that whoever he is, he's definitely dead. And has been for a while.'

'A fair assessment,' Gordy agreed. 'Forensics are on their way.'

'I know,' Margaret replied. 'Rebecca sent me a text. She'll be disappointed Harry's not here, though. He's one of the few she gets on with.'

'Few? You mean detectives?'

Margaret shook her head.

'No, I mean men,' she said. 'For a while, I thought she'd taken a shine to him. Might even have hoped she had, too, if you don't mind me saying so. But I read that completely wrong.'

'Harry and Rebecca?' Gordy laughed. 'Can you imagine?'

'I can, and the thought of it was mildly terrifying.' Margaret leaned in. 'She's got a new fella, you know.'

'Has she, now?' said Gordy.

'I'm not supposed to know; Rebecca's so private about anything like that. But I found out.'

'A bit of detective work yourself, there, then?'

'Mother's intuition,' said Margaret. 'I don't actually know anything about him, not even a name, but there's definitely a man on the scene now.'

'I'm thinking we've strayed a little from the subject,' said Gordy.

'Well, there's not much for me to say or do here, is there?' said Margaret. 'May as well make the most of the time with a little chinwag. Chocolate digestive?'

To Gordy's surprise, Margaret was holding out a packet of biscuits.

'You often carry biscuits around with you?' she asked, declining the offer with a shake of her head.

'No, I don't,' said Margaret, taking a nibble from one of the chocolate-covered treats, 'but I'm already viewing it as something I may do from now on. Do we know anything about who he is, then?'

'Not yet, no,' said Gordy. 'There's nothing jumping out from the scene itself. Maybe Rebecca's team will find something useful.'

'She usually does,' said Margaret. 'And speak of the devil ...'

Gordy saw two large, white vans coming along the lane.

Margaret glanced back at the body.

'It's an odd one, isn't it?' she said. 'Who does something like this?'

'It's the why as much as anything else that bothers me,' said Gordy. 'There's a reason for it, I've no doubt, otherwise why go to all this trouble? But what it is, I can't even begin to guess.'

Margaret left Gordy for a moment, walking around behind the body, still nibbling the biscuit.

'Well, at least he died with a view,' she said. 'Green fells, dry stone walls.'

'And a pile of rubbish,' Gordy sighed, glancing back at the blocked gated entrance to the field.

The vans had now parked up, the forensics team tumbling out of the vehicles to ready themselves for the job ahead. Another vehicle had joined them as well, and Gordy saw Jen making her way along the road to where Jadyn was acting as scene guard.

'I'd best get over there and speak to them,' Gordy said.

'I'll wait here for Rebecca,' said Margaret. 'Need to discuss a few things.'

Gordy paused at this.

'What? You mean you've spotted something?'

Margaret shook her head and lifted the biscuits.

'God, no,' she said, popping the rest of the biscuit she'd been nibbling into her mouth and pulling out another. 'I want to find out more about her man; she's been avoiding me like the plague, but she can't get away from me here. Not when I've got biscuits!'

EIGHT

Having sent a message to Grace, to let her know he was heading home to lie in a dark room and feel sorry for himself, Harry had driven back to Gayle.

Smudge followed him upstairs and jumped onto the bed, settling down at the bottom as Harry slumped onto the mattress, curtains closed, the room cool and dark.

Harry closed his eyes, desperate for sleep to take him. Whatever this was, it had been mooching around in the background for a few days now, and he'd done his best to ignore it, to force it to sod off by sheer force of will. But he'd woken up that morning feeling like death and, though he'd tried to battle through, the only thing for it was to rest.

Harry hated to rest. He had no time in his life for just sitting down and doing very little. He wasn't religious by any means, but he'd always thought that if there was ever a sin he despised, it was sloth. That wasn't to say it was any worse than all the others, it was just that he had a real problem with the conscious decision to waste your own life, to let it just drift on by, serving no purpose, each day like all the others. What the hell was the point of that?

As far as Harry was concerned, life was all about decisions. That's what it boiled down to in the end. The enemy of making the most of what you had was indecision; life was all about standing at those numerous forks in the road, deciding to go left or right, and accepting the consequences.

Yes, he understood that not everyone had the same opportunities, but what use was there in comparing? *Do that, and all you end up with is inertia,* he thought. He was and always had been fully signed up to making the best of what you had; decide what you're going to do with it and keep moving forward. And, above all, never do nothing, because making no decision was still a decision and time didn't wait around for anyone, good or bad, rich or poor.

Harry coughed, rolled over, coughed again, tried to shift his mind away from the sudden sky dive into the loose, and no doubt nonsensical, philosophies that drove him. Then he sat up, punched his pillows, flipped one over to the cold side, chucked the other off the bed, and thumped back down again onto the mattress.

Smudge huffed, wriggled, and let out a long, slow breath.

Harry tried to force his mind to empty. Meditation was good, or so he'd heard, and that's what it was all about, wasn't it, emptying the mind? But no sooner did he try, than more stuff pushed its way in. Whereas a few minutes ago he'd only been bothered about the body in the field, he'd now not only swept through philosophy, but quickly and unwittingly moved on to everything from Ben and Liz and their life together, the team, how Dave was doing as the new PCSO, how they'd all cope with Gordy moving away to Somerset, whether it was good or not to have two members of the team— Jadyn and Jen—dating, if it was okay to have Smudge and Fly in the office so much ...

Harry sat up and swore so loudly that bright lights burst inside his skull with the pain of it. Then he remembered something Gordy had said before he'd left the field and thought, *well, why the hell not?* He was on leave after all, wasn't he?

Swinging himself out of bed, Harry headed downstairs to the kitchen. He grabbed a sorry-looking lemon from the fruit bowl, a jar of honey and a bottle of whisky from a cupboard, and flicked on the kettle.

The whisky, Harry noticed, wasn't a single malt, but a bourbon, and a decent one, too, left over from Christmas. It had been a gift from Ben and Liz, and he decided it would probably be best if he kept that to himself, guessing that Gordy might not approve.

The kettle clicked off. Harry poured a healthy slug of the bourbon into a mug, sploshed in a little more for good measure, poured in plenty of honey, then added all the juice from the lemon, before topping everything up with boiling water. A good stir followed, and he lifted the mug to his lips.

The whisky-laced steam from the mug shot straight up Harry's nose.

'Bloody hell, Gordy!' he roared, pulling the mug away as he tried to deal with the sting in his nostrils and his now-watering eyes.

Harry tried again, this time a little more carefully, and took a sip. The liquid slipped down a treat, a warming, sweet and sour hit of something he had a sudden urge to spend the rest of the day drinking. Whether it was doing him any good, he wasn't really sure, but he was happy to give it a go, and shuffled his way through to the lounge to finish it.

With the hot toddy finished, Harry leaned back into the sofa. Smudge was sitting up next to him and she snuggled in, pushing her nose under his hand.

Harry closed his eyes, ignored whatever it was scratching at the back of his mind from what he had seen in the fields over by Kettlewell, and passed out.

BACK AT THE CRIME SCENE, Gordy was relishing being in charge. She loved working with Harry and respected his idio-syncratic approach to getting things done. His military bearing was impossible to ignore, and it gave him a certain power and authority.

She, however, didn't have that, and didn't want it, either. Instead, she liked to give people space to just get on, while keeping an eye on things. Ordering people about, getting them to do as they were told, had its place, and when the time was right, she'd step in.

Harry, on the other hand, was a warrior, a front-line soldier ready to take the fight to anyone who dared, and he certainly got things done. Gordy, though, kept her toughness a little more well-hidden, in no small thanks to her great aunt Maggie McPherson's husband, Uncle Charlie.

She'd spent many days during her younger years, staying with them in their small house in Glencoe village, either baking Maggie's famous porridge oat biscuits, or out in the hills with Charlie. He had stories to tell, did Charlie, his life as a ghillie for one of the estates in the highlands, of stalking deer, fishing, even hawking. He'd been in the war, but those tales he kept to himself.

Gordy could still remember the first time he had taken her out with one of his goshawks and the sense that something oddly mystical connected her to that bird as it sat on her gloved arm. But one of her most enduring memories of her time with him was when, coming down the glen late one evening in her uncle's car, they'd struck a bird. Charlie had stopped the vehicle to check on it, but then Gordy had opened her door to find an owl staring up at her, clearly stunned. Without thinking, she had reached down for it, and the bird had simply stepped up onto her arm. Sitting back up in the car with the owl, she'd watched her uncle check it over with his gnarled, gentle hands.

'Broken wing,' he'd said.

'Can you fix it?'

'I can try.'

With help from a friend, who was also the local vet, the bird had healed. When it was ready to fly again, it had shown little interest in heading back to the wild. It loved to be on the wing, dancing in the thermals, but would always circle back to Uncle Charlie. It quickly became his favourite bird, not to hunt with, but as a companion, perching on his shoulder, pecking at his ear. Gordy laughed at the memory of the old man asleep in his chair, the bird on his shoulder, eyes closed.

'You can learn a lot from an owl,' Charlie had said one day. 'They're whisper-quiet when they fly, and they're always observing, aren't they? Those great eyes of theirs, taking it all in. And they don't go around wasting time hunting this and that; they're patient, they know things, and when they're ready, they strike.'

Gordy hadn't really understood at the time, but as she'd grown older, that, and other lessons from Charlie, had started to reveal themselves. The old man had also been proud of his heritage, his family name, the history of it. Whenever she found him wearing the kilt, which was often, he'd touch the pin that held it and say, 'Remember the cat, Gordy; remember the cat!'

The pin was the shape of a claymore sword, and it was engraved with the clan motto, *touch not the cat bot a glove.*

Uncle Charlie had gone on to explain, 'Never touch a cat if its claws are ungloved.'

Gordy remembered just looking at him, confused.

'Ungloved?' she'd asked.

'An ungloved cat is a cat with its claws out,' he'd continued. 'It might look all fluffy and cuddly and calm, but if its claws are unsheathed, you could be heading for an almighty scratching if you piss it off, right?'

'Ummm, yeah, I suppose,' Gordy had answered, still looking a bit bemused.

Uncle Charlie had smiled back at her and jabbed her gently in her shoulder with a finger.

'What it really boils down to is that you don't need to look and act tough, to be tough,' he had said. 'So, if you can, be like the cat, quiet and unassuming, but always ready to strike if you have to. Another way to think about it is to walk softly, and carry a big stick.'

Which was why, when, after the photographer had finished his ghoulish task of recording the crime scene, and one of the forensics team had told her to shift it and let the real police through, she'd remembered that motto very clearly indeed.

'I've not seen you before,' Gordy said, voice calm.

'Why don't you take a sodding photograph, then?' the man replied, his voice muffled by the face mask over his mouth and nose.

The response, as odd as it was, had only served to have Gordy sharpen her claws and as he tried to push past, she stepped in front to block his way and in doing so noticed a faint whiff of alcohol in the air.

'Shift, I've a job to do,' the man said.

Gordy was very tempted to ask, *Are you sure this is the right one?* but leaned back into the wise words of Uncle Charlie and, like a cat, took control of the situation by way of being nice and cuddly.

'Are you okay?' she asked.

'What?'

'Are you okay? You seem on edge. Is there anything I can do?'

'Getting out of the way would be a start,' the man groused, and side-stepped Gordy.

Gordy matched his movements with her own.

'Let me through,' the man demanded, and jabbed a finger over Gordy's shoulder. 'That over there looks like a right bloody mess to me, so the sooner I can get on with sorting it out, the sooner you can get back to whatever it is you do up here to keep yourselves busy. Arrest a sheep or two, that kind of thing. No, scratch that, arrest the farmers instead; they're no doubt out there getting amorous with their fluffy little friends, aren't they? You know what people are like round here where it's all rural and remote ...'

To be on the receiving end of such unexpected and uncalled-for nastiness, from someone who was, for all intents and purposes, a colleague, took Gordy by surprise, but still she refused to move or raise her voice. Shouting had never really been her thing. And she had found often that as her anger and frustration grew, she became all the quieter. Unnervingly so, she had to admit.

'This isn't funny,' he said.

'You're right,' Gordy replied, and with a smile, held out a hand. 'Perhaps I should introduce myself? I'm the SIO, Detective Inspector Haig.'

'What do you want, a badge? A round of applause?'

Gordy's smile faded. She clenched her teeth behind pursed lips, took a long, slow breath in and out.

'No,' she said, her voice calmer still, and quieter, 'but just so you're aware, I'll have your badge if you continue to talk to me like that or refer to the victim as *a right bloody mess* again. Respect costs nothing.'

'For you or him?'

'Both.'

The man laughed, and Gordy was relieved for them both that she couldn't see beneath the face mask, or she would probably have been tempted to slap his lips clean off his face. Again, she noticed a sharp tang in the air from the man's breath.

'Heavy night last night?' she asked.

'What?'

'You smell like a distillery.'

The man's eyes widened.

'What? I do not! And no, it wasn't, not very anyway, but what's that got to do with you?'

Spotting someone approaching behind the man, Gordy leaned in. The man was taller than her, but height had never been an issue when it came to getting her point across.

'I'm going to be watching you,' she said, her voice now a whisper, her smile back on her face, though this time her eyes were very much not joining in. 'Not just right now, and not just today, but for a very, very long time indeed.'

'What? You can't, you're not part of the forensics te—'

'Hello, Ms Sowerby,' Gordy said with unreserved cheeriness in her voice, and completely ignoring what the man was saying, as Pathologist Rebecca Sowerby came to stand with them.

'DI Haig,' Rebecca replied, her eyes darting between the man and Gordy. 'Is everything okay?'

'Just getting to know your team,' Gordy said. 'Isn't that right, Mr ...?'

'What? Oh, Tippett,' the man said, blurting his name out.

'He was just telling me how important it is to maintain respect for the victim,' Gordy continued. 'Isn't that correct, Mr Tippett?'

'Respect? Yes, that's what I was ... I mean, it's very important.'

'Don't want to keep you from your work though,' said Gordy, and stepped back to allow Tippett to move past.

Tippett shuffled quickly away from Gordy and over to the crime scene.

'He's not very easy to like, is he?' Gordy said, turning her attention to Sowerby, but as she did so, a yell from behind yanked her around to where Tippett had headed. The man was sprawled on the ground, struggling to get back up onto his feet, his white paper overalls smudged with grass and mud.

'I'm okay, I'm okay,' he said, pushing himself up onto his feet.

'I've never fired someone this early in an investigation,' said Sowerby. 'But there's always a first time, isn't there?'

'Keep an eye on him,' Gordy said. 'I think he had one or two drinks too many last night.'

'What? He's pissed?'

Gordy shook her head.

'He's rude, and probably nursing a hangover, but I don't think he's drunk.'

Sowerby wasn't listening.

'Tippett?'

She beckoned him over with her hand.

'Breathe on me,' she said.

Tippett's eyes flashed at Gordy, then back at Sowerby.

'What?'

'I'm not one for repeating myself.'

Tippett breathed.

'Back to the van,' Sowerby said, and pointed back up the field. 'Now.'

'Why?' He stared at Gordy again, his eyes now narrow and mean. 'What did she say? I'm not pi—'

'Move!' said Sowerby, her voice a sharp bark.

Tippett hesitated for a moment, gave the impression he was on the cusp of saying something, then his shoulders sagged, and he slouched his way back to the vans.

'No Harry, then?' Sowerby asked, as they watched the man walk back across the field.

Gordy explained why.

'Probably good that he's not here, then,' said Sowerby, and nodded towards Tippett. 'Or we'd be dealing with two bodies, wouldn't we?'

Gordy laughed at that.

'If you need anything, let me know,' she said, and held up the cordon tape up for Sowerby to step under.

'Better staff, it seems,' Sowerby replied, then headed over to the body.

NINE

Harry woke to the sound of someone drilling into his head. It gave him such a start that he sat bolt upright, realised too late he was still in the armchair in the lounge, his head swam, he lost his balance, and he fell forwards to land on the floor on his knees beside Smudge.

The dog raised her head to stare at him, then slumped back down with a huff and a solitary thump of his tail.

The drill was still going, but the sound soon morphed into one that made a little more sense, and Harry reached for his phone.

'Grimm,' he said, answering the call.

'Harry? It's Jim.'

Harry heard tension in the PCSO's voice.

'Jim? Everything okay? I'm on leave today, and I'm rough as—'

'I know,' Jim said, 'It's Dad, Harry ...'

'What is?'

Harry was confused. Why had Jim called him, and not Gordy or Matt or anyone else on the team?

'He's had an accident, Harry. At the farm, I mean. Mum just called. She's in a proper panic, like. I'm heading there now.'

'An accident? What's happened? Is he okay?'

'I—' Harry heard Jim's voice catch in his throat. 'I don't know,

Harry. I called you because you were the first number I hit. Sorry. I just needed to let the team know. That I wouldn't be around, I mean. That's all. It doesn't sound good.'

'I'll let the team know,' Harry said, now very much awake.

'He fell or something, slipped, I think. Landed badly, managed to pull an old gate down on top of himself as he tried to catch his fall. Then the sheep panicked, and he got smashed about a bit. I don't even know when it happened. Mum only found him because he'd not come in for his tea. Sounds like he'd been lying there in agony for ages.'

Harry checked his watch, realised evening was creeping in through the windows, the air cold enough in the room to turn his breath ghost-like. Where the hell had the day gone? How could it be teatime already?

'Ambulance on its way?' Harry asked.

'Yes,' said Jim. 'I'm only in Bainbridge, so I'll be back before it arrives. I'm sorry, I just need to be there, you know?'

'You don't apologise, not for this,' said Harry. 'You've done the right thing, letting me know. Family first, Jim, family first.'

'I know, but—'

'Stop talking, hang up, and go,' Harry said. 'Your parents need you.'

'Thanks, Harry,' Jim said, then the line went dead.

Harry spent a moment or two just kneeling on the floor. He didn't feel any better, but he also didn't feel any worse, so he had to assume that in itself was a good thing. He reached out and gave Smudge a scratch. She thumped her tail softly on the carpet.

'You need a walk,' he said, pushing himself up onto his feet, and talking to himself as much as Smudge. 'Come on.'

A few minutes later, Harry was outside, Smudge walking to heel on the lead. The day was grey. A thick fog was gathering in layers on the sides of Wetherfell, thin fingers of it stretching over the walls to reach down into the valley.

The air was cool and flinty as he breathed it in deep to freeze the back of his throat. The chill of it made him cough, but he walked on, hopping over a stile to take a footpath across the fields just beyond the ford across Gayle Beck.

The path eventually led to Aysgill Force, a waterfall that seemed to almost keep itself to itself, happy to let the larger falls of Aysgarth draw the crowds. But it was no less impressive for that, and in spate after a storm, the forty-foot drop would be a thunderous caldron of water brown with peat, boiling through white horse tails as the fall threw itself down into the darkness below. But Harry would not be making his way there right now.

He was weary, a little unsteady on his feet, and the path was crisscrossed by tree roots that would, he was sure, take delight in tripping him up to throw him down into the beck far below.

With no sheep in the fields, Harry let Smudge off the lead, and she wandered off for a sniff and a snuffle. Watching her mooch around the tufts of grass, which stuck up out of the meadow grass like the badly buried heads of trolls, Harry paused, breathed, closed his eyes, and allowed himself to just be in the moment. He was cold, but that only helped to stir his mind, and he was soon thinking back on what he had seen at the field.

The call from Jim worried him, true enough, but there was nothing he could do about that for now. Jim was away to be with his mum and dad, and that was good. He had no doubt that the PCSO would be in touch soon to let him know how his dad was doing. They could hold off on talking about the time Jim would need off to help out back at the farm as and when; there was no rush.

Harry's thoughts then drifted to Grace. He would have to speak to her, let her know that he hadn't died of some awful and rare complication, ask about the houses, but even as he thought about that, his mind was tracking back across the field near Kettlewell. Something was bothering him still, and it wasn't just the whole scarecrow thing, either. But what?

Harry realised he was scratching his forehead, as though doing so would force the quandary to the front of his mind. It didn't.

Instead, he realised how cold he was getting, as a breeze cut through the field he was standing in, causing him to shudder.

'Smudge!'

Hearing his voice, Smudge trotted over to stand beside him as Harry reached down to clip in the lead. After checking his phone to see that he had no signal at all, and with no one else to speak with, Harry decided Smudge was better than nothing. She was a very good listener.

'There's something not right,' he said, as they made their way back towards Gayle, the grey stones of the houses now seeming to burrow themselves beneath thick shadows. 'And I know you're a dog, and I know you don't actually understand any of what I'm saying, but bear with me ...'

Harry fell quiet for a moment, casting his mind back to the crime scene. He'd not spoken with Gordy since she'd sent him off with a flea in his ear, so he had no idea what, if anything, Sowerby had uncovered, but no matter how he looked at it, no matter how many times he wandered around that field in his mind, it wasn't the body he was drawn to. Something else was there, but what?

Back at the stile, which would take them out of the field and back down to the lane into Gayle, Harry spotted something stuffed into the wall. He reached for it, prising it out from the gap in the stones it had been shoved in. It was a faded plastic bottle, one that had, at some point in its life, contained something fizzy and filled with sugar. Now all it had inside it was a slug or two and some brown, sludgy water.

Harry stuffed the bottle into his pocket.

'Who does that?' he said to Smudge as she followed him through the stile. 'How hard can it be to take your own litter home?'

And right then, Harry knew.

TEN

Harry was in his RAV, and on the phone to Grace.

'What do you mean, you're driving over to the crime scene?'

He could hear the frustration in her voice.

'There's something I need to look at,' Harry replied.

'But it's the evening, and it's dark!' Grace replied. 'You won't see anything! And, unless you've had a miraculous recovery, you're still ill! And don't go pretending you're not. I can hear it in your voice, you're coughing, and you haven't stopped sniffing.'

'It's just a cold.'

'Well, earlier today, your face looked like it was falling off,' Grace snapped back. 'Gordy sent you home because you were and are too ill to work. What makes you think you're any different now?'

'I've rested,' Harry said, then added for good measure, 'and I had a hot toddy.'

Harry heard Grace swear, though she had obviously pulled the phone away from her ear to do so, her voice distant, but no less pissed off.

'You're impossible, you know that, don't you?'

'I'm just going over for a look, that's all,' Harry said. 'I have to.'

'At what?' Grace asked. 'And no, you don't have to, do you? Can't you just ask the rest of the team who were there? Call Gordy, she'll help. If it's something you've remembered seeing, just call her and ask.'

'I need to look for myself,' Harry said. 'This is something that I don't think anyone else noticed.'

'And let me guess; only Mr DCI Harry Grimm did because he has extra special eyes which see things no one else can ...'

Harry allowed them both a moment of quiet before he spoke again.

'All I'm doing is going for a drive, Grace, that's all,' he said, trying to explain without saying too much. 'I'm not chasing down a murderer or anything like that. I'm not going to arrest anyone because there's no one to arrest. Not yet, anyway. I'm just going over there to look at something, that's all. I'm just looking.'

'Rubbish.'

'Exactly,' said Harry.

'What?'

'That's what I'm going to look at,' Harry continued. 'There's this big pile of rubbish blocking the entrance to the field. I think it's important.'

'And what's that got to do with anything?'

'I don't know,' Harry said. 'But it's an itch I have to scratch.'

Grace fell quiet. Harry listened to her breathing.

'So, what about the other houses, then?' he asked, eventually. 'How did you get on?'

'What about them?'

'Did you like any of them?'

'I think so,' Grace said, and the anger and frustration in her voice abated a little. 'They all need work, though.'

'Well, that just means we can make it how we want it,' Harry said. 'Put our own stamp on it.'

'But you hate DIY.'

'No, I don't.'

'You actually said, "*I hate DIY*," then went on to explain, in great detail, exactly why. You were very specific.'

'Then I'll just have to learn not to.'

Grace laughed just enough to break the mood even more.

'Look, I'll send you the photos,' she said. 'We ended up looking at a couple of places we'd not been told about because they only came on the market in the last couple of days. The details hadn't even been sorted out, so I can't send you a description or anything like that.'

'Photos are fine,' said Harry. 'Better actually.'

'You'd best be going,' Grace said. 'Make sure you're not late to bed, though, won't you? I can come over if you want?'

Harry smiled.

'And have me give you this?' he said, a cough crushing the end of his sentence.

'No, you're right, maybe not.'

With a final, *love you*, Harry stuffed his phone in his pocket.

Grace had a point, he thought; he could call Gordy, but he didn't want to. Not that he would ever have told Grace that. Anyway, Gordy had had a long day herself, so he was fairly sure the last thing she needed was him calling her and peppering her evening with questions. No, it made more sense for him to just drive over there himself and have a look around. It would also make him feel useful.

With Smudge tagging along for the ride, and Harry happy to have her with him for the company, he started the engine and turned the vehicle around. He'd parked in the area on the other side of the ford across the beck, and with his window down, listened to the water bubbling down into Hawes and beyond as he pulled away to head up Beggarman's Road, the ripples whispering secrets to the dark.

The night had grown darker still, and the drive up the valley was an ominous experience. No stars were breaking through, and the fell-side showed only a handful of twinkling lights, like distant sparklers, shining out from the windows of cottages and farms. Towards the top of the road, Harry became acutely aware of the steep drop-off to his right. He wasn't driving directly next to it, as he was heading up, not down, but it still seemed to yawn at him, as though it was trying to suck him down into its thick darkness to swallow him whole.

At the top of the valley, the road pulled Harry onwards and over into Wharfedale. Had it been daytime, and a clear day, then he would've been able to see far off towards the distant mountains of Ingleborough and Pen-y-ghent. Instead, all he was aware of was a vast space before him swathed in night, a sparsely populated dale where every corner, every wall, every tree and field and stream held tales and stories and memories no one alive could recall.

Rolling along the lane, bouncing from shadow to shadow between bends and dips and hills, Harry lost all sense of time. His head was still full of the cold and his mind focused on nothing but his headlights as they cut through the gloom ahead. From some fields, bright pairs of eyes glinted back, staring at him as he sped along. An owl on the wing danced over the road, its feathers aglow as it swept past on its hunt for food.

When Harry eventually found his way to Kettlewell, he was reminded of Hawes. It was a small town, but he could tell that there was life in the place. Slowing down, he passed the warm, orange glow oozing from the windows of a couple of pubs, both busy with people having a good night, sharing beer and a natter with friends, their laughter chasing them to the bar.

Harry wasn't tempted to stop, but he did find himself hankering after a pint of Wensleydale Gold or Gamekeeper at The Fountain in Hawes. That chair in the corner of the bar would welcome him, he was sure, and he could think of nothing he wanted more than to call Grace and tell her to meet him there in a couple of hours, if only for last orders. Then he sneezed, and the sneeze turned into a cough, and that comforting thought of beer and the woman he was buying a house with fizzled like a match flicked into a puddle.

Driving out of Kettlewell, Harry soon found himself on the

lane he had parked up on earlier in the day. Bringing the RAV to a halt, he left Smudge asleep in the back and pushed out into the night, which had grown colder still, a faint glimmer of ice now starting to form on walls and leaves and grass.

Walking towards the entrance into the field, Harry knew the crime scene would have been dealt with, all evidence collected, and Sowerby would be doing what she did better than pretty much any pathologist he'd ever worked with. He would call her in the morning to see if she had found anything of importance.

And yet, even though the body was now gone, there was still a somber air to the place. Harry had noticed it at many crime scenes over the years, and knew it was little more than his mind playing tricks, but death seemed to hang around places after such events, a spectre of the horror that had taken place still wandering, as though lost.

Harry stopped at the pile of rubbish dumped in front of the field, behind which the gate wasn't even visible from the road, pulled his torch out of a pocket, and lit the area up with a lightning-white beam.

At first, he wondered if he'd been making it all up, misremembering perhaps, imagining something in the pile of rubbish because he wanted, maybe needed, it to be there, rather than it actually being there at all.

The beam of his torch caught nothing of importance, and for a minute or two, all Harry could see was mud and soil and rotting vegetation. Then he spotted the reflection of something, and leaned in for a closer look, instinctively reaching into another pocket, this time for a pair of disposable gloves.

On closer inspection, Harry found himself teasing the broken remains of an electric bulb from a large pile of dark soil. As he did so, he saw another, and another, then spotted some grubby-looking coils of clear tubing beneath, no wider than five millimetres in diameter. Elsewhere he saw discarded plastic compost bags, and cheap, plastic plant pots.

Then, a little further off, and so decomposed that at a first, and even second glance, the observer would only see a rotting plant, he saw something he recognised. The leaf shape, though broken and crushed and brown, was distinctive. This was not a native plant, not by any stretch of the imagination. And Harry very much doubted that it had ended up here by accident. Admittedly, you did get instances of a random plant found in a cottage garden, grown from a bag of meadow flower seeds, which happened now and again, much to the surprise of the owners, who then found themselves suddenly in possession of a plant with a considerably higher street value than a handful of carrots and a potato or two.

Harry crushed the leaf and gave it a sniff just to make sure; the smell was faint, but there was enough of it still lingering to confirm what he had been thinking. He knew what he was looking at, what this pile of rubbish was, or at least some of it, at any rate: lamps, cabling, pots, compost, rotting plants … Somewhere in the Dales, someone was growing cannabis.

Judging by what had been dumped at this gate, it wasn't for personal consumption either—the remains of a plant or two cultivated in a greenhouse. This was waste from a considerably larger operation. Which made Harry turn just enough to stare into the quiet field beyond the gate and wonder just what the hell a scarecrow had to do with any of it.

Or maybe it's just a coincidence, he thought, as a cough ripped its way out of his throat. But the trouble with that was, Harry didn't believe in coincidences.

Collecting a few samples and stowing them in a number of evidence bags he always had to hand, Harry headed back to the RAV. Smudge didn't stir when he climbed back behind the steering wheel, placing what he had gathered on the passenger seat beside him.

He wondered what to do next. The pile of rubbish was another crime scene. He had no idea if it was connected to the body found in the field or not. The next course of action, then, was to call Sowerby.

Harry yawned. God, he was tired. And why did his eyes feel like they were about to crust over?

He'd give Sowerby a call in a minute or two. But first, though, he needed to close his eyes just long enough to recharge his batteries and give him the energy to talk shop.

Leaning back in his seat, Harry heard Smudge huff behind him, then closed his eyes.

ELEVEN

When Harry woke up, he was surprised by a bright light blasting into his eyes. His first thought was that someone was shining a torch at him, baffled and no doubt suspicious as to the reason why he had fallen asleep in his vehicle on a lonely country lane in the middle of the night. Then he realised it wasn't a torch at all, but the morning.

'Bloody hell, Smudge! Why didn't you wake me?'

Sitting up, Harry yawned, stretched, and heard his back crack. Behind him, Smudge pushed herself up onto her feet, then leaned back into the rear seat to regard him with an almost regal air.

Harry checked the time. Dawn had broken long enough ago for the sun to be riding the horizon clear and bright and orange.

He yawned again, rubbed his eyes, scratching away at something disconcertingly crusty around his eyelids.

First things first, he thought, grabbing his phone and calling Sowerby. There was no answer, so he left a message, quickly explaining what he had found, and that he needed her team back at the crime scene. Which, he added, was now two crime scenes. He then called Gordy.

'You did what?'

'Fell asleep,' Harry explained for the second time. 'Didn't

realise I was so tired. We need someone over here now to help me cordon off the—'

'What we actually need,' Gordy said, cutting in, 'is a DCI who listens to people when they tell him to stay at home!'

'I only popped over for a look, that's all, follow up on a hunch,' Harry tried to explain, but he knew Gordy wasn't listening.

'A hunch? And how did that go for you, then? Not that well, as far as I can tell.'

'Just because I fell asleep doesn't mean it was a wasted journey,' Harry said, then outlined what he had found, and what his thoughts were on it all.

'A cannabis farm?' said Gordy. 'Bit of a jump, isn't it, from a few odds and sods you've found in a pile of rubbish.'

'That's what it looks like to me,' Harry said. 'There's too much of it to be someone just growing a bit for themselves and a mate or two.'

'But why would they dump it there?'

'Because they're ignorant bastards, that's why,' Harry replied, surprising himself with the venom in his voice. 'Whoever they are, they don't care. Probably cuckooing someone, too, no doubt.'

'What makes you think that?'

'Like I said, this is a lot of kit,' said Harry. 'And it's probably only a small sample of what they've dumped elsewhere. No one running this much gear is going to risk using it on their own property.'

'So, you think they've bullied their way into someone's home, then?'

'It's the most obvious conclusion, isn't it? We've both dealt with this kind of thing before. All they need to do is find someone vulnerable, threaten them, exploit them, and take over their home.'

'What's this got to do with the body in the field, though?' Gordy asked.

'Something, nothing, I don't know either way right now,' said Harry. 'But it's odd that both are here in the same place, isn't it?'

'I know you don't believe in coincidences, Harry,' said Gordy, 'but there's every chance this could actually be one.'

'Only one way to find that out, isn't there?' Harry replied. 'I've left a message with Sowerby. Need her over here again to pick this pile of rubbish apart, see what she can find.'

Gordy said, 'I'm on my way. I just need to make sure Anna's okay, but I'll be there as quick as I can.'

Harry picked up on something in Gordy's voice. It was faint, but he heard strain there, worry, then he remembered what the DI had said the day before.

'Anna? She's no better, then?'

'Like you, she's still ill,' said Gordy. 'Maybe getting worse, but also like you, she's stubborn. Though today I don't think she has enough fight in her to argue with me, or anyone else for that matter, telling her she needs to stay home in bed. So that's where she is right now. And if I find she's left it at any point during the day for any reason other than a drink, a snack, or the loo ...'

'If she's feeling anything like I do, then bed's the best place to be,' Harry said.

At that, Gordy laughed, but the sound curled itself around her disbelief at what Harry had just said.

'Can you hear yourself?' she asked. 'You're impossible!'

Harry coughed, tried to contain it, but that only made it worse, and when it shot out of him, it felt very much like his lungs had ripped themselves out of his throat.

'I'm fine,' he said.

Gordy was quiet for a moment. When she spoke next, her voice was calm, but granite-hard.

'You'll wait there until I, or whoever else I send from the team, arrive,' she said. 'Then you will go home immediately. You will not stop on the way. You will not pass Go and collect two hundred pounds. You will not allow yourself to be distracted. You will go home, you will go to bed. And you will not leave your house until you are at least some ways back to being human. Do you hear?'

'You need me,' said Harry. 'We've two crime scenes now. We've got a body, we've got evidence of cannabis being produced in large quantities; this is a big thing to be dealing with.'

'And I'm a big girl,' Gordy said, 'with one of the best teams either of us has ever worked with. Go home, Harry. Get well. And if we need you, we can do a video call.'

'I don't do video calls.'

'You might just well have to,' Gordy said, then before Harry could say any more, particularly about his almost pathological hatred of speaking to someone on a screen, like some real-life Star Trek experience, she hung up.

Harry turned around to look at Smudge.

'That went well, didn't it?' he said.

Smudge wagged her tail, then stood up. Harry took that as a sign that she needed to get out of the RAV and answer the call of nature.

Walking Smudge down the lane on the lead, Harry's phone buzzed in his pocket. Sowerby had returned his call.

'What do you mean, you've another crime scene?'

Harry once again explained what he had found, though neglected to mention that he'd fallen asleep on the job and should've actually called her a good many hours ago.

'Have you got anything from yesterday?' he then asked.

'The photos will be sent through later, but I don't think they'll give us anything,' Sowerby said. 'Not for me to judge, obviously, but there wasn't much to see.'

'So, we've nothing to go on, then?'

'That's not what I said,' Sowerby replied. 'I'm doing the post-mortem now. Well, not right now, because I'm talking to you, but I'm about to go in and see what's what. Already looks like it's going to be interesting. Fancy joining me?'

'No,' Harry said. 'I would if I could, but feeling as I do, I'm not sure I'd make it all the way there without having to stop for a very extended nap.'

'Send someone, then,' Sowerby suggested. 'Gordy.'

'She's on her way to me now,' said Harry. 'I'll call her.'

'Then I'll be expecting her,' said Sowerby. 'I'll send the team over to deal with this second crime scene as well. Doesn't sound like I'm needed; I'm better here doing this.'

'Agreed,' said Harry.

Sowerby said, 'And you'll be doing the sensible thing and going back to bed, yes?'

'Doesn't look like I've much choice, does it?'

'None, actually,' said Sowerby, and killed the call.

Harry called Gordy again, who informed him that Jen was on her way over to him and would be there shortly.

'And don't worry,' she said, 'I'll report back to you if Sowerby has anything for us.'

With three phone calls in quick succession, Harry's tiredness seemed to increase exponentially. All he wanted to do was to get in his vehicle, drive home, and do as he should've kept doing yesterday and stayed in bed, instead of zooming off across the Dales, being all detective about things. But he wasn't about to change who he was, so he pushed the weariness down deep, and went to wait by the Rav.

Jen arrived a few minutes later bearing bad news.

'What, Joan's ill, and Mary-Ann?'

'And Liz and Ben,' said Jen. 'Matt's fine, he called in just to say he'd be a bit late, as he had to sort out Joan and Mary-Ann, but yes, they're poorly, and Liz has gone down with whatever it is you have as well.'

'We're dropping like flies.' Harry sighed, making a mental note to send a message to Ben, his brother, to check up on him. He didn't see him half as much as he used to, since he'd moved in with Liz. Strangely, he'd found that only made him care about him even more. 'Not the best timing, is it?'

'Not really, no,' said Jen. 'I'd go so far as to say downright inconsiderate even.'

Harry narrowed his eyes at the detective constable, looking for some telltale sign of illness in someone who was, without doubt, not only the fittest member of the team, but one of the fittest people he'd ever known.

'You're sure you're okay, though, yes? You're not just hiding the fact you're ill, too, only to then collapse as soon as I drive off?'

Jen straightened her back, then thumped a clenched fist against her chest.

'Strong, like bear,' she said, breaking into a passable Russian accent momentarily, which made Harry smile. 'You've heard from Jim?'

'I have,' said Harry. 'But nothing since yesterday. Any news on his dad?'

Jen shook her head.

'No news is good news, though, right? Matt said he'll be keeping in touch with him, though.'

'I was going to give him a ring, but no point inundating him with calls,' Harry said. 'I'll leave it with Matt. What are Dave and Jadyn up to? Please tell me they're both still fit enough to carry out their duties. We're running a skeleton crew as it is.'

'They're fine,' said Jen. 'Jadyn's on his way over here, and after what happened yesterday, Dave's doing a walk around in Leyburn.'

'What do you mean, what happened yesterday?' Harry asked, immediately irritated at not being kept in the loop.

Jen explained.

'A bit of police presence seemed sensible,' she added. 'And Dave is a lot of police presence for the money.'

'For a PCSO, he certainly provides plenty of bang for your buck,' said Harry, opened the driver's door to the RAV, climbed in, and started the engine.

With a nod to Jen, Harry heaved the door shut and drove away from what were now two crime scenes for his much-depleted team to be dealing with. All he could do was hope that things didn't get any worse.

TWELVE

Having taken Harry's second call, Gordy had continued on her way over to Kettlewell. She was there just long enough to have a quick chat with Jen and make sure she was happy to be in charge of proceedings, before heading off again to meet up with the pathologist.

The mortuary was cold and if she'd known before setting off that morning that this was where she would end up, Gordy would've packed a jumper or three. She shivered, the rubber boots, white overalls, and facemask providing no thermal protection at all.

'How's Harry, then?' Sowerby asked, as she and Gordy stood on either side of the body laid out on a stainless-steel slab, which was currently still hidden beneath a thin white sheet.

'Bear with a sore head, only worse,' said Gordy.

'He doesn't deal well with being ill? How surprising,' said Sowerby.

Though her mouth was hidden behind a facemask, Gordy could tell from the lines at the corners of her eyes that the pathologist was smiling.

'It's not so much that he doesn't deal well with being ill,' said Gordy. 'More that he refuses to accept when he is.'

'Bit of a martyr for the cause, then?'

Gordy gave a nod.

'He's not one for sitting still, is he? He seems to regard holidays or time off as an irritation rather than a necessity. So, the notion of actually having to stay away from work and get well?' Gordy shrugged.

'And I'm sure he took being told what to do really well.'

'Oh, he was all smiles and gratefulness.'

Sowerby laughed, the sound awkward in the surroundings, like it knew it didn't belong and wanted to get out as quickly as possible.

'Harry smile? That's never happened.'

'Oh, it has,' said Gordy. 'You just have to be quick to spot it or you'll miss it.'

Sowerby reached out for the sheet and pinched it between her fingers.

'Ready?'

'Not in the slightest,' said Gordy.

Sowerby eased the sheet downwards, revealing the head, arms, and torso.

Gordy, who was already very aware of the stink of the body, despite the liberal application of vapour rub under her nose, almost did a double take.

'Bloody hell ...'

'Not a pretty sight, is it?' said Sowerby. 'Interesting that he was displayed like a scarecrow, considering he's got the build of one.'

She had a point. The man was rake-thin, with ribs like the ridges of the old cast iron grill pan she had at home for cooking perfect steaks. He had the build of a jockey, but was tall with it, like he'd been stretched on a rack. His stomach, though, was swollen, like he'd swallowed an inflated beach ball.

'He's been dead a while,' continued Sowerby, as Gordy continued to stare at the body. 'Hard to be accurate with an actual time of death, but I've sent samples off for testing, and if we get anything conclusive from that, I'll let you know. I'd say, though, that it's around the five- or six-days mark.'

'You would? Why?'

'There are a few stages of putrefaction,' Sowerby said. 'During the first couple of days, decomposition begins, but discolouration of the skin on the abdomen, swelling due to gas formation, only starts after that.'

Gordy could see that it wasn't just the swollen abdomen that was discoloured. Veins were visible, too, like someone had drawn them all over the victim's body with a felt-tip pen.

'There's more discolouration, isn't there?' Sowerby said, explaining what Gordy could see herself. 'And we've got skin blisters, too. That's five to six days.'

'And then?' Gordy asked.

'Black putrefaction,' said Sowerby. 'Happens from ten to twenty days. At three weeks, tissues are soft, hair and nails fall off. After that, at about four weeks, though obviously these times vary on the environment and other factors, organs liquify, then—'

'I get the picture,' said Gordy.

Sowerby pointed to where the body was touching the metal slab.

'You'll see how this is all dark red and purple? That's where blood has settled due to gravity. That happens immediately after death, as the heart is no longer sending blood around the body, and it has to settle somewhere.'

Gordy took all the information in, then realised something wasn't right.

'Doesn't that mean that he was lying on his back when he passed?' she said.

'Yes.'

'But we found him strung up in a field like a scarecrow.'

'Doesn't make sense, does it?'

'Not in the slightest.'

'It gets weirder,' said Sowerby.

Gordy noticed how the pathologist said that with a notable tone of glee but decided to not point it out.

'Of course it does. But weirder how, exactly?'

'Salt,' Sowerby said.

'What?'

'On the body and in the clothing. Mostly rock salt, but some table salt as well.'

Gordy screwed her face up in confusion.

'You mean the brown stuff used on roads?'

'Exactly that,' said Sowerby.

'Are you saying he drove a gritter?'

Sowerby shook her head.

'Not unless he spent a lot of time rolling in it and filled gritters by hand. Looks like he was covered in it at some point after he died.'

'Why?'

'Salt can delay decomposition. He was buried, too. Lots of mud and peat, that kind of thing, in his clothing, on his skin, in various orifices, and in all the wounds, too, obviously. Oh, and I think he was wrapped up in clingfilm. Traces of it were found in various places, some caught in his nails, on his watch, that kind of thing.'

Gordy was growing increasingly confused. This was a body she had last seen standing in a field. Now she was learning it had spent a number of days prior to that covered in salt, wrapped in plastic, and buried.

'Why would someone bury whoever this is, then exhume them, only to then stake them out in a field?'

'I can think of healthier hobbies,' said Sowerby.

'I know I'm going to regret asking this, but have you found anything else?'

'The obvious thing is the eyes, or lack thereof. From the damage, it looks as though they were scooped out, then the optic nerve and everything else was severed by something sharp to remove them completely. That was done postmortem.'

'Not pecked out by crows, then?'

'No. And there's this, too.'

Sowerby pointed at the side of the man's head and Gordy saw a deep indentation.

'Most likely cause of death,' Sowerby said. 'Something solid and angular caused severe trauma to the brain.'

'He was struck?'

'Or fell against something. But that right there is enough to kill anyone.'

Sowerby reached behind her for a folder. She handed it to Gordy, along with some plastic, sealed bags, their contents clearly visible.

'Driving licence,' said Gordy, reading the name Mark Armitage next to the small black-and-white photo. 'And bank cards.'

'Wallet was in his pocket,' said Sowerby.

Gordy looked at the next file. It contained a number of sheets of paper, the first being a photocopy of a blurry black and a white image on a small piece of creased paper.

'That's a twelve-week baby scan,' said Sowerby. 'You'll see that it has the patient's date of birth, hospital number, and it was done only a week or so ago.'

'No name, though.'

'If our friend here is local, then my guess is, so is the owner of that scan, and a quick call to the hospital should clear that up. It was all scrunched up in the pocket of his jeans.'

'Aren't these usually kept as souvenirs?'

'All I can do is tell you what we found,' said Sowerby. 'So, I've no idea. Anyway, that's about it, really. Wasn't easy to get him down from those stakes. Whoever did it certainly know their knots.' Then she added, 'A couple of the bits of rope were joined together with a double fisherman's, and they'd used a trucker's hitch as well, to make sure he was held up good and tight.'

'I have no idea what either of those knots are.'

'Neither did I until a few hours ago,' said Sowerby. 'I've printed them off for you, as you'll see, and there's a photo in there as well of some scraps of material we found close to the body. Not sure what they're from, but might be something, might not be.'

'Anything else?'

Sowerby said, 'There's scuff marks from the gate and across the field, and we found blood from the victim on the gate itself. My guess would be he was hauled over it, then dragged across the field.'

Gordy flicked through the papers in the file, then allowed herself another look at the body. She'd been to numerous post-mortems, and it always amazed her to be in the presence of something that had once been a living, breathing human being, but was now just a dead sack of flesh, albeit a sack that carried bones and very little else.

Is that all people are, she thought, *or is there more to it?* She knew Anna would tell her yes, of course there was, but then she was a vicar and believing in the soul, in God and all the rest of it, was part of the job. It was also an essential and inescapable part of who she was as a person. Gordy, though, still wasn't sure. Was there more to existence, or was this all there was at the end of it for everyone, just a breathless, rotting thing, with no true evidence of the life that had been lived, the thoughts and feelings, the fears and dreams and loves?

'You okay?'

Sowerby's question brought Gordy out of her brief contemplation on mortality.

'I'd best be getting back,' she said.

'Well, you've certainly got plenty to tell Harry,' said Sowerby.

'I have, but do I really want to?'

'No,' Sowerby replied. 'But we both know you will. And as soon as you're back in your car, too, no doubt.'

A few minutes later, Gordy was in her vehicle, phone on speaker.

'Well, what did Sowerby have for you?' Harry asked.

'A lot and not enough,' said Gordy, and told him.

THIRTEEN

Harry stared at Matt. Whatever the detective sergeant had just said, he'd not heard a word of it.

'What?'

Matt spoke again. His lips moved, but Harry couldn't hear a thing.

'I can't hear you!' Harry said, his voice raised.

He watched as the rest of team all looked at each other, as though trying to decide who should speak next. Then they all started talking at the same time.

Still nothing.

Harry's phone buzzed.

'What?'

'You've got your microphone switched off.'

'My what now?'

'Microphone,' said Matt.

Harry stared at his laptop, an old machine he generally did his best to avoid getting out and using at home. Still, needs must. So here he was, staring at the thing like it was a lump of junk that had just fallen out of the sky. He was sitting in the lounge, the laptop resting on a low coffee table.

Matt was on the screen, phone to his head, and his voice was on the other end of the line.

'How can it be switched off if there isn't one?' Harry asked. 'I've never had one, either. Never had the need. Where would it plug in, anyway?'

Harry saw now that some of the team looked like they were trying not to laugh, Gordy especially so, shaking her head as she smirked.

'Your laptop has a built-in microphone,' Matt explained. 'Have you really never done a video call before?'

'Not on this, no,' Harry said. 'Always managed to avoid it.'

Matt then explained to Harry how to get the mic working.

After a few moments of muttered swearing, Harry eventually found the icon on the screen and click it.

Laughter erupted in his lounge.

'I can hear that,' he said, staring hard at the screen.

The laughter only grew louder.

'You're all set,' said Matt, hung up, then spoke to Harry from the laptop. 'You can hear us now, yes?'

'A little too well,' said Harry. 'But yes.'

The team erupted into spontaneous applause, and the grumpy, annoyed side of Harry softened quicker than he expected.

'Now that we've got that all sorted, shall we get on?'

Smudge appeared at Harry's side and stared at the computer screen.

'Hello, Smudge!' said Jen, and waved.

Smudge wagged her tail, let out a soft woof, then lifted a paw to the screen. Before Harry could do anything about it, she managed to dislodge the laptop and send it toppling off the table.

'No!'

Harry grabbed for the laptop and caught it before it crashed to the floor, screen first. He turned to stare at Smudge, who was now sitting, staring at him, tail thumping the floor.

'Not helpful,' he said, placing the laptop back on the table, and commanded Smudge to go and lie down. 'Let's start again, shall we?'

Matt had positioned another laptop back in the office so that Harry could see the team and also the board. Jadyn was standing beside it, pen at the ready.

'Do you want to lead this?' Matt asked.

Harry shook his head.

'Gordy's better placed than me.'

Gordy laughed.

'My guess is you already have a load of questions, so why don't you do what you do best, and ask them?'

'You're sure?' Harry asked.

'I'd hardly have said so if I wasn't.'

Harry asked, 'Is there anything from Leyburn? And what's going on with ukuleles over in Swaledale?'

Dave Calvert said, 'Nowt in Leyburn. I did a bit of asking around, to find out if anyone had seen the group Jadyn chased, but nothing I'm afraid. Nice to be there, though, meeting folk.'

Matt said, 'With regards to Swaledale, someone's taken up playing the ukulele and their neighbour isn't too happy about it.'

'How's that even possible?' Harry asked, thinking of the size of a ukulele. 'Not exactly an amped-up electric guitar, is it?'

'No, it's not,' said Matt. 'But the person in question has been playing it outside in his garden rather a lot because his wife can't stand the sound of it. And now, neither can the neighbour.'

'Fair enough, though,' said Jen. 'Awful twangy things, aren't they? I think I'd be having words if my neighbour started doing the same.'

Harry hacked up a cough.

'Can we get on? Sounds like there's nothing else exactly pressing.'

Gordy said, 'You've read what I sent through from what Sowerby and her team found?'

After speaking with Gordy following her visit to the patholo-gist, Harry had then received everything they'd discussed as a quickly typed email, with no punctuation and a lot of spelling mistakes. He'd managed to decipher most of it and guess the rest. And everything he'd learned had already been neatly written up on the board by Jadyn.

'I have,' said Harry. 'You've an address for the victim?'

'Yes,' said Gordy. 'And we'll be heading over as soon as this meeting is done.'

'Where?'

'West Burton.'

'That's nowhere near where he was found, is it?' Harry said. 'So, why the hell was he in that field?'

'West Burton's half an hour from Kettlewell,' said Jen, backing up what Harry had just said. 'Main road goes through both.'

'What about next of kin?' Harry asked, knowing that attempts had already been made to trace relatives, but to no avail.

'No phone was found with the body, so we've no contacts to trace via that route,' said Gordy. 'Property has no landline associated with it, either. If there's no one there when we arrive, but his vehicle is there, we can do an insurance check for contact details, see if there's any mention of a named driver, that kind of thing. And we'll do a door knock as well, see what the neighbours can tell us.'

'Hopefully a lot,' said Harry. 'You don't just end up dead in a field, half an hour away from home, do you? What about that baby scan?'

'Now that, we do have something on,' Gordy said, and looked over at Jen.

'We've a name,' Jen said. 'And an address. Miss Helen Nevill.'

'Is she his partner?' Harry asked.

'Not a clue as yet,' said Jen. 'She lives in Leyburn.'

Harry scanned through the email Gordy had sent.

'Any thoughts on the salt?'

'Yes, actually,' said Matt. 'There are bins of the stuff all over the dale, but not as many as you'd think. I've managed to get a list of them from the highways' folk, so we can start checking.'

'But check for what, exactly?' Harry asked. 'We're in February, so those bins will all be well used, won't they? Most are probably half empty.'

'I figured we could narrow it down to the ones around West Burton and Kettlewell,' Matt said.

'We've no idea where he was buried, though, have we?' said Harry.

'No,' said Matt. 'But we need to start somewhere.'

'Is there anything else?' Harry asked. 'What about those knots that were used to tie him to the stakes in the field? And wasn't there something about a few scraps of material?'

He felt like he was clutching at straws now, but also that he had no other choice than to do so. And straws were better than nothing at all.

'Not sure where the knots can get us,' said Jen. 'They're knots that maybe the average person in the street might not know, but a lot of people do, for all manner of reasons.'

'Like who?' Harry asked.

'Take me as an example,' Jen replied. 'I know those knots because I've done a bit of climbing, and I used to have a kayak, and the trucker's hitch is what I'd use to secure it to my roof. My guess is every builder in the area, anyone who uses a ladder as part of their job, most farmers, would know those knots and use them daily.'

Harry decided to move on to the other crime scene.

'Have we got anything back yet on the stuff fly-tipped in front of the gate?'

'Too early,' said Gordy. 'Won't be till tomorrow for anything on any of that.'

Harry's frustration was only growing now. Not only was he stuck at home feeling ill, but the team also didn't seem to have much to go on with either investigation. It wasn't anyone's fault, he was just impatient. Then he remembered something.

'Mr Dent, the farmer whose field the body was found in, he

didn't actually find the body, did he? Someone told him about it, right?'

Jadyn said, 'Aiden Hunt. I've already had a quick chat with him on the phone.'

'And?'

'He confirmed he told Mr Dent about the scarecrow.'

'Nothing else?'

Jadyn shook his head.

Harry wasn't sure what he'd been expecting.

'Well, we've not got much to go on, have we? But then, it is early on in all of this.'

'I was going to go and speak to him face-to-face anyway,' Jadyn said. 'Lives over in Preston-under-scar.'

'He does?' Harry said. 'That's nowhere near Kettlewell. What was he doing over there so early in the morning?'

'I'll ask him,' Jadyn said.

'Yes, you will,' Harry agreed, his voice suddenly breaking into a hacking cough. 'So, Gordy, what next?' he finally managed.

Asking the DI to lead things was almost painful, but Harry knew it was for the best. He wasn't about to step on her toes by trying to control things from his armchair. He'd asked enough questions. Now it was over to Gordy to set things in motion.

'Plenty,' said Gordy, sounding considerably more positive than he felt himself. 'But there's no point going through it all with you right now, because you need to get yourself back to bed.'

'I'm fine,' Harry said, and heard a knock at a door, only it wasn't his, but the one in the office. 'Who's that?'

Matt stood up and went to the door as Gordy leaned into the screen till her face filled it.

'I'll be in touch,' she said, then Harry's screen went blank.

Harry was a little taken aback by the abrupt end of the meeting. So much so, he almost grabbed his phone to call Gordy. But then another cough burst out of him, turning his throat into razor blades, and he found himself agreeing with Gordy's suggestion.

A few minutes later, and with another hot toddy clutched in

his hands, Harry wandered upstairs to the bedroom, Smudge slinking along behind him.

Sitting down on the bed, and with Smudge already curled up on it, he sipped the drink, enjoying the warmth as it slid down his throat. Then he placed the mug on the bedside table, fully intent on finishing it once he'd got himself comfortable.

He was asleep in seconds.

FOURTEEN

In the hall outside the office was a man dressed in an ankle-length waxed jacket, jeans, and a jumper.

'Can I help you, sir?' Matt asked.

'Clearly not,' the man said, 'but it's not like I've got any choice, is it?'

Matt was confused.

'I'm sorry, but I'm not sure that I—'

'I called your lot yesterday, was told that someone was coming out to help me with what I've been dealing with, then I was told there was a delay and that someone else would be in touch, but nothing, not a damned thing! It's not good enough!'

'I don't think I'm entirely up to speed with the issue you're talking about,' said Matt. 'We've just had something that has required the whole team, you see, and—'

'Oh, so the little man gets left behind, is that it? Bloody police these days, hopeless. I blame political correctness, that's the real problem, always too worried about what someone might think or say, rather than just getting on with the actual job you're supposed to do, which is to catch criminals!'

Matt hadn't expected the man's rant to take such a sharp turn.

'Perhaps we should have a chat somewhere more private?' he suggested.

'Why?' the man asked. 'Afraid I might start spouting a few too many truths, is that it? Don't want the public knowing what a mess things are? How you don't care about the Englishman and his castle?'

'You live in a castle?' Matt asked, the words out of his mouth before he could stop them.

'Of course I don't!' the man replied. 'The point I'm making is—'

Matt stepped to one side and gestured along the hallway.

'If you'll just follow me,' he said, and before the man could do anything about it, had ushered him along to the interview room.

Sitting the man down at the table, the door closed behind them, Matt asked if he would like some water, maybe a mug of tea or coffee.

'Bribery, is it?' the man said. 'Unbelievable!'

Matt took a long, slow breath, in and out, took out his notebook, and smiled.

'Now, perhaps I can take a few details?'

'You already have them,' the man said. 'I gave them to your officer yesterday. What a waste of time this all is!'

'Name?' Matt asked.

'Fine,' the man said, rolling his eyes. 'Mr Howes.' He then gave Matt his contact number and address, before adding, 'I'm surprised you don't know who I am, but then again, you're probably a lefty, aren't you?'

'Name doesn't ring a bell,' Matt said, then listened as Mr Howes explained who he was. 'Oh, so you're a politician.'

'That I am,' Howes said. 'I got rather sick of all the other parties and set up my own.'

'Not really into politics,' said Matt. 'All that shouting and argu-ing. Seems to me it's more about personality and power than anything else now, isn't it?'

'Not to me it isn't,' said Howes. 'I'm here for the man in the street, people who are tired of being ignored. People who—'

'Now, back to why you're here, then,' interrupted Matt, having no interest at all in being dragged into a political debate.

'These,' Howes said, and from an inside pocket of his jacket pulled out some folded bits of paper, placing them in front of Matt.

'And what are they?' Matt asked, sliding the papers over to unfold them.

'Threats, that's what,' said Howes.

The first sheet of paper had the words *Fish Don't Belong In Farms* written very neatly in felt-tip pen, and was decorated with various sketches of fish. The one beneath it said something about pollution and rivers. The next was more of the same, and the one after.

'Can you give me some background?' Matt asked.

'Shoved through my door,' Howes said. 'Stapled to trees on my land, stuck under the windscreen wipers of my car. It has to stop! I want you to stop it! That's your job, yes? Find who's responsible and throw them in jail where they belong.'

Matt wasn't one for jumping to conclusions about people, certainly not in the first few minutes of meeting them, but Mr Howes was making it very difficult for him to do anything else. Politeness, after all, was free.

'Do you know who sent them?'

'You're the detective, not me,' Howes replied.

'Have you seen anyone on your property? Anyone trespassing?'

'They think they can just stop a man trying to make an honest living, don't they?' Howes said, seeming to ignore Matt's questions. 'I own the land, the rights to the river. I've done all the paperwork, had everything checked. I'll be bringing employment to the area, you know, improving the local economy.' He jabbed a finger down on the sheets of paper. 'This? This is just the rantings of someone who wears clogs and thinks biking everywhere is going to save the planet!'

Matt decided that on this occasion he was happy to jump to a conclusion about Mr Howes.

'So, you've not seen anyone on your property?'

'I didn't say that, did I? And what I've seen is neither here nor there,' Howes said, which was an odd sort of response, Matt thought, as Howes continued speaking. 'And it's not just happened to me, either, you know? A colleague of mine is building a house, as he has every right to do, and he's had leaflets shoved through his door as well, telling him trees are homes, too, or some such rubbish.'

'This been happening for long, like?' Matt asked, keen to get to the end of the chat.

'The leaflets, at least a month,' Howes said. 'And I ignored it until now, but with this trespassing, well, I decided I needed someone from your team to come and monitor things. I need a police presence, my property protected from these ... these terrorists!'

'Terrorists?' Matt said, repeating the word, simply because it was so ridiculous.

'That's all they are. People with an agenda. People who think they can bully the rest of us into, well, I don't know what into, but I won't have it. So, what are you going to do?'

Matt took a moment to compose himself and folded up the pieces of paper.

'I think it's probably best if one of the team comes out to have a chat with you at your property, see what's going on, that kind of thing.'

'When?'

'We'll try and have someone over later today. And if you could let me know the contact details of this colleague of yours you say has also been dealing with similar, that would be useful.'

'Try? Oh, there'll be no try,' Howes said, jotting down a name and address on a clean page of Matt's notebook, before standing up. 'I'll be expecting a visit by the end of the day, or I'm going to the press.'

Matt stayed in his chair.

'I'm sure someone will be over today,' he smiled.

Howes said nothing more, turned on his heel, and stormed out of the interview room.

Matt stared at the door, listening to the man's retreating footsteps.

'There are some people I like, and there are some people I do not like,' he said to himself. 'And you, Mr Howes, are definitely one of the people I do not like.'

He then rose out of his chair, exited the interview room, and headed back down to the office.

HAVING DISPERSED the team to the various jobs, which had been discussed at the meeting, Gordy, with Jen in tow, headed off to Leyburn.

Matt and Dave were on their way to check out the address of the victim, Mark Armitage, and had a warrant to search the premises, assuming they were able to get in. Matt had briefly explained the chat he'd had with Mr Howes, and Gordy had agreed that they were best to send someone over sooner rather than later, if only to prevent the man from calling in again. So, Jadyn was given that job as well, in addition to tracking down Aiden Hunt, as the two addresses were only a couple of miles apart. In the car with Gordy,

'What's the news, then?' Gordy asked Jen, who'd just received a message from Jim.

'Sounds like his dad is fairly smashed up,' Jen said, reading the message on her phone, and Gordy heard the worry in the detective constable's voice. 'Broken leg, cracked ribs, broken arm and wrist. He's not in a good way.'

'His dad will be out of action for a while, then,' said Gordy. 'All of that sounds like months rather than weeks, doesn't it?'

'It does,' agreed Jen. 'There's a lot of stuff Jim's going to have to think about now; not just about his dad, but his mum, the farm, everything.'

'That's a lot to be dealing with.'

Gordy was quiet for a moment, focusing on the road ahead while she gathered her thoughts.

'He's going to be needed, isn't he?' she said eventually. 'On the farm, I mean.'

'Running a farm isn't something you can just stop doing,' said Jen. 'Farmers aren't renowned for taking time off or going on holiday.'

Gordy could only agree. 'Vocational jobs, they're all the same. Anna's no different. Seems to think if she takes time off, she's letting people down, or that she'll be most needed when she's away.'

'Shepherds and their flocks, right?' said Jen, and Gordy caught the smile in her voice.

'Well, she's having forced time off right now, isn't she?' Gordy said. 'Thanks to whatever illness it is that seems to be sweeping through the Dales.'

'I didn't realise,' said Jen. 'How's she doing?'

Gordy wasn't sure what to say. Anna had seemed worse, but in an odd way. She still had the temperature and headache, but that morning she had seemed a little confused and disorientated. She'd thought that maybe she'd just had a bad night's sleep, woken in the middle of an odd dream, but it had still caught her off guard. She'd be checking up on her later in the day, that was for sure.

'She's in bed, and rough enough not to have to tie her up to stop her escaping,' she said, deciding to keep the disorientation stuff to herself, because she didn't want to sound paranoid. 'I'm fairly sure that she's been sick for a few days, but she's just been ignoring it. I think that's made it worse.'

Gordy noticed Jen was staring at her.

'You sound worried,' Jen then said.

'I'm sure she'll be fine,' said Gordy, as convincingly as she could, then added lightly, 'Just so long as she doesn't suddenly decide to get up to go and check on the bells in the church, or something equally ridiculous.'

'And everything now sorted for the move? You're really going to be missed.'

Gordy smiled, though she couldn't quite hide the sadness

behind it. They were both excited about the move south, but it was still a huge thing they were taking on, both of them throwing themselves into new jobs in a new area.

'Same,' she said. 'It's a big step we're taking, but that's what you do when you love someone, isn't it? Take a risk?'

'Couldn't agree more,' said Jen. 'You'll be getting married next!'

Gordy smiled at that, her hand drawn to something she'd been carrying around in a pocket for a while, but she kept it hidden.

'I've enough to deal with as it is, being in a same-sex relationship with a vicar,' she said. 'I don't think I want to go throwing a ring-shaped spanner in the works as well, do you?'

'You've thought about it though, haven't you?' said Jen with a wink. 'And don't go saying you haven't. Everyone knows you're a diehard romantic.'

'And there's nothing wrong with that at all,' said Gordy.

'Didn't say there was. Anyway, what about Jim?' Jen asked. 'If he's going to be needed at the farm, then ...'

Gordy heard the unvoiced question.

'I'll have to have a chat with Harry once he's a little more human,' Gordy said. 'Work out what time Jim will need at the farm, how best to manage it with the team. I'm sure it's doable.'

'Hmm,' said Jen, clearly uncertain.

'You don't think so?'

'I think,' said Jen, 'and this is me speaking openly, that the draw of the farm on Jim will be too much for him to do that and his role as PCSO while his dad is out of action. The farm's always there with him, isn't it? Pulling at him. After they lost his older brother all those years ago, I think he's always it known that the farm would hook him back somehow. That's where his heart is.'

'You think that's what might happen?'

'Hard to say,' said Jen. 'He loves his job, and everyone loves him doing it. But what if his dad just can't get back to health again? Then what?'

Gordy had been so focused on what she and Jen were talking

about that she hadn't realised how far they'd travelled. They would be rolling into Leyburn in just a few minutes.

'Might be best if we try not to think about it right now,' she said. 'We're nearly at Helen's, so time to focus.'

When they pulled up outside the address, Gordy led them both from the vehicle and down a short path to the front door of an unassuming bungalow, a thin card file under her arm.

The garden was neat, given over to gravel and various pots and a small ornament in the shape of a well. A few other ornaments were scattered around, including one of a squirrel and another of a bright red toadstool, carved from wood. Not Gordy's taste at all, but there was something faintly quaint to it all that she could appreciate.

Jen rang the doorbell, footsteps approached, and the door was clicked open.

A middle-aged woman stood in the open door. She was dressed in a purple fleece jacket and jeans, her skin pale, eyes sunk deep beneath lank, brown hair.

'Oh God, what's happened? Is she okay? She's not dead, is she? She can't be! Not my Helen. I knew I should've been more worried, but she's a grown-up, isn't she? I'm her mum, not her keeper! I can't keep her on a leash!'

Gordy quickly introduced herself and Jen.

'We're looking for a Miss Helen Nevill,' she said.

'What? So, she's not dead, then? Oh, thank God ...'

Gordy was a little taken aback.

'So, Helen does live here?'

'Yes, she's my daughter,' the woman said. 'I'm Pam Nevill. Just me, no husband. He died a few years ago, bless him. He was out for a walk to buy a newspaper, and just dropped down dead.' She clicked her fingers in the air. 'Just like that! Can you imagine? One minute you're out for a stroll, and the next, well, that's it, isn't it? You're gone! I won't lie, I do miss him, not that he was exciting to have around, really, but then who wants exciting? I certainly don't.

Far too exhausting. He was a safe bet, a lovely husband and a great father.'

'Perhaps it would be better if we came in?' Gordy suggested, interrupting before Pam could say anything further about her husband, as she was fairly sure that the details weren't entirely relevant to what they were there for.

The woman stepped back from the door and gestured for Gordy and Jen to follow.

Inside, the dwelling seemed to carry on the ornamental theme of the garden. It was neatly decorated, in an old-fashioned way, and Gordy had the impression of being transported back to the early eighties, with the patterned carpet and wallpaper.

Small shelves on the walls of the hall held various knick-knacks in residence, most of them china, all of them animals. In the lounge, more shelves were on the walls, but there were display cabinets here, too, all similarly filled, though the items had grown in range and now included numerous tiny houses, as though a model village had been carefully distributed around the room. There was even a thimble display rack and another for decorative teaspoons. Neat still, but overwhelming, as well. One wall was turned over to a photo gallery, all of them of a girl growing into a woman. Helen, Gordy assumed.

'Grab yourselves a seat,' the woman said, as she fell into an armchair, then picked up a vaping device from a small coffee table and took a huge lungful. When she breathed out, she disappeared momentarily behind a cloud of raspberry-scented cloud, which billowed out into the room.

'You don't mind, do you?' she asked, holding the vape up.

Gordy decided it was best to offer no preference, and instead get on with the reason they were there in the first place.

'Mrs Nevill,' she began, but the woman interrupted.

'Sorry if it all seems so busy,' she said, waving a hand around the room. 'I've always collected things, can't stop myself.'

Gordy smiled.

'Nothing to apologise for,' she said. 'Collecting things is a harmless hobby and a lot of fun.'

The woman pointed to a small display cabinet.

'Those are Helen's, though,' she said. 'Poor thing, she must've caught the bug from me! Started when we had a little trip to a zoo, back when she was a toddler. All she was interested in was the chimpanzees and the gorillas. Couldn't drag her away. In the end, I had to bribe her with a stuffed gorilla and a funny little keyring!'

Gordy realised that Mrs Nevill was someone who could happily talk for hours to anyone, and most likely about anything, but she needed to move on with the reason she was there in the first place. This wasn't a social call.

'I'm going to assume, from what you said at the door, that Helen isn't home right now,' she said.

'I don't know where she is,' Mrs Nevill said. 'And please, call me Pam. It's short for Pamela, but I've never really liked that. Makes me sound posh. And I'm not, am I? Not saying I wouldn't like to be, though, given the chance.'

Pam took another lungful of the vape.

'When was the last time you saw her?'

'But why are you here if it's not bad news or to tell me Helen's been arrested or something? What's happened? Where is she?'

'How long has it been since you saw your daughter?' Jen asked, asking the same question as Gordy, but in a slightly different way.

'I see her every single day thanks to those photos,' Pam said, gesturing at the wall, confirming Gordy's assumption as to who they were. 'She's everything to me, all I have, if that makes sense. But I know that's not what you mean, and it's been a week at least. She usually calls me, which is why I'm so worried. I thought, you know, she's a big girl, isn't she? I can't go chasing her, need to give her the freedom she needs. So, I waited and today I was going to call you, anyway. Well, not you specifically, like, because I don't know you, do I? But the police, that's who I was going to call, because she's never done this before.'

'And you've no idea where she is?'

'Where, no,' said Pam, shaking her head. 'Who she's with, though? Now, that I do know.'

'You think she's with someone?' asked Gordy. 'Do you have their details?'

'I do,' said Pam. 'Her boyfriend, Chris Hogg. Been seeing each other for six months, that's all, but it got very serious very quickly, if you know what I mean. They're never apart. She's said she's moving in with him next month. He's a lovely lad, though.'

Gordy opened the file she had with her and handed something from it to Pam.

'What's this, then?' Pam asked, staring at it, bemused.

'It's a twelve-week scan,' Jen explained. 'And it belongs to your daughter.'

Gordy watched Pam's eyes widen to dinner plates.

'What? This? It's Helen's? This ... but ... It can't be! She can't be pregnant! I mean, I'd know, wouldn't I? I'm her mother!'

'We need to talk to Helen in connection with a case we're investigating,' Gordy said.

'Case? What case? Why have you got this scan? How can you have it and not know where she is? Doesn't make any sense at all.'

'The scan was found on the body of a man,' Gordy said.

'Chris? Oh, God, no, is he dead? He can't be! Helen will be heartbroken!'

'No, it's not Chris,' Gordy said, jumping in quickly, before Pam spiralled out of control.

'You're absolutely sure? Tall lad, thin as a stick of bamboo, nice smile though, and always smells good, like he's just jumped out of the shower.'

'The identity of the person who we found the scan on is a Mr Mark Armitage,' Jen said. 'Obviously, we can't provide you with any further deta—'

'Armitage?' Pam held the scan up in the air for Gordy and Jen to see, as though it was her that was showing it to them, rather than the other way round. 'That bloody man had this, our Helen's scan that even I, her mother, didn't know about, never mind the fact that she's pregnant in the first place? Are you serious?'

'It was found in his possession,' said Gordy, noting Pam's clear dislike for the man they'd found in the field. 'Though we are unable to say how or why. Which is why we would like to speak to Helen as soon as possible.'

'But why would he have it?' Pam asked. 'And he's dead now, is he? You're sure about that? Well, I can't see him being missed, but even so; dead? I can't believe it. How? What's happened? And what's Helen got to do with it?'

Gordy said, 'You know him, then, Pam? You know Mark Armitage?'

'Of course I do,' Pam replied. 'He's Helen's boss!'

FIFTEEN

Matt climbed out of the old police Land Rover and took in his surroundings.

'I've always had a bit of a soft spot for West Burton,' he said, as Dave Calvert came around to join him. 'There's just something special about the place, isn't there? And the pub's good.'

'So's the butcher,' added Dave. 'Their lamb is very, very special. And now that the thought's in my head, I may have to head over there and get some for dinner later.'

Matt had parked them up on the left, just before the old Methodist Chapel, and near enough opposite the small children's play area. Those old swings had sat on the green for decades, and Matt remembered playing on them himself as a child. The Methodist Chapel was also stowed away in his memory, from harvest festivals, a christening or two, and a funeral. He was almost tempted to pop into the place and have a look, suspecting it wouldn't have changed much—the pews all in a semi-circle, like some mini amphitheatre.

'Always looks so neat and perfect, doesn't it?' Dave said, breathing deep the cool air of the day. 'There's a fair bit of money in some of these houses, like, isn't there?'

'It's like walking into a postcard, isn't it?' said Matt. 'Whenever

I come here, it always seems so perfect, like you said, pristine almost. Time stands still in West Burton, I think.'

'You ever seen the falls when there's been a storm?' Dave asked. 'If you can manage to get yourself behind them when it's hammering down, it's awe-inspiring. By which I mean, bloody terrifying!'

Matt laughed.

'It's been a long time now, but I've even gone swimming in the pools just under the bridge. Don't think I'd fancy doing it now, like. You don't feel the cold when you're young, do you? Just strip off down to your pants, and in you go. Now though, even just the thought of it is enough for me to want to go home and light a fire.'

'Where's the house, then?' Dave asked.

Matt pointed up the road and to the right.

'We head up there,' he said. 'If I'm right, then I think there's a lovely little footpath that goes right past the house. One that takes you through the fields and eventually round to the falls from the other side, rather than from the bottom of the village itself. It's a smashing walk, if you ever get the chance.'

'I know it,' said Dave. 'Lovely in the spring, when the weather's cool, but the sun's bright. Last time I was walking it, I heard a cuckoo.'

'You lucky sod,' said Matt. 'Can't remember the last time I heard one myself.'

'Beautiful sound. The day was so quiet, and then the cuckoo started calling from those little woods in the valley, and just for a moment I couldn't help but think how bloody wonderful this planet is.'

'Pity we humans seem to be buggering it up so much.'

'There is that,' Dave agreed.

Matt led Dave up through the top end of West Burton and brought them to a stop outside a house.

'Yep, it's the one that I thought,' he said, noticing then how dark the house was, the windows reflecting the day, but the rooms behind them hidden in darkness. A black SUV was in the drive.

Looked expensive, too, he noticed, very shiny, leather interior, which meant that it kind of fit in well with its surroundings.

The house itself was a stone-built property, a traditional Dales' building, old and weathered and obviously with a lot of money spent on it, judging by how neat and perfect everything was. The garden was neat, but in a low-maintenance, landscaped way. A little too modern for Matt, who preferred things to be a little rougher around the edges than all straight lines. Well, that was his excuse, and he was sticking to it. Not that Joan minded, and they'd made sure their garden was plenty enough accessible for her and the wheelchair.

The thought of his wife, and then of his daughter, gave Matt's gut a twist. He didn't like being away from them both like this, especially when they were both so ill. But Joan had insisted he head to work, independent and stubborn to a fault. Didn't do anything to still his concern, though.

Yes, this was a neat house, and the owner had money, and with that being the case, it looked as much as Matt would've expected, especially with it being situated in West Burton.

But what Matt certainly hadn't expected to see and couldn't pull his eyes away from no matter how hard he tried, was the word BASTARD slapped across the bright white front door in lurid red paint, the letters dripping down like blood.

'Well,' said Dave.

'Indeed,' said Matt. 'Looks like our Mr Armitage might not be all that popular.'

Matt walked up to the front door and, seeing no bell, gave the wood a sharp rap with his knuckles, careful to avoid the paint.

Nothing.

He tried again; still no answer.

One last go, and all he heard was the knock disappearing into the silent void on the other side of the door.

'Either he lived alone, or whoever he lives with isn't in,' Matt said.

'Car's there, though,' said Dave.

'Which makes me wonder how the hell he ended up where he did, in a field over by Kettlewell.'

'Someone must've taken him there,' said Dave.

'Or someone drove him there in that, and brought it back,' said Matt. He touched one of the paint drips, found it to still be tacky. 'And this is recent,' he added. 'It's thick, so would take a while to dry. Couple of days, maybe longer.'

'Before he was found in the field, then?'

'Looks that way,' said Matt.

A voice called from somewhere behind them.

'Now then ...'

Matt and Dave turned around to see an older man leaning over a garden wall of a cottage hunched up on the other side of the lane. It was sandwiched between two other similar-looking cottages. Though his bottom half was hidden from view, Matt saw that the man was wearing a jacket that looked as though it had once belonged to a rather natty-looking tweed suit, but was now rather threadbare, beneath which lay a checked shirt and a dark, woolen jumper. This was a man dressed for the cold, but not necessarily to impress.

'Hello,' Matt said, waving to the man.

'You'll be wanting Armitage, then,' the man said. 'Wasted trip, mind; I've not seen that man in days.'

Matt noticed a faint edge of flint to the way the man said *that man*, and asked, 'Does anyone else live at the property?'

The man snorted a laugh, at the same time taking a small, silvery tin out of a pocket in the old jacket he was wearing and popping open its lid.

'Live with Armitage?' he said and dipped a thumb and finger of one hand into the tin to take a pinch of the contents. 'You're having a laugh! Awful man, he is, like. Awful.'

Matt took out his notebook, just in case.

'That's a no, then, correct?'

The man lifted his pinched finger and thumb to his nose and took a sniff into each nostril.

'It's more of a *not a bloody chance of it* than a no,' he said, giving his nose a quick wipe with a knuckle, before popping the lid back on the tin. 'Don't know many folk who have a good word to say about him. No, actually, they do, and that word is git. A very good word, in my opinion. As is that one painted on his door there.'

Matt didn't quite know what to say to that, so he responded with a question.

'Has this happened before?'

'No,' said the man, 'which is a surprise, really.'

'Why's that?'

'Let's just say that he gets plenty of visitors, but that none of them stay longer than a night.' He then tapped his nose as though what he was sharing with Matt and Dave was very hush-hush indeed. He then added, 'If you know what I mean,' winked, then sneezed with an almost operatic zeal. 'That's the stuff!' he said, clenching a fist. 'Really hits the spot.'

Matt walked over so that he wouldn't have to continue shouting from the other side of the road.

'I'm Detective Sergeant—'

'Dinsdale,' the man said. 'I know who you are, and this fella here, too, like.' He looked at Dave. 'Calvert, isn't it? I like to know what's going on. And this is the Dales, isn't it, so it's not like no one knows nowt? I'm Terry Thwaite, not that it matters.' He held out the tin. 'Fancy a pinch?'

'Of what?' Dave asked, coming over to stand with Matt.

'Snuff,' replied Terry. 'Menthol, this one. Clears the sinuses out like a blast from a shotgun! Doesn't half make your eyes water. I always like to offer it to folk I see around and about. It's nice to share, isn't it?'

'You take snuff?'

'I do,' Terry said. 'Did you know it's the only type of tobacco you can use in parliament? In fact, there's even a special wooden snuff box at the door to the House of Commons.'

'Why?'

'Why not?' Terry replied.

Matt decided to step in and move the conversation on quickly from Terry's strangely old-fashioned habit and asked if he had seen any visitors to Armitage's property over the last few days.

'Seen anyone? No,' Terry said with a shake of his head, stowing his snuff tin away, and tapping the pocket as he did so, as if to reassure himself that it was there. 'Heard a car though ... When was that? A few nights ago, anyway. Light sleeper, you see. I usually hear the cars that come and go. And there's plenty of them, like.'

'But no one at the property at all, then? Just Mr Armitage?'

'Not even him,' Terry said. 'It's been maybe a week since I've had the misfortune of having to share oxygen with him.' Another sneeze, but not as violent, caused him to pause for a moment, after which he said, 'If you want, I can give you a call and let you know when he shows up again. I'm bound to notice. I'm a nosy old bugger. Hard not to be with him opposite.'

Matt said, 'And you're sure that you've not seen anyone over at the house over the last couple of days, just heard a car?' He pointed at the front door. 'That looks fairly recent.'

'Just the car,' Terry said. 'I didn't get up to look. Been suffering with this cold or flu or whatever it is going round. Only just come out the other side of it.'

'Yeah, it's not great, is it? My wife and daughter have it.' Matt reached out and laid a hand on the small gate that opened on a path leading to Terry's front door. 'Touch wood.'

Terry leaned forward a little.

'You know, if I was the suspicious type, Detective Sergeant Dinsdale, which I am, obviously, I'd be seeing you two here asking questions about a man I've not seen hide nor hair of in a good few days, and I'd be thinking something was amiss.'

Right then, Matt wasn't entirely sure he wanted the news spreading of Armitage's death, especially by Terry. That kind of information was best kept close early on, and really only discussed with anyone closely associated with the case and the victim. He'd be following Harry and Gordy's lead on that. Terry wasn't close enough to what had happened to be party to that information quite yet. But he couldn't help but be intrigued by what the man had said earlier, and especially with the way he had said it.

'You mentioned that Mr Armitage would have a lot of visitors,' he said. 'Mostly at night.'

'Always at night,' Terry said. 'Always. If you know what I mean.'

'Not sure that I do,' said Matt, though he had a suspicion of what Terry was implying, and also wondered if '*if you know what I mean*' was a favourite phrase of Terry's.

'Well, once you meet him, you'll understand why he has to pay for it, because no bugger would ever want to sleep with him out of choice, that's for sure.'

'Escorts, you mean?' Matt said.

'If you like,' said Terry. 'Though he does have a certain charm about him, and it works on some, I suppose, and I reckon a few he picks up through those dating sites on the internet that folk use now. It's all an act, though. Most end up out on their ear in the early hours, or a taxi whisking them away if they've not been sensible enough to turn up under their own steam. They're the ones I feel the worst for, having to wait for a lift just so they can get away from the man.'

Matt thought about the scan the SOC team found. There was a link there for sure. Had this all been done by someone who'd fallen pregnant after a night they regretted, with a man who, according to Terry, no one liked? Perhaps on finding out, they'd gone to Armitage for financial help, he'd refused, and things had got out of hand.

Matt shook his head at that. There was getting out of hand, and there was staking someone out in the middle of a field and scooping out their eyes. Neither could he see how a young, pregnant woman would be able to murder someone, bury them, dig them up, then drag them to a field and hitch them up on a makeshift cross, no matter how stick-thin they were. It also didn't explain the salt and everything else they'd discovered. Still, though, it was a line of enquiry they'd not considered until now.

'Will there be owt else?' Terry asked. 'Only I'll be heading down the pub now, you see. Got myself a game of dominoes lined up. Can't be missing that, now. League games are important when there's nowt much else going on.'

'We'll let you get on,' Matt said, then took down Terry's contact details.

'You're sure you'll not be wanting a pinch?' Terry asked, once again bringing out the small tin.

'Very kind, but no,' said Matt.

'You're sure? I've a few tins spare, you know. A few different flavours, too; peach is a bit of a favourite, but I've also got peanut butter, whisky—'

'You keep them,' said Matt, but before he could do anything, Terry had leaned over the wall and popped a small, round silvery tin in Matt's hand.

'Honestly, I don't—' began Matt, but Terry was already walking back towards his front door.

'My pleasure,' Terry called back, then was inside his house, door closed behind him.

Matt was about to turn away, when the door opened again.

'You'll be wanting to get inside? Armitage's house, I mean.'

'We've a warrant to search the property, but there's no one in,' said Matt.

Terry waved away Matt's words.

'There's a rock to the right of the door. Except it's not a rock, is it? It's a key safe. It was put in when the gardener was there. No external tap, you see, so they had to water plants from the kitchen.'

Half jogging back to Armitage's front door, Matt soon found the rock, a key set inside it behind a plastic flap. He went to say thank you, but Terry had already disappeared back inside his house.

Matt slipped the key into the lock.

'Away then, Dave,' he said, opening the door. 'Let's see what we can find, shall we?'

SIXTEEN

Inside the hallway of Armitage's house, all Matt could really think about was how expensive everything looked, and they'd not even seen the rest of the house yet. Not just the furniture either, and right now the only piece of it they could see was an antique settee against the wall, but the décor, the wallpaper, the hugely pointless glass ornaments on display on a simple wooden shelf, the artwork hanging from the walls which Matt neither understood nor cared to, because whatever it was it didn't look like anything he'd ever seen in his life.

This was a house where only the best would do. It wasn't a huge place, and in many ways quite modest in size, but what it lacked in grandeur, it certainly made up for with everything else.

'I think we've walked into a show house,' Dave said, standing beside Matt. 'I couldn't live somewhere like this; too many things to break.'

'That doesn't fill me with confidence having you here,' Matt laughed. 'Should I ask you to go and stand outside, or can you be trusted?'

'I'll make sure that I only break stuff that won't be missed.'

Matt looked around. Everything was very just-so, like it had been placed with care and attention to every detail.

'Not sure that's possible.'

'I'll be careful, then.'

'Not sure that's possible, either,' Matt said.

'You'd be surprised.'

'You're not wrong.'

Matt watched as Dave deliberately crossed his arms slowly.

'You know those wildlife cameras I have?'

'The ones you've got up Snaizeholme?' Matt asked, remembering him mentioning of them a good while ago now.

'Well, I can't just go tramping up to them making a racket, like, can I? And I don't just depend on them to keep an eye on badgers and squirrels and such like.'

'You don't?' Matt asked, not really sure where Dave was going with this.

'Of course I don't! You know, you can't beat being out in the middle of the night, hiding out in the hills, just watching nature do its thing.'

'Hiding out?'

'It'll surprise you, I know, but I can be quiet and sneaky,' Dave said. 'I fell asleep one night, out watching a badger set, woke up with a red squirrel sitting right in front of my face, just staring at me.'

'There's a difference between sneaky and asleep,' said Matt. 'And a very big difference between any of that and making sure you don't knock into something in here and break it!'

With that, Matt led them through to the first room, a lounge populated by a deep blue sofa, a large, wafer-thin television, and very little else.

'Minimalist,' he said.

'You mean empty,' said Dave. 'What are we looking for, anyway?'

Matt gave his chin a scratch, trying to come up with an answer.

'Hard to say, really,' he said. 'Often, with things like this, you don't really know until you've found it, if you know what I mean.'

'Not really, no,' said Dave.

'You'll just have to trust me, then.'

With little else to see in the lounge other than some more very confusing artwork, Matt led Dave back out into the hall and along to the kitchen. The room looked out over the rear garden.

'That is a very nice garden indeed,' Dave said, coming to stand at his side. 'Not my cup of tea, like.'

As with the smaller garden at the front of the house, the area at the back was also something low on maintenance and high on cost, with lots of paving and gravel, dotted with pots filled with plants, strange ornaments of rusting metal, which bowed and twisted in the breeze, and even a fountain. A small patch of grass was central to the whole affair, and Matt had a sneaking suspicion that it wasn't grass at all, but Astroturf, because something told him Armitage had not been the kind of person to own a lawnmower, never mind use one. On top of the turf was a metal table corralled by four metal chairs, and to the side, an outdoor burner for logs.

'Not very kid-friendly, is it?' Matt said, thinking about the scan found in Armitage's pocket.

'Not wildlife friendly either,' said Dave.

A quick scooch around the kitchen, and a look in the dining area off to the side, they headed back out into the hall and made their way upstairs. Darkness enveloped them as they climbed, the walls a deep, matte blue, and dotted here and there with more art, and the occasional brass-framed mirror.

On the landing were four doors. The first was the bathroom, which provided nothing other than a bath so huge, its polished copper sides rose from the wooden floor like a metallic cliff face. Dave could only stare at it slack-jawed.

'It's only a bath,' Matt said.

'But look at it,' said Dave. 'It's bloody enormous! Who needs a bath like that? You could go swimming in it.'

Matt laughed.

'I'd pay good money to see that,' he said, then added, 'On second thought, maybe not.'

The next door was empty. No bed, nothing at all, which struck

Matt as odd. But then, perhaps Armitage had no call for a spare room. If what Terry had told them was true, it didn't sound as though he was a man with a large circle of friends.

The next room was a bedroom and was taken up by a four-poster bed sitting smack bang in the middle of the room, and a wardrobe. The curtains were closed, but a thin dagger of light cut through where they met in the middle, slicing the bed in two.

Matt walked around it, while Dave stayed over by the door.

'Why's it not pushed up against the wall?' Dave asked.

'Maybe to make it look more impressive?' Matt said and opened the wardrobe. 'Oh ...'

'Oh?' said Dave, walking over to join Matt. 'What've you found?' And then he saw. 'Oh, right ... *that* kind of *oh*.'

A rubber mask stared vacantly back at Matt. It had eye and mouth holes and was decorated with silver studs. Next to it were various other garments, all of them running wild with the theme of rubber and leather, or both, joined with chains, and a whip or two. On some hooks at the back of the wardrobe were an array of hand-cuffs, ropes, ribbons, and something that looked like a very large table tennis bat, but clearly wasn't.

The blunt spikes on it would probably render it useless, Matt thought, and definitely go against whatever rules there were in the sport.

'Each to their own,' said Matt, and closed the wardrobe.

With the room giving up nothing else of interest, he then went to head back out onto the landing, but something caught his eye, glinting in the sliver of light from between the curtains. Crouching down he found a key, the brown, plastic, and strangely shaped fob it was attached to was worn with years of use. He pulled an evidence bag from a pocket and slipped it inside.

'What do you think that is, then?' he asked Dave, holding it up as they left the bedroom and walked over to the last remaining door.

Dave leaned in for a closer look and shook his head.

'Probably Armitage's,' he said. 'Back door key, maybe. Looks like a camel.'

Matt laughed.

'A camel with no legs, no head, and three humps?'

'It's brown,' said Dave. 'Camels are brown.'

Matt stuffed the key into a pocket and reached for the door handle.

'What do we think's in here, then?' he said.

'Well, judging by what we've seen so far, I can't say I really know how to answer that,' sighed Dave, 'and the wardrobe makes me a little afraid of guessing.'

Matt gave the door handle a twist. The door swung open without even the faintest of squeaks to reveal a thick darkness.

Stepping into the room, Matt quickly found the curtains and heaved them open, surprised at just how good they were at blocking out the light. Then, as he stared out into West Burton, Dave called him over.

'Matt, you're going to want to see this ...'

Matt turned from the curtains to find himself in what was undoubtedly Armitage's office. Against a wall was a large desk, the surface home to three large computer screens and a keyboard. Tucked under the desk was a comfy-looking leather chair. But neither of these drew Matt's eye. What Dave was standing in front of did that.

The notice board was huge, taking up much of the wall opposite the window. But it wasn't so much the board that drew the eye, more what it had on display.

'Well,' Matt said, searching for something a little more accurate and coming up blank.

'I can only second that, really,' said Dave, stepping back from the board to stand beside Matt.

The board was split into two sections by a length of thin, red ribbon pinned down its centre. The left side was covered in photographs, all of them of women, the right side comprised several brown envelopes, all pinned to the board, each one numbered.

'Jesus Christ,' Dave said, then immediately apologised, adding, 'What the hell is this, Matt? What on earth was Armitage up to?'

Matt said nothing and moved in for a closer look, though he would have preferred to have done the exact opposite, given the choice.

'I guess this explains why that massive bed is in the middle of the room,' he said.

The photos were all from the bedroom they had just left, each showing the bed itself but from various angles. Matt guessed that a closer examination of the other room would uncover various hidden cameras.

Dave reached for the photographs.

'Don't,' said Matt. 'Don't touch a thing.'

'We can't just leave them up there,' said Dave. 'It's ... well, it's wrong, isn't it? What kind of sick bastard was he?'

Matt had never heard Dave talk with such seething anger before and if he hadn't known the man as well as he did, he would've been not just concerned, but alarmed.

He left Dave's question unanswered and did his best to stay calm.

Each photograph was of a different woman. They were all either fully naked or in different stages of undress. Armitage was in all of the images as well. He was naked, his pale physique like the wandering bones of a skeleton caught in the camera's glare on a Hammer Horror movie set.

The women, Matt noticed, weren't simply lying on the bed. It looked to him as though they had been posed somehow, pushed and pulled into various positions for the camera. And none of them had their eyes open.

Not one.

'You okay?' Matt asked.

'No, I'm not okay,' Dave replied. 'Not in the slightest.'

'You don't have to be here. A bit beyond the call of duty for a PCSO, really. If I'd known, then ...'

'Bit late for that now, really, isn't it?' said Dave.

'A little.'

Matt was bothered by the eyes. He was bothered about everything else, yes, because what was in front of them was horrific and wrong on so many levels, he doubted there was an area in his mind he would ever be able to hide it in to forget about it completely. But those eyes ... something wasn't right ... He was fairly sure he knew why as well, but to help him get his head around what Armitage had been doing, he turned to Dave.

'Why do you think they've all got their eyes closed?'

'How do you mean?' Dave replied.

'I mean,' Matt explained, 'that every single one of them looks like they're asleep, right? But they can't be, can they? Not with what's happening to them.'

'People close their eyes when they don't want to see what's going on around them, or what's being done to them,' Dave suggested.

Matt shook his head. Yeah, he knew why, because no other explanation fitted what they had uncovered.

'It's more than that. They look ... unconscious.'

'What? Why would they be—' Dave's voice snapped in two. 'You think he drugged them.'

'I do,' said Matt. 'We don't know that from what we've got here, but I can't see there being any other explanation, can you?'

He forced himself to examine the other side of the board, this time slipping on a pair of disposable gloves pulled from a pocket and taking down one of the envelopes.

'There's something inside it,' he said, and opened the envelope, tipping the contents out onto his open palm.

An SD card slid out and he held it up.

'I really don't want to know what's on that,' said Dave.

'Neither do I,' said Matt, and called Gordy.

SEVENTEEN

Arriving in Preston-under-scar, having driven over from Hawes, Jadyn parked up just beyond the small children's play area, tucking his vehicle under a tree still bare from winter, though he could see buds forming on the grey branches, dancing enthusiastically in the wind.

Climbing out, the wind decided to change dance partners and grabbed Jadyn, almost spinning him on his heel. He laughed, hunched his shoulders up against the chill, and made his way under the tree to the lane above.

Just opposite, he saw what he thought must be one of the smallest parish churches in the country. The small, single-storey building sat quietly on the side of the road, its pretty lattice windows staring out into the valley of Wensleydale.

He'd never been a churchgoer, but for some reason, Jadyn found himself wondering what it was like inside, intrigued by how something so unassuming could have anything at all to do with the larger, grander churches he was used to associating with the Church of England. He'd maybe ask Anna about it, or Gordy anyway, see if he could have a nosy.

The address he was looking for was just along to the left of the church, and a few steps later, Jadyn was outside and knocking at the door.

A blast of wind rushed at him down the lane, catching him hard at the same moment as the door opened. Stumbling against the gust, Jadyn tried to catch himself against the wall, but missed.

'Woah there,' said a voice, as a pair of strong hands grabbed Jadyn. 'Nearly had you there, didn't it? You alright?'

Jadyn managed to steady himself.

'Thanks,' he said. 'Wasn't really expecting that.'

The man in front of him was mid- to late-thirties, Jadyn guessed, shirtsleeves rolled up despite the month and the cold. Skin tanned, he looked fit, a physique born from a physically demanding day job rather than the gym. Jadyn may have been bigger, but he wouldn't have been surprised if there was little, if any, difference in their strength.

'Wind's a bugger along here some days.'

'Isn't it, just?' said Jadyn, and introduced himself.

'Don't get many visits from the police,' the man said. 'But then no one knows my secret identity, do they? And that's the way I like to keep it!'

'Secret identity?'

'I'm not saying another word.' The man grinned. 'So, how can I help you, other than to catch you when the wind comes along and tries to sweep your feet out from under you?'

'I'm looking for a Mr Aiden Hunt.'

'And you've found him. Ta-Dah!'

The wind shot down the lane once again, buffeting Jadyn.

'Why don't you come inside?' Aiden offered. 'I've just made a fresh pot. Having a break between jobs that for once are close enough to home to allow me to pop back.'

Once inside, and with the door firmly shut against the day, Jadyn followed Aiden along a short hall, the flagstone floor polished smooth from years of use, and into a small kitchen with a vintage, Formica-topped leaf-top table against the wall, a couple of chairs perched either side.

'How do you take it?'

'Just a bit of milk,' Jadyn said, as Aiden nodded at the chairs for him to take a seat.

Tea poured, and with a packet of biscuits pulled from a cupboard, Aiden plonked himself down in the other chair.

'Cheers,' he said, lifting his mug and taking a sip.

Jadyn returned the gesture.

'Is it just you, then?' he asked.

'Happily married,' said Aiden. 'Izzy's at work. She's a teaching assistant at the primary school in Middleham.' He then fixed Jadyn with a firm stare. 'Best you get on with telling me why you're here, then. Because if this is my final meal before I'm locked up for good, I'm not going to be very happy. Izzy's an amazing cook and I'd be asking for her carbonara, that's for sure.'

'It's about a scarecrow,' Jadyn explained.

'What?'

'A scarecrow,' Jadyn repeated. 'Over in Kettlewell.'

He saw realisation dawn in Aiden's eyes as he gave a nod in recognition.

'You mean the one in Sam Dent's field?'

'That's the one.'

'Why on earth would you be here about that?'

A very good question, Jadyn thought, wondering how best to go about explaining without saying too much.

'You've not spoken to Mr Dent since yesterday, then?'

'I've no need to. I only know him in passing, really,' Aiden said, shaking his head and taking another biscuit, and holding the packet out for Jadyn. 'I did some work for him a couple of years back, just a bit of a garden tidy really, so I usually say hello when I see him. It was a present for his wife, I think, paying me to make the place a little more suitable to have friends over for a barbeque, that kind of thing. He's not really a gardener, too busy with the farm, and it all got a bit out of hand. Not so much couldn't see the wood for the trees, as all you could actually see was nettles.'

'How did you know it was his field?'

Aiden laughed.

'Well, back when I was working for him, we ended up having to help him with a few sheep that'd made a break for it. Somehow, they'd managed to find a weak section of a wall and had done a runner. We got roped in to help gather them back in. Made the day a little more interesting. Turns out, I'm not a very good sheepdog.'

'You were over there early, though,' Jadyn said. 'And you live here.'

'I was passing through to drop my lad off at another job over that way. Needed to give myself enough time to get back here to get on with something else. We cover more than just Wensleydale in this line of work. And I've built a decent reputation, too, so if a job's big enough and pays well, I'm happy to travel a bit further if required. Follow the money, right? So, I'm over here, he's over there.'

'He doesn't drive?'

'His car's in the garage.'

Jadyn asked for the address of the job Aiden had mentioned.

'You're being very mysterious,' Aiden said, as Jadyn jotted down the details.

'Just gathering information, that's all.'

'About a scarecrow.'

'Yes.'

'And there's nothing more you can tell me about it?'

Jadyn shook his head, and finished his tea.

'Thanks,' he said, and rose to his feet. 'This has been really useful.'

'It has?'

'Very.'

Aiden walked Jadyn out of the kitchen and back along the hall to see the front door burst open and a small woman dressed in a large down jacket and woolen hat, fall into the house.

'Izzy?' Aiden said and dashed past Jadyn.

'God, I feel awful,' the woman said, then saw Jadyn. 'You're ... you're a police officer.'

Aiden had hold of his wife and was guiding her through another door and into a small lounge.

'What's happened? What's wrong?'

Izzy dropped down onto a sofa.

'I felt fine when I headed off this morning,' she said. 'But I think I've caught that bug going around. I feel like death.'

'My boss has it,' said Jadyn.

'He has my sympathy.'

'Not sure he'd accept it,' Jadyn laughed. 'He's not one for anyone making a fuss.' He stood at the front door and opened it. 'I'll leave you to it.'

'Well, thanks for coming round,' Aiden said. 'It's been ... different.'

Jadyn stepped back outside into the day. A small car was now parked next to Aiden's van; Izzy's, he guessed.

Walking back to his own vehicle, Jadyn realised how empty his stomach felt. He needed a bite to eat, but he had a feeling that delaying a visit to Mr Howes for a quick lunch wasn't the best plan, so he did his best to ignore it and allowed his mind to drift onto something else: Jen.

How long had they been seeing each other now? Jadyn wasn't really sure, was terrible at dates and anniversaries, and Jen didn't seem to be very much bothered by any of that either. But it had been a good while, now, hadn't it? And he was enjoying it.

Jen was amazing. He loved her lifestyle, the way fitness wasn't just something she did because it was important to be healthy, but because she loved it. Running was her happy place, her haven, and she was good at it, too.

He'd been out with her a few times, just on short runs. He was more of a weights person but did a bit of cardio as well, though usually only when the weather was good. And on each of those runs, he'd been blown away by her easy grace on the roads and trails. How she looked so relaxed, like she was putting no effort into it at all.

He would return from those runs blowing like a steam train,

but Jen would be fresh, beaming, alive. Throw in the fact that he fancied her something terrible, and most days, Jadyn could hardly believe his luck. She was a couple of years older than him as well, and he couldn't help thinking that was kind of cool, too.

And then there was Steve. The creature was definitely the first Lizard Jadyn had ever got to know. Usually, they were behind glass in zoos, or in little tanks in pet shops. But Steve was large enough to occupy the whole of Jen's sofa, and was never too happy about relinquishing it, either.

For the first few months, Jadyn had been very sure Steve didn't like him. Dislike had eventually thawed, and now? Well, Jadyn didn't want to jinx it, but as Steve had actually started to come over to greet him, he was thinking that perhaps he had finally been accepted. And if that was the case then—

Jadyn's phone buzzed.

It wasn't the office this time, but Gordy. He went to speak, but the DI got in first.

'Where are you?'

'I've just finished meeting with the gardener, and I'm now on my way to see that Mr Howes,' Jadyn said, remembering what little Matt had shared with him about the discussion they'd had, and not really keen to get going. 'Why? What's happened?'

'Matt's just called from Armitage's place. I need you over there with him right now. Jen and I are on our way, but you're closer. I need you on-scene, sharpish.'

'Why, what's happened?' Jadyn asked, already dreading the answer. 'And what about Mr Howes?'

'I'm going to send Dave instead,' Gordy said. 'And as for what's happened, let's just say Matt's uncovered something a little more pressing to deal with than an irate politician ...'

EIGHTEEN

Dave Calvert was beginning to think that dealing with what he and Matt had uncovered at the house belonging to Armitage would have been a much better use of his time than having to spend even a single minute more in the presence of a certain Mr Howes. He had someone else to visit after this, as well, someone Matt had described as a colleague of Mr Howes.

Well, Dave thought, *if Howes himself was anything to go by, then that visit isn't going to be much fun either, is it?*

Having left Matt in West Burton to secure the house and wait for the SOC team to arrive and give the place the once over, he'd arrived half an hour ago at the man's property, a recently renovated farm with land that bridged the River Ure. He would either pick Matt up once done with the jobs Gordy had given him, or one of the others would.

So far, Dave had yet to get a word in. He'd tried, really, really, tried, but Mr Howes was having none of it, having somehow managed to talk constantly from the moment Dave had climbed out of his vehicle and met the man outside his front door, which is where they were still standing. He wasn't even sure he'd had a chance yet to introduce himself.

Though he absolutely understood why DI Haig had requested

Constable Okri over to West Burton, and for him to carry out the task he was now undertaking, it didn't lessen at all his urge to shut the man up by dragging him down to the river and throwing him in, and as unceremoniously as possible.

'So, you can see my problem, can't you?' Howes said, but in such a way that Dave knew he wasn't expecting an answer. 'Here I am, trying to establish a business, to provide employment in an area that very much needs it, and a sustainable source of food, I might add, and what do I have to put up with? Well, ignoring all the red tape and the bureaucracy, and all those who have no idea at all as to what it is that I'm trying to do here, but seem intent on getting in my damned way, I now have some idiot running around my property, my own private land, and leaving these ridiculous signs and messages everywhere! I mean, what is the point? What? Have they really got nothing better to do? No, probably not. My guess is that whoever it is, they're unemployed, a university dropout, someone in patchwork trousers who thinks veganism will save the planet. It won't, you know. It can't. And I should know because ...'

Dave wasn't listening. He may have been giving the blustering Howes the impression that was exactly what he was doing, with lots of nods, and the occasional nonsensical scribble in his notebook, but that was all. Howes' words were bouncing off him like rain off a flysheet, and all Dave could really think about was those photographs. How could he not? They had, in moments, burned themselves into the back of his skull, seared his memory with their hellish awfulness. That was the only way to describe them, how the girls had been positioned, what Armitage had been ...

No, he thought, he had to focus. Thinking about it, dwelling on it, was going to help no one. Had to do the job at hand, do as Gordy asked.

'... on security camera, too, you know? Thought they'd snuck in unseen, didn't they? But they were wrong. Had them installed last week.'

'Pardon?' Dave said, bringing himself back online.

'The cameras,' Howes said. 'Had them put in last week.

Caught the little sod, too, didn't I? Come on!'

Dave watched as Howes turned on his heel and marched into his house, leaving the door open, and clearly expecting him to follow. So, Dave did exactly that, wondering what it was that Mr Howes had managed to catch on to his cameras.

'Here we are!' Howes said, ushering Dave into a small room at the far end of the house. 'Used to be some kind of gun room or something, I think. Now it's the nerve centre of my security system.'

Nerve centre, thought Dave, staring at a single computer screen, a keyboard, and a very modest collection of various other bits of electronic equipment and wires surrounding it. Bit of a grand statement, all in all. Especially when compared with the hi-tech stuff he and Matt had stumbled upon over in West Burton.

Howes sat down on a swivel chair at the desk the screen was perched on and tapped a few keys.

'Just you wait and see,' he said, leaning close enough to the screen for his nose to almost touch it. 'If evidence is what you need, then evidence is what I have!'

Dave stood behind Howes as various boxes flashed up on the screen. Various passwords were typed in, interspersed with swearing as he got them wrong, until at long last, Dave was staring at a screen now divided into four.

'There, you see?' Howes said, jabbing a finger at the screen.

'See what, exactly?' Dave asked.

Each of the four segments showed a grainy, black-and-white image of what Dave assumed was somewhere on the property.

'I've had four cameras placed to cover the drive, the house, the site where I want to put the tanks, and the woods,' Howes said. 'And I'm having more put in next week, too. Got to be thorough with these things, haven't you?'

'Always helps,' said Dave, though he wasn't really sure why. 'Are these live now?'

'They are,' Howes said. 'Impressed?'

Not really, thought Dave.

'You said you had evidence of an intruder on your property,' he said.

Howes didn't answer. Instead, he tapped a few more keys, swore at the mouse, and eventually brought up a file on the screen. Clicking on it, he revealed various other files, said, '*Bugger,*' under his breath a few times, before eventually finding what he was looking for.

'There!' he said, clicking a small, white triangle on another grainy image, which now filled the screen.

Dave leaned over the man's shoulder as nothing at all happened.

Minutes passed.

'Won't be long now,' Howes said.

'What are we looking at, exactly?' Dave asked.

'Can't you tell? It's the woods.' He jabbed a finger at the screen. 'See? Those are the trees, that's the fence and— Wait, there they are, look!'

Emerging from what Dave now understood to be trees on the left of the screen, something blurry slipped into view. It then made its way over the fence and seemed to drift across the screen until it disappeared off to the right.

'And what do you say to that, then?' Howes asked.

'Can you play it through again?' Dave asked.

A few minutes of muttering and swearing later, Howes managed to work out how to rewind what they had just watched and play it again.

Dave watched as the thing on the screen once again made its way over the fence and across the field.

'Pause it there,' he said.

Howes tried, failed, swore, rewound it again, and managed to do what Dave had requested.

'There he is,' Howes said, and didn't just point at the screen this time, but pressed the end of a stubby finger up against it, causing it to wobble.

Dave stared. Then stared some more.

'Do you have anything else?' he asked.

'Is that not enough?'

'Not really, no,' said Dave. 'It's quite hard to tell what it is we're looking at, isn't it?'

'We're looking at someone trespassing, that's what we're looking at!' Howes said, turning round to stare up at Dave.

'Can you zoom in?'

'What?'

'Zoom in,' Dave said. 'Make the image bigger.'

'I know what zoom means!'

'Well, can—'

Howes swung back around in his chair and faced the screen, muttering under his breath.

'There,' he said at last. 'Is that any better?'

The image was certainly larger, Dave thought, but it was no clearer. As far as he could tell, whoever it was just looked like a massive blob on the screen, the edges rough and loose, like the head of a mop.

'I'll be honest,' Dave said, 'I'm not really sure we can do much with that.'

'You can act on it, that's what you can do,' said Howes. 'I need a police presence on my property, don't I, to protect me? I'm in danger!'

'In danger? You didn't mention that before. What's happened? Did they attack you? Damage your property?'

'What? No! Of course not. But they could, couldn't they?'

'Look,' said Dave, 'I can understand your concern. However, what you're asking for is—'

'I've seen them with my own eyes!' Howes said, on his feet now, pointing out of the room and, Dave guessed, at the world outside his front door. 'Out there, running across my fields!'

'Do you have a description?' Dave asked. 'That would be very useful, I think.'

At this, Dave saw Howes falter for the first time since he'd arrived.

'A description?'

'Yes,' said Dave. 'You say that you saw whoever this is. Can you give me some idea of what they looked like, what they were wearing, their height, that kind of thing?'

'You want to know what they look like?'

Dave gave a nod, wondering why Howes seemed to be stalling suddenly.

'Yes,' he said, and made a point of poising his pen ready on his open notebook.

'That's a little difficult,' Howes said. 'You see, it was dark, and, well ...'

'Anything at all will be of use,' Dave said, trying to encourage the man to say whatever was now stuck in his larynx.

Howes cleared his throat.

'Well, whoever they are, I don't think they were very tall,' he said. 'Though, that's hard to tell, isn't it, from a distance, I mean?'

'And what were they wearing? Did you catch a hair colour, perhaps?'

'It was nighttime,' Howes said. 'And it's difficult to see at night, isn't it, even with the security lights on?'

Dave said nothing, just waited.

'And you won't believe me anyway if I tell you,' Howes said at last, his voice quieter now.

'I just need a few details,' Dave said. 'Then, maybe I can arrange to do some random spot checks, that kind of thing, see if we can't catch them in the act.'

He had no idea if that was possible, but he was happy to say anything to get Howes to finish what it was he was reluctant to say.

'They ... they were covered in ...' Howes' voice faded.

'Covered?' Dave asked. 'Do you mean dressed?'

Howes shook his head.

'No,' he said. 'I don't.'

'Not sure I understand.'

'Hair,' Howes said eventually. 'Whoever that is, they ... they were covered in hair.'

NINETEEN

When Harry woke the next morning, he had hoped to feel considerably better than he did. If anything, he felt worse, but couldn't work out how that was possible. Neither could he remember going to bed, and yet here he was, waking up in it. He sat up, yawned, and stretched so violently that his back cracked loud enough to make Harry briefly think he might have broken it. He saw that Smudge had vacated the room, then he heard something downstairs.

Harry froze, his eyes now focused on the open bedroom door.

'Smudge?'

His voice caught in his throat like a stray carrier bag blown by the wind and snagged on barbed wire.

No, it isn't Smudge, Harry thought.

Another sound. Clattering, like someone was rummaging through his cupboards.

Harry couldn't think straight. He was still ill, barely awake, couldn't remember going to bed, his dog was missing, and now someone was downstairs in his house.

Sliding his legs off the side of the bed, Harry pushed himself to his feet. His world swam, a wave of nausea slammed into him, and he stumbled forward, catching himself against the wall.

Harry squeezed his eyes shut, took a slow breath in and out, opened them again. With a not inconsiderable amount of effort, he pushed himself away from the wall and started to shuffle towards the door.

More sounds from downstairs. Whoever it was, they were clearly intent on having a good old look around, but for what? And who the hell was it? And what had they done with Smudge?

Closing in on the door, Harry's mind scanned back through all the faces of those he knew would love the chance to get one over on him, to turn his place over. *Most of them would also probably happily slot me,* he thought, the old phrase from his Paratrooper days popping into his mind out of the oblivion of the night before.

Outside the bedroom, Harry made his way to the stairs, then came to a dead stop. If someone was in his house—and it certainly sounded like they were—there was no way in hell he was going to face them without something to protect himself with. But what? There was nothing in the bathroom other than a bottle of shower gel, some toothpaste, a toilet brush ...

Quietly, he slipped back into the bedroom, only to appear back on the landing, clutching the only things he could find with any chance of fending someone off; his belt, which he had wrapped around his left hand and now hung loose like a whip, and his bedside lamp upside down in his right, minus the lampshade and bulb. As clubs went, it was next to useless, but it was better than nothing. At least Harry hoped it was, though as he caught sight of himself in the bathroom mirror, he wasn't so sure.

Making his way slowly down the stairs, the sounds from below only grew louder. Harry gripped his belt and lamp, white-knuckle tight.

'Whoever you are, I'm coming for you,' he muttered, as Smudge appeared at the bottom of the stairs, tail wagging.

Harry stopped halfway down.

Smudge sat down and stared up at him.

Now Harry really was confused. Just what the hell was going on?

With Smudge eyeballing him, Harry continued on his way down, desperately trying to avoid every spot he knew would elicit a creak.

Something moved in the corner of Harry's eye. He snapped around, lamp raised above his head.

'What the bloody hell are you doing?'

Harry stared at Grace over the banister.

'I ... I thought ...'

'And why are you carrying that lamp?'

Harry let his hand drop to his waist.

'I woke up and heard something,' he said. 'I didn't know what ... who ...'

Smudge had padded up the stairs to greet him and was pawing at his thigh for some fuss.

'What are you talking about?' Grace asked. 'I left you in bed and came down to make some breakfast. Thought I'd make you something tasty, see if that didn't get you going a bit.'

Harry screwed up his face in confusion.

'You slept with me? In the same bed?'

'That's what sleeping with someone usually involves, yes,' said Grace.

'But when?' asked Harry. 'I mean, when did you get here? I don't remember.'

Grace's face fell dramatically.

'You don't remember me being in bed with you?' she said. 'Way to make a girl feel good about herself, Harry ...'

'No, that's not what I meant,' Harry began, then saw a faint smile break across Grace's lips. 'Oh, right, you're taking the piss.'

Grace laughed.

'You really don't remember?'

Harry made his way to the bottom of the stairs.

'Not a thing,' he said. 'When did you get here? I remember a video call with the team back in the office, but that's it. No, wait ... I came up to bed immediately after; I remember now. But I don't remember you turning up at all.'

Grace came over to Harry, placed her hands on either side of his face, then kissed him gently on his forehead.

'Yuck,' she said. 'Sweaty. Hungry?'

Letting go, Grace turned and led Harry into the kitchen.

Harry followed, aware then of the smell of bacon, the rich tang of it filling the air, mixing with steam from a teapot on the table.

'Yes,' he said, sitting down at the table. 'Actually, I am. First time since I got the plague, too.'

The radio was on just loud enough to be heard, but not so loud as to barge into the conversation. Classical music, too, Harry noticed, rather liking it.

Grace placed two plates on the table, then sat down opposite Harry and poured out two mugs of tea.

'Thanks,' Harry said, staring down at the plate of food in front of him. The bacon was accompanied by an egg, some toast, and a couple of slices of black pudding.

'I popped down to Cockett's early doors,' Grace said. 'You didn't stir.'

Harry tucked in, savouring every mouthful, almost sensing every part of his body turning the food into fuel as soon as it was in his mouth.

'When did you get here, then?' Harry asked. 'And nice though this is, and I do appreciate it, what if you get what I've had?'

'If I'm going to get it, I've probably already got it,' said Grace. 'Anyway, I missed you. Well, Smudge, anyway.' Hearing her name, Smudge switched her attention from Harry, whom she had been staring at since he'd started eating, to Grace. 'How are you feeling?'

Harry paused eating, took a swig from his mug.

'I felt rough when I got up,' he said, 'which wasn't helped by thinking someone was downstairs doing my house over.'

Grace laughed.

'You genuinely thought that? How paranoid are you?'

Harry pointed at the now half-consumed plate of food with his fork.

'This, though? It's helping me feel human again.'

'Thought it might,' said Grace. 'Can't say you look ready to go back to work quite yet, though.'

'I'll give it another day,' said Harry. 'Tomorrow, I should be fine.'

He lifted one of the slices of toast and dipped the corner in the egg, went to take a bite, when his phone buzzed.

'You don't have to answer it,' Grace said. 'But I know you will.'

Harry saw the number.

'Gordy,' he said, and answered.

'Harry?'

'If you're calling to check up on me, and to make sure I'm resting, not only can I confirm that I am, but I even have a witness.'

'I'm not,' said Gordy.

'Then why the call?'

'Two things,' said Gordy. 'First being we've got a positive lead on who dumped all that stuff in front of the gate.'

'What? How?'

'Long story, which I won't bore you with now. The edited version is that, while searching Armitage's house, Matt and Dave found something. The SOC team have been over the place. Blood and hair were found at the top of the stairs on the banisters and have been matched to Armitage.'

Harry remembered what Gordy had told him about the postmortem, the wound to Armitage's head.

'He was killed at the house, then,' he said.

'And then covered in salt and buried before being pegged out in that field,' said Gordy. 'Don't try to make sense of it, because I can't.'

'What did Matt and Dave find?'

'SD cards,' Gordy said. 'Quite a few of them, actually, and photographs, too, but that's something else entirely. Looks like Armitage was into a few things, none of them nice.'

'Not sure I follow.'

'Following analysis by the SOC team, we have a lot of footage relating to the photographs I just mentioned, but what we also have is the footage we have of a truck.'

'Truck? You mean we've a positive ID on who dumped all that stuff?'

'We've got a numberplate, model, and manufacturer, so yes.'

'Address?'

'Matt and Jadyn are heading there now.'

Harry leaned back in his chair, wishing he could be more involved in what was going on.

'But how is it you've got this footage?' he asked. 'How was it taken?'

'Jen's on her way over to the field,' said Gordy. 'Only way it could have been taken is by some cameras set up near the gate.'

'Put there by the farmer, you think?'

'If they were, then how is it that Armitage had the footage?' Gordy asked. 'Doesn't make any sense.'

'Only way to find out is to speak to the farmer,' said Harry. 'Get Jen to head over after she's been to check out the field.'

'I will,' said Gordy.

'What's the other thing, then?' Harry asked.

'We've got news on the missing couple; Helen and Chris.'

'It's all go, isn't it?' said Harry, unable to hide the tone of disappointment at not being involved.

'A little,' said Gordy. 'They've been holed up in a little Airbnb in Sedbergh. They're on their way back to Helen's mum's as we speak. I'm heading over there once I've finished talking to you.'

Gordy paused then, and Harry noticed a certain weight to it.

'Something wrong?'

'What we found at Armitage's house,' Gordy said. 'Firstly, Helen, the missing girl, she worked for Armitage. Secondly, she was there, at his house. We've found footage of her from a room he had set up with a bed, cameras, the works. There are also photos of her taken at work, we think, and very clearly without her knowledge, considering their nature.' Gordy paused, took a breath, and when she spoke again, her voice was quieter, darker somehow. 'He ... he did things in the bedroom, Harry. To lots of girls. To her.'

Harry didn't need Gordy to say anymore.

'Drugs?'

'My guess is he was an expert in spiking drinks. Though he hired escorts, too, apparently. He had an appetite, that's for sure, one that I wish I could scrub my mind clean of. Liked to pay for it, but obviously also liked to do things that weren't consensual.'

'Don't let me keep you, then.'

Gordy said, 'I'll let you know how I get on with Matt and Jadyn, and I'll have Jen keep you up to date on what's what over at the field, and if she gets anything from her chat with the farmer.'

Conversation over, Harry placed his phone on the table, then yawned uncontrollably, which only served to make him swear, frustrated at not being involved with what was going on, being useful.

'I need to head off to work,' said Grace, standing up. 'Reckon you should get yourself back to bed.'

'But I don't want to,' Harry said. 'I should be out there, helping Gordy, leading the team on this.'

Grace came over and, leaning down, rested a kiss on his cheek.

'Stop being a grump and get upstairs,' she said.

Harry raised an eyebrow.

'Ha, fat chance!' Grace laughed, catching Harry's implication. 'But if you do want a little bit of slap and tickle, then you need to be fit and well, don't you? So, finish your breakfast and get back to bed. And once you're well, I'll maybe be able to take that look you just gave me a little more seriously.'

A few minutes later, with breakfast finished and Grace on her way to work, Harry had done as she'd said and pottered back off to bed. Lying there in the gloom, sleep refused to come to him. He couldn't get comfortable, and he was either too hot or too cold. His conversation with Gordy was bouncing around in his head, as was the rest of the investigation. None of it made sense, and now with this footage of a truck dumping all that rubbish at the field? Why was nothing simple?

Closing his eyes once more, he tried again to drift off, but his restlessness got the better of him. Then he had an idea, and before he could stop himself, was on the phone with Jen.

TWENTY

Pulling up outside the house, which sat far back from the lane leading through Constable Burton, Jadyn let out a whistle.

'Quite a place,' said Matt, staring at the shiny, black gates in front of them, which were guarded by large, white lions atop brick posts on either side.

'My guess is that whoever they are, they're doing a little better than either of us.'

'You've never been to my house,' said Matt. 'For all you know, I could live in a mansion with a tree-lined gravel drive.'

'Do you?'

'No,' said Matt, staring through the gates at the house beyond. 'Not sure I'd want to, either. Big houses are overrated.'

'Wouldn't say no, though, would you?' said Jadyn.

'I would actually, and so would you once you saw the heating bill, the maintenance costs, the insurance, the council tax ...'

'Even so.'

Matt shook his head.

'Trust me,' he said. 'A place like this? It'll be a money pit.'

'It'll go up in value though, won't it?' Jadyn said.

'It will,' agreed Matt. 'But you'll have spent all of that extra cash on making sure the whole thing doesn't just crumble into the

ground. No, you're much better off with something smaller, something sensible, a house that when you turn the heating on you don't
have to sell a kidney.'

Jadyn laughed.

'Not into the grander side of life, are you?'

Matt shook his head.

'A house should be a home,' he said. 'Simple as that. And why
would you want to draw attention to yourself like this, anyway? All
it does is shout, *Look at me, I'm a rich git*, doesn't it? And if you are,
and you're happy, why would you need to shout about it? Doesn't
make sense to me, or Joan, for that matter. Which is a good job,
really, because there's no bloody chance of my ever buying her
something like this!'

'I guess,' said Jadyn. 'Shall I see if anyone's in?'

He didn't wait for Matt to answer, and instead, opened his
window and pressed a button on a small telecom device set on top
of a metal pole just to the side of the gates.

A faint bleep sounded, then a moment or two later, a man's
voice crackled through a small speaker above the button.

'Yes?'

'This is Constable Okri and Detective Sergeant Dinsdale,'
Jadyn said. 'Just wondered if we could come in for a chat about
something?'

'We're chatting now, aren't we?' the voice replied.

Jadyn glanced at Matt.

'He's got a point.'

'Face-to-face,' said Matt, and nodded back at the small
speaker.

'Can we come in, please?' Jadyn asked.

'What is it you want to talk about?'

Matt leaned over Jadyn to make sure he could be heard by
whoever it was they were speaking to.

'This is Detective Sergeant Dinsdale,' he said. 'Open the gates,
please. This won't take long.'

'I'm busy.'

'So are we,' said Matt. 'The sooner we get this done, the better, then, don't you think?'

The voice went silent.

'Don't think he wants to let us in,' said Jadyn.

'Gates like that, I don't think he wants to let anyone in,' said Matt. 'Give it a second, then we'll try again.'

The gates started to swing open.

'Sensible decision,' said Matt, and Jadyn rolled them through the opening and on towards the house.

Climbing out of the vehicle, Matt took in the grand Victorian villa, with vast bay windows staring down at them like the glaring eyes of some very hungry monster. The driveway was lined with neatly manicured hedges, and beyond it sat a well-cared-cared-for lawn, which swept around the house, giving the impression of it floating on a pool of green. Trees reached up around the house, casting shadows over it and the grounds like artistically placed drapes of grey and black. One vehicle was parked outside, an imposing Mercedes 4x4.

'That's not the truck in the footage, is it?' said Jadyn, coming around to join him.

Matt didn't get to reply as the front door was opened and a man walked out. He was neatly dressed in beige chinos and a jumper and looked altogether rather unassuming. His slight build and thin face gave him more the air of someone who spent their days pouring over spreadsheets and their nights reading books, rather than driving trucks in the dark to fly-tip rubbish in front of a gate.

He hardly looks big enough to drive the one currently sat in front of the house, Matt thought, and raised a hand in greeting.

'You said this wouldn't take long,' the man said, approaching Matt. 'I'll hold you to that. I'm a busy man.'

He was soft spoken, which only added to the man's unassuming air. Except there was a notable edge to his voice, one that Matt suspected was razor sharp if it needed to be.

'I'm sure you are,' Matt said. 'Can we go inside, out of the cold?'

'Of course,' the man said, turning and heading back inside.

Matt led Jadyn through the door, following the man into the house and then left into a large, airy office lit by various lamps, and the gloopy light leaking in through the bay window.

The man gestured to a huddle of comfortable chairs around a low table, taking a seat himself as he did so.

Matt and Jadyn sat down.

'I'd offer you a coffee,' the man said, 'but I'd rather we just got this over and done with. What's this all about?'

Matt took out his notepad. Jadyn did the same.

'Can we take a few details first, please?' he asked. 'Just a name and a contact number, that's all, in case we need to follow up with anything.'

'I can't see that there's anything you have to discuss that would need following up,' the man said.

'Even so,' said Matt, making it very clear that he was insisting on being given the information he'd just asked for.

'Bacon,' the man said eventually, sitting back, crossing his legs, his hands resting on them, fingers entwined. 'Edward Bacon.' He then gave them his phone number.

'There, that wasn't so painful now, was it?' said Matt, then looked at Jadyn to continue.

Jadyn said, 'We just need to check if you own a vehicle linked to an investigation we're currently working on.'

As Jadyn shared the vehicle's make, model, and registration number, Matt kept an eye on the man in front of him. He seemed calm, collected, and unfazed by the unexpected arrival of two police officers in his house.

'Yes, that's my vehicle,' Bacon said. 'Can I ask what it is you need to know about it?'

Jadyn said, 'We have reason to believe that the vehicle used in connection with the illegal dumping of waste on a public road.'

'Ridiculous.'

'Is the vehicle here?' Matt asked.

'No.'

'Do you know where it is?'

When Bacon went to answer, Matt noticed the briefest of hesitations and a flick of his eyes to the window before he spoke.

'No,' he said. 'It was stolen a week ago.'

At this, Matt again looked at Jadyn, and this time said, 'Did that come up when we ran a search on the vehicle?'

'No,' said Jadyn.

'You didn't report it?' Matt asked, turning his attention back to Bacon.

'What would be the point? The police are hardly going to spend time trying to find it, are they? I couldn't see the point.'

'What about an insurance claim, then?' Matt asked. 'If it was stolen, you would need a crime reference number for that.'

'Again, more hassle than it's worth,' said Bacon. 'It was easier, and cheaper I might add, for me to just class it as a business loss and move on.'

'Cheaper?' said Matt. 'Really? A vehicle like that isn't cheap.'

'And neither is my time,' said Bacon. 'It's better spent on other things, things that actually bring in money, rather than wasting it. Spending hours on the phone with an insurance company, then more hours with someone in a bad suit interrogating me about what happened? Simply not worth it.'

'What is it that you do?' Matt asked.

'I'm a trader,' said Bacon. 'Stocks and shares, Bitcoin, that kind of thing. Work for myself and a small number of private clients. I do well enough to know that a stolen car is easier and cheaper to replace than spending my valuable time trying to prove to my insurance company that it was stolen in the first place.'

'Where was it stolen from?' Jadyn asked.

Matt watched Bacon's eyes snap around to stare at the constable.

'The marketplace in Leyburn,' he said.

'How did you get home?' Matt asked.

'What? My assistant came to fetch me.'

'Are they here now?'

'No.'

'Would it be possible for us to contact them to verify this?'

'I'm not going to give you their personal details,' said Bacon. 'Not without their permission.'

'Will you be speaking to them today?'

'Of course.'

'Then can I ask that you have them call me?' said Matt, rising to his feet. He looked at Jadyn, who followed his lead. 'We can let ourselves out.'

Outside, Matt dropped himself into the passenger seat as Jadyn joined him. Edward Bacon had already closed the front door on them.

'Rushed out of there a bit quick, didn't we?' Jadyn said, starting the engine and then turning the vehicle around to head back up the driveway.

'Well, we're not going far,' said Matt.

Jadyn stopped the vehicle, waiting for the gates to open.

'How do you mean?' he asked.

'Something's not right,' said Matt. 'He hesitated when I asked if he knew where the vehicle was, glanced out of the window, too.'

'Maybe he's just a bit twitchy,' said Jadyn.

Matt shook his head.

'He didn't seem bothered about us being there, did he? Not at first, anyway. Most people are surprised to have the police turn up on their doorstep uninvited. He only grew irritable when we asked about the vehicle. I think that took him by surprise.'

'Why, though?' asked Jadyn. 'If it was stolen, then—'

'Exactly,' said Matt. 'If.'

Outside the gates, Jadyn came to a stop.

'Where to now, then?' he asked.

Just down the lane, Matt spotted an entrance to a field which was barely visible due to trees hanging over it, and an overgrown verge.

'Right there will do,' he said.

'Really? Why?' asked Jadyn, a confused frown furrowing his brow.

'Well, for a start, I don't for one minute think that the vehicle was stolen.'

'There's something else though, isn't there?' Jadyn said. 'I can tell.'

'There is,' said Matt. 'I don't think that our Mr Bacon was alone ...'

TWENTY-ONE

Jen was sitting at a large, wooden dining table, directly opposite Mr and Mrs Dent, in a kitchen that had seen its best years at least a decade ago, and holding her phone screen out towards them.

An old sheepdog, grey around the muzzle, was curled up on a rug in front of an Aga belting out enough heat to melt the icecaps. A mug of tea was to her left, and a large plate of biscuits was close enough for her to help herself. In a vase on the table sat a fresh bunch of flowers, alongside a card with a sheep on the front.

Mr Dent was probably around five foot nine, she guessed, with the build of someone who worked a farm day in, day out. He had broad shoulders beneath a head of dark, thinning hair speckled with grey. His hands were thick and meaty, with fingers like sausages, and she could tell he carried enough extra weight to make her think his calories erred on the side of meat and potatoes and a beer or two.

Mrs Dent was a little shorter, with light brown hair, bright eyes, and ruddy cheeks from the wind and weather. What surprised Jen, though, was how fit she looked, and strong. Her clothes seemed to be loose in places and tight in others, as though she'd changed physically, and for the better, but not as yet got around to adjusting her wardrobe accordingly.

Jen could see the love between the two of them, which seemed to radiate out into the room.

The journey over had been swift, at one point a little too much so, as black ice had caught her sharp and sent her sliding. But she had handled the skid well, her police driver training kicking in, and, after quickly stopping by at the field where Armitage had been found, had arrived in one piece about fifteen minutes ago.

The day was bright, but no less cold because of it. Harry had insisted on being on video call as soon as she arrived in the yard in front of the Dent's farmhouse and had asked how the journey over was.

'A little dicey,' Jen had answered. 'With it being so cold, the roads aren't thawing at all, so there's ice patches all over the place.'

She'd then watched Harry actually lean in towards the screen.

'Doesn't look icy there, though.'

'That's because it isn't,' said Jen.

The only vehicles they'd seen parked in the yard were Sam's truck, which they'd seen at the field the day the body had been found, and a little yellow hatchback.

Jen reached for a biscuit, but was interrupted by Harry.

'Right then,' he said from the screen of her phone. 'Shall we get on?'

Jen could tell by the looks on the faces of the couple in front of her that neither of them knew quite how to respond.

Mr Dent raised his right hand.

'Do you normally do interviews like this?' he asked, his eyes flicking between Jen and Harry.

'No,' said Harry. 'Can't say that I do.'

'And it's a first for me as well,' Jen added.

Mr Dent lowered his hand.

'Can I ask, then, why you're here?' he said. 'I've already given a statement about what I found. I thought it would all be dealt with by now.'

'This won't take long, Mr Dent,' said Harry, and Jen hoped he was right, because this really felt very strange, holding Harry's scarred visage out in front of her to talk to the Dents. Not quite Star Trek, but the Dents were certainly staring at her as though she was from another planet.

'Call me Sam,' Mr Dent said.

'And I'm Debs,' his wife added with a wave, which seemed to drift in direction between Jen's phone and Jen herself, until it finally faded away, and Debs put her hand back in her lap.

'This isn't actually about what you found in the field,' Harry said.

Jen saw a look of confusion flash between Sam and Debs.

'It's not?' said Debs. 'Then, now I'm really confused.'

'It's about the fly-tipping,' said Jen. 'The pile in front of the gate?'

'You mean something's going to be done about it?' Debs asked. 'About bloody time! We can't just be clearing it up again and again, can we?'

Harry said, 'We're currently following up on details of the vehicle we know was involved in the illegal dumping. However, it's the way those details came to our notice that's brought us back here.'

'Did someone see who it was, then?' Sam asked. 'And if so, why've they taken so long to come forward and say anything?'

'It's been there for at least three weeks now,' added Debs. 'I tell you, if I get my hands on who did it ...'

Jen could feel the heat in Debs' voice, her anger at what had been done as clear as it was understandable.

'You won't be getting your hands on them or doing anything,' said Sam, looking at his wife. 'That's what the police are for, remember? And here they are.' He glanced at Harry on Jen's phone. 'Well, sort of.'

'Can I ask if you've ever used anything like a wildlife camera?' said Harry.

'That's an odd question,' said Sam. 'How do you mean?'

'Something you could hide in a bush or up a tree,' Harry explained, clearly struggling to explain.

'And why would I want to do that?' Sam asked.

'I know the kind you mean,' said Debs.

'You do?' said Jen.

Debs gave a nod.

'I've a few of my own, actually. Why?'

'Can I ask what you've used them for?' Harry asked.

'I do a little bit of pest control,' Debs said. 'It's not a full-time thing or anything like that, but it brings in a bit of extra cash, which, when you're running a farm, is something you always need, isn't it, Love?' She smiled at Sam. 'The cameras are useful to monitor a site before I decide what to do, how to deal with what the problem is, that kind of thing.'

'Can you explain?' Jen asked.

'Of course,' said Debs. 'If you've a rat problem, you can use traps, poison, shooting; all three, or a combination, it all depends.'

'On what?'

'Not everyone wants traps left all over the place for a start,' said Debs. 'And bait boxes are okay, but they're not exactly wildlife friendly. Shooting is surprisingly effective. Once I know what I'm dealing with, I can set up a nicely camouflaged place to hide in and stake a place out.'

'She's a crack shot,' said Sam.

'And where are these cameras right now?' Harry asked.

'I can get them for you if you want?' Debs said. 'I've a few out at a barn over by Hawkswick, like, but there's probably half a dozen in with all my gear.'

'Have you ever placed any out in the field where the fly-tipping is?'

Debs shook her head.

'Why would I?'

'We found footage of the vehicle used to dump the rubbish from a camera like the ones you describe using,' Jen said. 'I popped over to the field on my way here, and my guess is that the camera was situated in the wall somehow. Obviously, it's not there now.'

Jen saw confusion on both Debs' and Sam's faces.

'Wait,' said Sam, 'you're not suggesting that Debs here put the camera there, are you?'

'Wish I had, actually,' said Debs. 'But I've not enough cameras to cover every single bloody gate we have for all of the fields we own, have I? And thinking I'm going to catch anyone with a random camera is never going to work.'

'And yet it seems to have done just that,' said Harry. 'Which is why we're here now.'

'Well, I didn't put a camera in the gate to the field,' said Debs.

'And neither did I,' said Sam. 'Wouldn't know how to use one, even if I had done.'

Debs laughed.

'He's still confused by the TV remote, aren't you?'

'Have you ever noticed anyone in the field before?' Jen asked. 'Maybe hanging around the gate, or parked there at night? I noticed there were no stiles in the walls, so I'm assuming there's no footpath.'

'There isn't,' said Sam. 'Though, that's not stopped some from thinking there is then having a go at making their own. Honestly, some people have no respect, do they? A few stones knocked down, a sheep spots it, and they'll be over it as quick as you like, followed by every other sodding sheep in the field, and that's your wall gone, and a real headache getting it patched up again, I can tell you.'

'I saw someone in the field a couple of nights ago,' Debs said.

'I meant to go and check straight away,' said Sam, 'but I forgot. Which is why I was round there that morning and found what I found.'

Jen turned her phone so she could speak to Harry's actual face, rather than just his disembodied voice.

'I don't think that was in Mr Dent's statement,' she said, and glanced up at Sam.

'It wasn't,' said Sam. 'Sorry, I didn't think it was important, or I forgot. Can't remember really. I had a migraine coming on, and that can be a little distracting.'

'But you saw someone in the field, yes?' Jen asked, looking now at Debs.

'Not sure what I saw,' Debs replied. 'I was driving past, coming back from a bit of pest control late one night, and I thought I saw something. I was too tired to stop.'

'And when was this again?' Harry asked.

'The night before I found what I found,' said Sam.

'And you saw it as you were driving past?'

'Yes,' said Debs.

'Were you able to get a good look at whoever it was you saw?' asked Jen.

Debs shook her head.

'Honestly, I'm not sure what I saw. It was a blur. I was driving, I was tired, it was dark. I only mentioned it in passing to Sam. Neither of us expected any of this.'

Jen looked at Debs and said, 'So, to confirm, then, you've not placed any cameras at the gate to the field. Also, you saw something in the field the night before the body was found by your husband, yes?'

'It's not much, is it?' Debs said, then added, 'If you've the vehicle details, then you'll be able to catch whoever dumped the rubbish, won't you? And someone will come and clear it up?'

Jen could tell from the look in Debs' eyes that she knew the answer.

'I'm afraid it's the responsibility of the landowner to clear fly-tipped waste,' she said. 'The council can help, but they'll charge.'

'Thought you'd say that.' Debs sighed. 'Seems a little unfair, don't you think?'

'I don't make the rules,' said Jen. 'But in this case, yeah, I do think it is.'

Harry said, 'I think I've run out of things to ask.'

'Same,' said Jen, once again looking at Harry on her phone's screen. 'Shall I finish off here?'

'That would be appreciated, yes,' said Harry, and Jen's screen went blank.

Jen thanked the Dents for their time, and let herself out, though she was accompanied to the door by the old dog.

Outside, she hunched her shoulders against the frosty bite in the wind, quickly jumped into her vehicle, and headed back to the office.

TWENTY-TWO

Gordy was back in Pam Nevill's lounge.

'You're sure you don't want a brew?' Pam asked.

For once, Gordy wasn't in the mood for more tea. Or coffee, or indeed any kind of refreshment. She simply wanted to get on with the real reason she was there, to find out exactly what was going on, what had happened at Armitage's house, because right then, all that she had were questions.

'No, I'm fine, thank you,' she said, then turned her attention to the other two in the room with her, Helen, Pam's daughter, and her boyfriend, Chris. Helen's head was tipped forward, almost as though she was unable to lift it to meet Gordy's stare, her coal-black hair hanging long on her shoulders. Next to her, and holding her hand, Chris was just as sheepish. 'So,' she said, 'where shall we begin?'

The question was as much to herself as it was to the young couple who had been missing for the better part of a week.

Helen lifted her face, and where Gordy had expected to see worry and fear, she instead saw a hardness that caught her breath.

'What do you want to know?' Helen asked, lifting a hand to wipe a tear from her cheek.

Gordy stared at the tear, wondering what had caused it, what

Helen would be able to tell her about what had happened at Armitage's house, in the field …

'First,' she said, 'can you confirm where you were two nights ago?'

'Yes,' said Chris, though his eyes seemed to be filled with horror more than Helen's. Anger was there, though, like he was keeping it at bay for now.

Gordy waited, found herself staring at the young man's shoes, spotted something, but decided to leave it for a while.

'You need to actually tell me where you were,' she said, trying to coax the information from the young couple.

'It's an Airbnb over in Sedbergh,' Chris said. 'I can give you the address.'

He did exactly that, and Gordy jotted it down, then asked, 'You were there alone?'

'Yes.'

'So, can anyone confirm that you were there on the night in question?'

'Me,' said Helen. 'I was there. We were there together.'

'I need something more than that, I'm afraid,' said Gordy.

She needed to get through this part so that she could get on with what had been haunting her since she'd seen the photographs from the house, watched some of what was on the SD cards.

'Like what?'

'Did you do anything? Did anyone come round? Did you go out? Is there anything at all that can place you where you say you were?'

Gordy waited while Helen and Chris exchanged looks.

'My brother,' Chris said. 'He visited. He was with us the whole night.'

'Your brother? Why was he there?'

'Broke up with his girlfriend,' said Chris. 'Seemed really cut up about it, so we invited him over.' He gave Gordy his brother's contact details. 'Call him,' he said. 'He'll confirm what I've said, where we were.'

'You weren't in West Burton, then?'

That got their attention, Gordy thought, noting a flicker in the couple's eyes, a twitch that said they knew more than they were letting on.

'West Burton?' said Helen. 'Why?'

And there it was, Gordy thought: *Why* ... If they had never been there at all, then the response would've been a simple no, because there would be no reason for it to be anything else. An answer like that would be instinctive, the truth would just fall out. But *why* was different. It was answering a question with a question, and that always made Gordy feel uneasy. She didn't want to press on because she knew where it led. She'd seen the photos, the footage, and a face from that wall was staring back at her in that very room.

'Helen ...'

'What?'

Gordy was momentarily lost for a way to progress. She knew, at least to some degree, what had happened to Helen, what Armitage had done. Whether or not Helen and her boyfriend had had anything to do with the man ending up in the field was as yet to be uncovered, but the only way to do so was to press on.

'Can you tell me what you do for a living?' Gordy asked, changing tack a little, if only to unsettle Helen.

'What? Yes, I'm a personal assistant.'

'And who is it you are a personal assistant for?'

'Mark Armitage,' Helen said, her voice flat.

'Can you tell me what Mr Armitage does?'

'He's an environmental officer for the council,' Helen said.

That was news, Gordy noted, jotting the information down.

'Do you have much to do with him outside of work?'

'No. What? Why would you ask that?'

'So, you wouldn't regard him as a friend, someone you'd see socially outside of work?'

'Of course I fucking well wouldn't!' Helen spat back. 'He's—'

Gordy waited for Helen to finish what she'd been going to say, but she clamped her mouth shut.

'He's what?' Gordy pressed, but Helen said nothing more.

Gordy reached into a pocket and removed an evidence bag. She leaned over and handed it to Helen.

'Mr Armitage's body was found in a field near Kettlewell two nights ago,' she said. 'This was later found to be in his possession. It's a twelve-week scan. Your scan, to be precise, Helen.'

Chris and Helen's reaction were enough to tell Gordy that Pam had shared the news of Armitage's death, as she would've expected her to.

Helen's hands shook as she stared at what they now held, but she said nothing, her jaws clenching, her lips tight.

Then Pam was on her feet.

'You think Helen had something to do with it? Is that why you're here? Is it? I don't believe it. I can't. I won't! It's impossible!'

Gordy waited for Pam to calm down and sit back down in her chair then focused her attention on Helen.

'Can you tell me why he had your scan with him?' She leaned forward, her eyes fixed on Helen's face, looking for a response. 'Please?'

Helen opened her mouth to speak, but the only sound that came out was a strangled cry so full of pain that before Gordy knew what she was doing she was in front of the young woman, her arms wrapped around her so tightly she heard her joints crack.

To hell with being professional, she thought, *this kid needs this ...*

Helen cried then, the cry turning into a wail so filled with pain that Gordy felt tears well in her own eyes.

'It's okay,' Gordy said, her voice the softest of whispers. 'It's okay ... You just need to tell me what happened, that's all.'

Pam joined in as well, leaping out of her chair to throw her arms around her daughter. Chris leaned in, but couldn't make it through the barrier of Gordy and Pam.

Eventually, the sobbing subsided, and Gordy sensed Helen

pulling away, so she released her, and sat back in her chair, Pam doing the same.

'In your own time, Helen,' she said. 'But you need to know that I've seen photos of you taken by Armitage. Not only in his house, but I assume at work.'

'What?' said Helen. 'How? He's never taken a photo of me. I'd never let him!'

'And judging by what I saw, you didn't know they were taken.'

Helen was already pale, but she grew paler still.

'There are videos, too,' Gordy said. 'I've not seen them myself, but the forensics team has. We know what's on them, what Armitage was doing in that house. I need to know everything, Helen; how this happened, how he did what he did, and what you did about it.'

That last question she directed not just at Helen, but at Chris, too, whose look of horror she noticed had now burned away into a potent cocktail of sorrow and rage.

'We didn't do anything about it!' Helen said. 'We just got the hell out of there.'

'How did you end up there in the first place?' Gordy asked.

'He ... I think he must've spiked my drink,' Helen said. 'While I was at work. Something in my coffee maybe.'

Pam was on her feet again.

'He did what?'

'He drugged me, Mum,' Helen said. 'He must've done. I mean, it's the only way any of this could've happened.'

Helen's voice broke, and Chris stepped in.

'She would work late quite often,' he said. 'Mark ... He's a bullying bastard; he'd have her working mad hours, doing stuff he should've been doing himself, I reckon. I think he thought he could get away with it.'

'I don't understand any of this,' Pam said. 'Why would he drug you, Helen? What are you talking about? Just what is this?'

Gordy held up a hand to calm Pam down.

'Please,' she said.

Pam hesitated, went to say something else, but managed to sit back down.

'His office is on a trading estate on the edge of Leyburn,' Helen said. 'I never go to his house. I've never been, not once. All I ever knew was that it was in West Burton. I used to like visiting the falls, but I stopped going because there was always the chance I might bump into him, or see him as I drove through. But that's where I woke up, in his house.'

Gordy saw Pam go to stand again, but a quick look was enough to have her stay where she was.

'You woke up in his house?'

Helen's nod was barely noticeable, but it was enough for Gordy to press on.

'Are you able to tell me what he did?'

Helen shook her head.

'It's not that I don't want to, it's that I don't remember,' she said. 'Not all of it. I get flashbacks, images of being in a bedroom, but they're fuzzy. Really, all I actually remember is waking up on a bed, and realising that I was wearing ...'

'You don't have to tell me all the details,' said Gordy. 'You only have to share what you can, okay? I know this is hard.'

Helen took a moment to gather herself.

'When I woke up, I didn't know where I was. I saw my clothes folded on the floor. I got dressed, then the door opened and there he was—Mark—just standing there, staring at me. He looked surprised, not at me being there, but at me being awake. He was as close to being naked without it making much difference, considering all that he was wearing was a black pouch. He was carrying a mask and some rope. It's something I can't stop seeing, like the image has been burned into my mind of this pale, thin, sweating man, ... God, it was awful. No, it was worse than that. It was terrifying. I've never been so scared. And he was carrying this ... this *thing* ... and ... and the next thing I know, I'm no longer in the room. I'm downstairs. I can't remember getting there.'

'But you remembered all of what you just told us,' said Gordy.

'I needed to get out of there,' said Helen. 'I just ran at him and the next thing I know I'm downstairs. I've no idea what happened between those two things. I just wanted to escape. And I still didn't know where I was, so I ran outside and ... it was the middle of the night!'

'What did you do?'

'She called me,' said Chris. 'And I fetched her.'

'My phone, it was in the back pocket of my trousers,' Helen said. 'It has a button flap on it, so I always put it in there because it doesn't fall out. Chris came to get me.'

'But why did you run away to that Airbnb?' Gordy asked. 'Didn't Armitage come after you? And how did he end up with your scan?'

'I've carried it with me every day since it was done,' Helen said. 'That was three weeks ago. It must've fallen out of my pocket when he ... when he undressed me.'

'And the baby's father is ...' Gordy began.

'It's Chris's,' said Helen, interrupting. 'I've been keeping it quiet, didn't want to say too much, not early on. Didn't want to jinx it.'

That news was a relief to Gordy, who had been carrying around a dark thought about the scan, wondering if the baby had been Armitage's.

A cry broke from Helen again, and she rocked forward. Pam went to her, throwing her arms around her daughter.

Gordy turned her attention to Chris.

'Can you tell me what happened when you arrived at the house?'

'There's nothing to tell,' Chris said. 'I took Helen away, as far away as I could and as quickly as I could.'

'Why didn't you call the police?'

'I panicked. We both did. We were in shock.'

'Did you see Mark yourself? Did you do anything to him?'

Chris looked genuinely shocked by the question.

'All I cared about was Helen. She didn't want to go home,

didn't want to tell her mum, tell anyone, what had happened. She wouldn't listen. What was I supposed to do? Force her? I knew I had to give her time.'

'You didn't answer the question,' said Gordy, pressing harder.

'Did I do anything to him? Like what?'

Gordy remained quiet. Waited.

'I know we should've called the police,' Chris said. 'I wanted to, but Helen ... she ...'

'I didn't want to talk about it, okay?' Helen said, her voice raised this time, and directed at Gordy. 'But it wasn't just that. I knew I'd have to talk about it eventually, even though I just wanted to forget it all, but I didn't know what I was trying to forget, because I couldn't remember any of it! And I needed time to remember so that I could have something to tell you because no one would believe me, would they? It would just be my word against his.'

'I've seen what's at the house,' said Gordy. 'If you'd have gone to the police straight away—'

'Mark would've cleared everything away,' Helen said. 'He would've made it all look normal, I'm sure. Because that's what he's like.'

'He's a bastard, that's what he is,' said Chris, and he said it with such venom that Gordy remembered something else.

'You went back though, didn't you? Not both of you, but perhaps just you, Chris. Am I right?'

Gordy saw Chris's eyes widen with guilt at the accusation.

'Your shoes,' she said, pointing at Chris's feet. 'Spots of red paint. I'm guessing you never noticed them. Doesn't take much to match them with the paint used on the front door of Mark's house.'

'I had to do something,' Chris said. 'I know it was stupid, but I wanted him to know. I wanted everyone to know.'

'Know what?'

'That we were coming for him,' Chris said. 'That he was finished. I don't know ... a warning, maybe? I wanted him to be frightened.'

Gordy's phone buzzed in her pocket. She ignored it.

'You think we did it, don't you?' Chris said. 'Like Pam said, that's why you're here. You think we killed him.'

'After what was found at the house, your disappearance, we needed to—' Gordy began, but her phone buzzed again, cutting her off. She looked at the number, saw that it was the office. 'I need to take this,' she said, then excused herself from the room, shutting herself in the hallway.

'Gordy? It's Jen. I'm back in the office and—'

'Look, I'm in the middle of something ...' said Gordy, cutting Jen off. The last thing she needed right now was any kind of interruption.

'I know,' said Jen. 'But something's come up.'

'Can't you handle it? What about Matt? I'm right in the middle of something.'

'I know you are,' said Jen. 'That's why I'm calling you.'

That got Gordy's attention.

'This is to do with what we're on with now?' she asked. 'What is it? What's come in?'

Jen didn't reply right away.

'Jen,' Gordy said, a chill settling over her now at Jen's silence. 'What is it?'

'We've another body,' said Jen.

And the chill Gordy felt froze her blood.

TWENTY-THREE

'Another? Bloody hell! Where?'

Harry was sitting up in bed, with Smudge down by his feet, staring up at him, clearly annoyed to have been woken up by Harry's roar of shock and frustration. He could see from his bedroom window that the day was turning grey. Night would be drawing in soon.

'Over near Agglethorpe,' said Gordy. 'Jadyn's already on the scene. Matt and Dave won't be long behind.'

'What about you?'

Gordy explained where she was.

'It won't take me long to get there, either. And Jen's on her way as well, and no doubt at a pace that would terrify us both.'

'She's as bad as Liz.'

'By which you mean worse.'

Harry rubbed his eyes in a poor attempt to squeeze out the weariness he felt all the way to the marrow of his bones. Not just from the illness either, but from not being involved, from being stuck at home and useless. The conversation with the Dents had worked well, but it had knocked him flat.

'What do we know?' he asked.

'Not much,' said Gordy. 'The body was found by a couple of

ramblers out on a day's walk. Their dog disappeared, but all they had to do was follow the barking, then the smell. They were very keen to point out that bit, the smell, I mean. I think it was the shock of it. And that their dog was … well … chewing.'

Harry rubbed his eyes again, gritted his teeth.

'Sod this for a game of soldiers,' he said, and swung his legs out of bed. 'I'm on my way.'

'You'll stay right where you are is what you'll do,' ordered Gordy. 'We've already lost you and Liz to this sickness, and I certainly can't have you sharing your diseased miasma with the rest of us and risk someone else going down with it.'

'Miasma?' said Harry.

'I'm as surprised as you that I just used that word, but don't think I'm in any way going to shift from telling you to stay the hell away.'

'But I'm no bloody use here, am I?' Harry snapped back. 'I'm a police officer! You need me!'

'And you'll be a damned sight more use when you're well, rather than turning up now, coughing over everyone like some plague-carrying fool, only to be sent home again with my boot up your arse!'

'Yes, but—'

'There are no buts,' said Gordy. 'If you turn up, I'm calling Walker.'

The mention of the detective superintendent made Harry even more annoyed.

'You wouldn't …'

'Perhaps you should call her anyway,' suggested Gordy. 'Keep her abreast of what's happening.'

'You're telling me how to do my job now, is that it?' Harry said, though the thought had crossed his mind.

Gordy laughed.

'Don't you go getting all huffy with me. You know I'm right.'

Harry did, but that didn't make the pill any easier to swallow.

'What about an update, then?' he asked.

'Too much to share now,' said Gordy. 'But I can give you the bullet points.'

'I'm listening.'

Gordy gave Harry a run-through of everything that had happened so far, covering as much as she could about what she had learned from the rest of the team and what they'd been up to.

There was little to report from Jadyn's visit to the gardener, and she touched briefly on Dave's chat with Mr Howes, though it didn't escape Harry's attention that she was clearly not telling him everything about that, but he decided not to press it.

He listened quietly to what she said about the horror of Armitage's house in West Burton, this time sharing more than she had before, and he sensed the heat of her anger through the phone.

When she went through what had happened with Helen, Pam, and Chris, he said nothing about how she had reacted to Helen, because he wondered if he might have reacted the same way. Not that he was one for dramatic demonstrations of feelings and emotion, but in that situation, he wasn't so sure, not anymore anyway. Age was a funny thing, and he knew his harder edges had been smoothed off by time. And perhaps by Grace and Smudge as well, and the rest of the team, for that matter. The Dales had changed him, and he knew it had been for the better.

'What about the rubbish at the gate to the field?' he asked. 'Anything from that?'

Gordy explained about the SD cards found at Armitage's house and how, though many had contained recordings of what had been going on in the bedroom, the rest had comprised recordings of activities that blatantly suggested blackmail. Not just the dumping of rubbish, but secretly recorded conversations. Things Armitage was using for leverage, though to what end they didn't know yet. Harry suspected money. It was always money. Crime, in almost every form, boiled down to that in the end.

'We've followed up the fly-tipping case first, because that's the one we know the most about,' she said. 'But there's plenty else there to be looking into. Armitage was a piece of work, Harry.'

'So, lots of suspects for his death, then.'

'It looks that way,' said Gordy.

'Helen and Chris, though; they were there where it happened.'

'They were, but I just don't see it.'

'We both know what people are capable of when pushed. And they were pushed harder than most people would ever withstand.'

'I don't think they've told us everything,' said Gordy. 'But honestly, Harry, I can't see them behind it.'

'Then there's the blood and hair on the banister,' Harry said, 'and Helen not remembering how she ended up downstairs.'

'Whatever happened, it'll take a hell of a lot of work to unpick,' Gordy said, then changed the subject. 'Anyway, Matt and Dave were staking out the house of the owner of the truck that dumped the rubbish. They'd just followed him to another property when I called them about this other body.'

'Why were they staking out his house?'

'Matt was fairly sure that the owner wasn't being entirely truthful,' Gordy answered.

'What other property?'

'A bungalow in Bellerby,' said Gordy. 'Matt said there was nothing spectacular or suspicious about it at all.'

'Which in itself is suspicious,' said Harry.

'He said that, too. Great minds, right?'

Harry shivered. He was hot and cold at the same time and didn't know whether to get out of bed and go outside for some fresh air or just hunker down in bed and get cosy again.

He hated being ill.

'That it?'

'It is, for now,' Gordy said. 'I'll call you when we have more.'

Harry went to hang up, but then remembered the video call he'd had with the team, and his little chat with the Dents, aided so deftly by Jen.

'You know, there is a way I can still be involved in this,' he said. 'And it would stop me getting more and more frustrated and then pestering you with grumpy questions.'

'And what would that be, then?' Gordy asked.

'We can do another video call,' Harry said. 'When you arrive at the crime scene, call me, put me on the screen, and I'll be able to see what you see.'

For a moment, there was nothing from Gordy.

'You know,' she said eventually, 'that's not actually too bad an idea.'

'Not actually too bad? It's brilliant,' Harry said. 'Admit it.'

'I wouldn't go that far. But yes, we can certainly give that a try, can't we?'

'Already have,' said Harry. 'Jen didn't mention it?'

'Mention what?'

'I'll await your call.' Harry smiled.

'Yes, you will,' Gordy replied, and hung up.

Harry did the exact opposite and immediately punched in a call to Jadyn.

'Boss? Something up?'

'Tell me what we've got ...'

'What?'

'The crime scene,' Harry said. 'I've just spoken with Gordy and all I know so far is that a body was found by a pair of hikers.'

'Actually, it was their dog that found it.'

'I know it was their dog!' Harry snapped back, but caught himself just in time to make his next sentence not so fierce. 'How are they?'

'They're currently in the back of my vehicle drinking tea,' Jadyn said.

'Where's their vehicle, then?'

'It's parked up a couple of miles away. Thought it best to keep them on-site until Gordy arrives.'

'Sensible. Have you had a look at what they found?'

'Only briefly,' said Jadyn. 'I've cordoned off the area. That's where I am now. It's not pretty.'

'Describe it to me.'

There was a pause in the conversation.

'Really? Are you sure?'

'I generally only ask people to do things if I'm sure,' Harry said.

'I know, but—'

'But nothing,' said Harry, cutting Jadyn off. 'Just tell me what you see.'

He heard Jadyn take a long, slow breath in and then out.

'He's tied to a tree,' he said, his voice quieter, solemn. 'He's upright, feet on the ground, arms round the back of the tree, head taped back against it as well, round the forehead.'

'God almighty,' Harry sighed. 'Go on ...'

Another pause from Jadyn.

'There's a lot of blood,' he said eventually. 'It's kind of hard to see what's happened exactly. But then I'm not forensics, am I?'

Harry sensed that Jadyn wasn't being entirely open, like he was censoring what he was saying.

'What else?' he asked. 'And there is something else, isn't there? I can hear it in your voice, something you're not sure you should say.'

'There is,' said Jadyn. 'I could be wrong, though, couldn't I? All that blood? It's hard to tell what's what, like I said.'

'Constable ...' Harry said, hoping the edge of frustration in his voice was encouragement enough.

And it was.

'I think ...' said Jadyn, his words hesitant and quiet, 'that whoever he is, he's had his ears cut off.'

TWENTY-FOUR

Harry was once again staring at the screen on his phone. He couldn't quite get the distance right. Too close, and it was out of focus and his eyes would start to feel like they were attempting to implode. Too far, and the opposite was the case, and just as out of focus.

Age, he thought, *was a bit of a bugger.* And he wasn't old anyway, was he? Fifty was still far enough away for him to ignore it. But still, it was creeping up on him, the signs were there, with the odd ache in the mornings, his feet seeming to be further away than expected when he tried to put on his socks, and now this.

'Can you see alright?' Gordy asked.

'Yes,' Harry lied, doing his best to work out what all the fuzzy stuff was on the screen. Definitely trees, he knew that, but they all seemed to blend together to create a deep brown gloom. The growing darkness wasn't helping either, though Gordy's torch was at least bright enough to bring whatever it was pointed at into sharp relief.

Maybe he needed to get his eyes checked? It was a few years now since he'd been to an optician, and that visit hadn't gone very well, what with falling asleep in the chair within moments of the lights being turned off.

'The body's just ahead,' said Gordy. 'I've not had a look myself yet, but from what Jadyn's told me, I'm fairly sure it's not going to be pleasant.'

'Dead bodies generally aren't.'

'You know what I mean.'

I do, Harry thought, wondering then if he should worry more that he was becoming increasingly desensitised to death, regardless of the violence which had brought it about.

In his kitchen, Harry was nursing a mug of tea and attempting to nibble at a slice of bread and butter. Every swallow was painful, but he was hungry, so he persisted. He'd also lit a fire in the wood-burning stove, and the warmth from it was welcome. Not just for him, either, but Smudge, who was stretched out on the floor and breathing slowly, letting out the occasional softly expelled snore.

Harry saw cordon tape.

'Jadyn scene guard now?' he asked.

'He is,' said Gordy. 'He's been first on the scene to two bodies in a very short space of time, so I'm keeping him downwind of it, if you will. Jen is with him, and she will liaise with the SOC team when they arrive.'

'An astute move,' said Harry.

'Astute?'

'I've no idea where that came from either,' said Harry. 'What about Matt and Dave?'

'They're dealing with the couple who found the body,' said Gordy. 'Ambulance is also on the way. And Margaret as well, obviously.' Her voice cut off suddenly with the faintest of gasps.

Harry couldn't yet make out much from what he could see on his phone screen, but as Gordy walked on, everything soon came into view.

'Dear God in Heaven,' Gordy said, her voice almost a whisper. 'How does this ... Harry, can you see this?'

'Yes,' Harry said, though he wished the opposite was true.

Gordy walked closer and soon Harry was able to make out a

good amount of detail, but he asked Gordy to describe it to him just the same.

'Male,' she began. 'No way I can put an age on him, not with his face like ... I mean ...'

'Jadyn said something about the ears,' Harry said.

'Well, it doesn't look like he has any,' said Gordy.

'That's what he mentioned.'

'You'll see that he's standing, but it doesn't look like he had much choice in the matter; his ankles are tied together and lashed to the tree. His hands are pulled behind him round the other side of the trunk, and they're tied together with rope. His head has been lashed to the tree with duct tape. Only way he was ever getting out of this was if someone cut him free.'

'That obviously didn't happen.'

'No.'

Harry narrowed his eyes, working hard to see everything that he could, even though the strain was starting to make his head hurt.

'What else?'

Gordy circled the body, clearly being careful not to disturb anything. The image on Harry's phone was shaky and blurred.

'Right now, it's hard to see how he even ended up here,' she said, coming to a stop and scanning the area with her phone. 'There's no footpath to this section of the wood, and the ground is all leaves and mulch and twigs; I can't even see where I've been, never mind the route someone else took, goodness knows when.'

'Why's he there, though?' Harry asked. 'Why string him up in a woodland? And while we're on with asking questions we blatantly can't answer yet, just who the hell is he?'

'Do you think it's connected to what we found over near Kettlewell?' Gordy asked.

'To Armitage?' Harry said. 'Do you?' he asked, throwing the question back at the DI.

'They're a fair distance apart,' said Gordy. 'But if we ignore the fact that two bodies turning up in as many days is odd in itself, the fact that they're both strung up and have been mutilated makes me think that yes, they are.'

'Totally different though, aren't they?' said Harry. 'Armitage was out there for all to see; wasn't exactly going to take long for him to be found. But this poor bastard? He could've been out here for days and days, months even, before anyone found him.'

'Months is probably stretching it,' said Gordy. 'You think that could be the point, though?'

'Could be,' Harry said. 'But then, if they are connected, why would one be purposefully easy to find, and this one not? Maybe we're reading too much into what we're seeing because we're not actually seeing what's right in front of us.'

Harry was confused by his own sentence, but hoped Gordy knew what he was trying to say.

Gordy had made her way back around to where she'd started when the body had first come into view.

'Maybe there's no purpose to it, not like that, anyway,' Gordy suggested.

'How do you mean?'

'The locations, they're completely different, aren't they? Open field, gloomy woodland; could be that's more important here than the bodies being discovered.'

'But Armitage was clearly meant to be discovered, wasn't he?' said Harry. 'That's not killing someone and hiding it, or an argument that went a little too far; that's deliberate. He was out in the open for all to see.'

'I know, you're right about that,' Gordy said, 'but still, you can see my point, can't you? All I'm saying is that maybe the locations are important.'

'And we're still coming up short on suspects,' said Harry. 'When you told me about Armitage and all that footage found on the SD Cards, I dared to think this might all start to make sense. But this body? It's like throwing a hand grenade into a chicken coop.'

'We've Helen and her boyfriend,' Gordy suggested. 'Her scan

connects them directly to Armitage. And there's the blood and hair found at his house as well, which links directly to how Sowerby says he was killed.' But Harry heard the DI's disbelief tainting her words as she spoke, and he knew she didn't believe it for a minute.

'Not to what we're looking at right now though, it doesn't,' said Harry. 'Although, we obviously don't know that for sure, not yet.'

'They went missing,' Gordy said, and Harry suspected she was just trying to tease out some new revelation.

'What you've told me about what happened at Armitage's is enough to make anyone want to disappear,' Harry said. 'Especially if you were at the centre of it. So, I don't think we can go judging their reaction to it, can we? They buggered off for a few days, no doubt unable to deal with what had happened.'

'That kind of argument won't hold up well under serious questioning,' said Gordy.

'It will with me backing it up,' said Harry. 'When you've been in a combat zone, really seen just how bloody awful man can be to his fellow man, you get an understanding of how, sometimes, the mind just can't cope. If it decides it's had enough and needs to escape, there's nowt you can do to stop it.'

'I know,' Gordy said. 'I'm just playing devil's advocate, that's all.'

I guessed right, then, Harry thought, and Gordy had a point. But he was finding it hard to see a young pregnant woman and her lover responsible for what they were dealing with; two very brutal slayings. These were not done in the heat of the moment. Thought had gone into them, planning. And that was deeply concerning. As was something else.

'Say they killed Armitage, perhaps Helen threw him against the banister, or knocked him against it as she made her escape. But if they were in Sedburgh when we found him in that field ...'

Harry left the rest of what he was going to say hanging in the air.

'Clear as mud, isn't it?' said Gordy.

'Investigations always are at this stage,' Harry nodded. 'Anyway, whatever this all is, I think the young couple are linked to it, because of course they are, but not to the bodies; that's too much of a stretch. If we can use the *how* they were killed to work out the *why*, then we might be getting somewhere. But right now—and even though we both know there's a better than good chance these crime scenes are linked—we have to analyse each in situ.'

'Try and ignore the other until something becomes too obvious to ignore,' Gordy said.

'Exactly that. We can't go making connections where there might be none.'

By now, Gordy was out of the woodland and making her way across a field towards the vehicles in the distance.

'How soon before Sowerby arrives?' Harry asked.

'Not soon enough,' said Gordy. 'Never is though, is it?'

'Fair point,' said Harry, then added, 'And thanks for doing this, having me on-screen, I mean.'

'It was a bit weird, but I figured it was best to do as you suggested, rather than have you sitting at home growing more and more frustrated, then doing something Harry-like and just turning up anyway, regardless.'

'I'd never do that.'

'You did exactly that yesterday. How are you feeling?'

Harry thought about that for a moment.

'Better than I was,' he said. 'Should be fine for tomorrow, touch wood.'

'Do you need anything?'

'Yes,' said Harry. 'To be back at work.'

'You're impossible.'

Harry smiled. 'I know.'

Conversation over and having made Gordy promise to keep him in the loop with everything that was happening, Harry sent a quick text to Grace, then leaned back in his chair. The warmth from the fire was already making him sleepy, so with nothing better to do, he gave in to it. And on the floor, Smudge rolled over and rested her head on his feet.

TWENTY-FIVE

A while after the conversation with Harry, and with Margaret Shaw having confirmed that the victim was indeed dead, and the pathologist, Rebecca Sowerby, busy chivvying her team into action, the one sound Gordy really did not want to hear was a sniffle.

'Jen ...'

The detective constable glanced up at Gordy. They were standing out on the lane, having just had a final chat with the couple who had found the body, a Mr and Mrs Barnes, who were on holiday from Norfolk, and their moderately annoying terrier, called Biscuit. Gordy had just asked Jen to take them back to their own vehicle, and Jen's response had been a sneeze.

'I'm fine,' said Jen. 'Really, I am. It's probably just tree pollen or something.'

'In February?' said Gordy.

'Actually, yes,' said Jen. 'Hay fever isn't just a spring and summer thing.'

'But you don't get hay fever.'

Jen gave her nose a scratch.

'It's nothing, I'm sure,' she said. 'I'm not at death's door, am I?'

'No, true,' said Gordy, 'but if you start feeling ropey, you do the sensible thing and head home, you hear? I don't want any martyr-like behaviour.'

'And you won't be getting any from me, either,' said Jen. 'Tried to do an ultra marathon with a cold once. Nearly died.'

'I'm hoping that's an exaggeration.'

Jen held her hand palm up in the air and gave it a wiggle.

'I managed eight miles before my body gave up. Marshalls had to rescue me. Felt like an absolute idiot, and rightly so, too, because that's exactly what I was, trying to do that. Never again, believe me.'

And Gordy did.

'Best you get the Barnes and their dog back to their car,' she said. 'My guess is they weren't expecting their late afternoon dog walk to turn into any of this.'

'I'll give them a call tomorrow as well,' said Jen. 'Check that they're okay.'

WITH JEN GONE, Gordy was able to focus on everything else that was going on. And that was plenty. Sowerby's team were busy with their to-and-fro between their large, white vans, and the crime scene, their procession in white overalls strangely eerie in the evening light. Margaret was still on scene as well and having just finished having a natter with Matt and Dave, Gordy saw that she was making a bee-line for her.

'Biscuit?' Margaret asked, holding out a packet of Rich Teas. 'Not the best, I know, but it was all I had to hand.'

'They called their dog that, you know,' Gordy said, taking one from the packet. 'The couple who found the body.'

'Really? I rather like that,' said Margaret. 'Poor little bugger must've had the fright of its life finding what it did.'

'Not so sure about that,' Gordy laughed. 'My understanding is that they had a job and a half dragging it away.'

'So, what do you think?' Margaret asked.

'About this?' Gordy shook her head despairingly. 'I think it makes me wonder sometimes about what the hell is wrong with us.'

'It takes all sorts to make a world,' said Margaret. 'I just don't see why it can't be all sorts of lovely, kind, friendly, fun people. Why should it also include the unexpectedly large number who end up doing something like this?'

'People ...' said Gordy.

'I've met enough to know I really don't like many of them at all.'

'I find myself thinking the same. Sad really, isn't it?'

Margaret smiled, then reached out a hand and gave Gordy's arm a squeeze.

'It's a little too easy to let the darkness win. Which is why we never can. How's that lovely lady of yours? I've heard she's a bit under the weather. Works too hard, if you ask me. Doesn't half do a bloody good sermon, though. Rousing! Good pair of lungs on her, too, you know; voice of an angel.'

'You should hear her in the shower,' said Gordy, then felt herself blush so quickly said something else. 'She does work too hard, and I think that's probably why she's ill now. She's a bit run down, I think, and that makes you more vulnerable, doesn't it?'

'And what about my favourite scarred face?'

'Grumpy,' Gordy said. 'But at least he's listened to reason and stayed home.'

Margaret narrowed her eyes.

'You shouted at him, didn't you?'

'Yes,' said Gordy.

'Good!' Margaret clapped her hands. 'Well, my work here is done. The evening isn't getting younger, and neither am I. Best get myself home and watch something awful on the telly, maybe have a generous glass of red, too, while I'm about it.'

Farewells said, Gordy watched Margaret head back to her Range Rover and was secretly pleased she wouldn't be meeting her on the roads; she was surprised Margaret could even climb into the thing, never mind see over the dashboard. Rumour had it that she sat on a couple of cushions to bump herself up just enough to do so. Gordy hoped the rumour was based in truth.

'Detective Inspector Haig ...'

Gordy turned towards the voice to find Sowerby in front of her, though it was only her voice that gave away her identity, the white overalls, facemask, and gloves hiding her identity with ease. Behind her, Gordy watched others from her team carrying a stretcher towards the ambulance that had arrived a few minutes ago, clearly weighed down by what was on it and hidden from sight by a white sheet.

'How's it going?' she asked.

'Well, although this body was found two days after that other one, I think this one has been outside a while longer.'

'How so?'

'Nature has a way of dealing somewhat enthusiastically with a body,' said Sowerby. 'And this one has certainly been nibbled at. That one in the field had hardly been touched.'

'You think they're connected?'

'Not for me to say, but there are similarities.'

'Like what?'

'The knots,' Sowerby said. 'The ones used to tie him to that tree. They're the same ones used with the other body. Then there's the fact they've both been strung up; one on some kind of makeshift cross, the other against a tree.'

'Coincidence?'

Sowerby laughed.

'You're only saying that because Harry's not here. It's always a possibility, but in reality, I'd be very surprised if we had two completely unrelated murderers going round mutilating their victims and stringing them up.'

'What else?'

'Your constable, he was right about the ears.'

'Gone?'

'Looks like they've been cut off, though I'll be able to have a better look when I get to the postmortem. And we've not found them anywhere at the scene, though they're just skin and gristle; easy for a fox to snaffle those. Or a buzzard.'

'Buzzard?'

'You must've heard them? Reckon there's a load of them nesting in the trees.'

'Aren't they predators rather than scavengers, though?' Gordy asked.

'They're more opportunistic,' said Sowerby. 'They'll take road-kill, so I don't see why they'd turn their beak up at a free ear or two. The things you learn on the job!'

Gordy sighed.

'Eyes, and now ears; perhaps Harry was right.'

'About what?'

'Souvenirs. Maybe whoever's done this is collecting body parts.'

'What a truly lovely thought.'

'Isn't it just? Anything else?'

Sowerby was quiet for a moment.

'There was something attached to a rope around the victim's neck, and we've found a few scraps of material caught in some of the trees nearby. No idea what they are.'

'I didn't see anything round their neck,' said Gordy.

'It was tucked down inside his jumper. A bag of something, not sure what yet. I doubt that it's pleasant. It certainly wasn't there to mask the smell.'

'ID?'

Sowerby shook her head.

'Whoever they are, or were, right now, that's a mystery.'

'Add it to the list. Anything else?'

'Not for now. We'll be having a final check, then clearing up. I'll be in touch tomorrow as soon as I have anything more.'

Sowerby said goodbye and headed off to join her team.

Gordy yawned, a little louder than she had expected to, and only just managed to cover it when Matt came jogging over, worry in his eyes.

'They've been trying to call you,' he said. 'Couldn't get through.'

'Who has?' Gordy asked, pulling out her phone to see that the battery was dead.

'I didn't catch his name, but it was the choirmaster, I know that.'

'What? Why was Geoff trying to call me?'

'He popped round to pick something up from the vicarage. No idea what. But it's Anna, Gordy ... she's ...'

'Anna? She's what, Matt? What's happened?'

'He, Geoff, I mean, he found her unconscious in the lounge. I think he spotted her through the window.'

'Is she okay?'

'She's been rushed to hospital,' said Matt.

Gordy's heart stopped.

'Go,' said Matt.

And Gordy ran.

TWENTY-SIX

By the time Harry arrived at the hospital, all memory of his illness had been burned away by the singular concern he had for Gordy.

Matt had called him, full of apologies for doing so, moments after Gordy had left the crime scene. All Harry knew was that Anna had been rushed to hospital, and that Matt had, without any hesitation, stepped in as SIO, and sent Gordy off to follow her. Because that's the kind of person Matt was, and Harry was glad of it, not least because he'd learned a thing or two from the man since moving to the Dales. Not that he would ever admit such to his face.

The last thing Harry had heard about Anna had been from Gordy herself, back when she'd sent him home, and he was glad now that he had listened to her. Though not firing on all cylinders quite yet, he was certainly feeling a lot more human now. But it was a different story with Anna.

A quick call to Grace and he had dropped by to deliver Smudge, not wanting to leave her home alone. Then he had raced on, worry raking at him like lightning on a rough, dark sea.

The journey was a blur, forgotten the moment he arrived at the hospital and marched through the main doors, crashing through them like an armoured truck through a barricade.

The hospital was a warren of corridors, and Harry thundered

his way through door after door after door, trying to follow the various maps pinned to the walls, the directions given to him by the person he'd spoken to at reception clearly little more than guesswork.

When he finally found the wing where Anna had been taken and had blurted out breathlessly who he was there to see, Harry was brought to an abrupt halt by a male nurse no older than Jadyn.

'You'll have to wait here,' he instructed, holding a gentle hand up to Harry's chest.

'Why?'

'I'm hoping I don't need to say *because I say so*,' the nurse said.

Harry pushed against the hand, and its gentleness gave way to strength.

'Please,' the nurse said. 'Take a seat. I'll go and see what I can find out.'

Forcing himself to do as he was told, Harry walked over to a row of chairs and sat down. A table in front of him held a sorry-looking pile of magazines, most of them little more than glossy gossip columns, interspersed with a car magazine or two, and a few others about living the country life.

Harry ignored the magazines.

He stared at the walls, read posters about how to wash your hands, felt himself getting fidgety so he stood up and marched over to the vending machines slouching against the far wall.

'Soup, tea, or coffee?' he muttered to himself, staring at what was on offer, and being deeply unimpressed.

A quick check of his pockets and he was surprised to find he had enough change rattling around to get himself a coffee and a bar of chocolate.

Refreshments purchased, he sat back down, sipped the coffee, winced at the taste, and bit into the chocolate.

Harry tapped his feet, scratched the back of his neck, reached for the magazines and shuffled them. He took out his phone, found that he had no signal, attempted a game of solitaire, but that only made his agitation worse.

Chocolate finished, the coffee drained, Harry stood up and walked over to the bins.

'Harry ...'

Gordy was standing in front of a set of double doors, which led from the waiting area to the ward beyond. She was pale, her eyes red from tears.

Before Harry knew what he was doing, he'd closed the distance between them and taken the DI in his arms. He said nothing, just held Gordy as she wept.

When she eventually pulled away, Harry led her over to the seating area.

'Usually, I'd ask if you wanted a drink,' he said. 'But having just had a coffee myself, I can only see it making you feel worse.'

Gordy managed a weak smile as she wiped her eyes.

'God, just look at me,' she said. 'I'm never like this.'

Harry sat back, giving Gordy the space and time to gather herself.

'The symptoms are just like flu,' she said at last, her voice a little stronger. 'That's why neither of us thought anything of it. And Anna's not one for being told anyway, is she?'

'No, she's not,' Harry replied. 'Probably why I like her.'

Gordy smiled at that.

'I should've spotted something wasn't right though, shouldn't I? She's seemed a little confused, disorientated almost, but I just thought it was tiredness.'

'You need to stop that right now,' Harry said, spotting where Gordy's thoughts were taking her. 'Whatever this is, it's not your fault. There's no blame here. You know that full well, so don't listen to that whiny little voice that wants you to think otherwise. Shut it down, right now.'

Gordy sat back, shoulders sagging.

'If I'd just said something though, Harry. Called a doctor ...'

'No,' Harry said. 'Don't. This isn't on you.' He changed tack. 'Do we know what's wrong with Anna?'

'The doctors think it's encephalitis.'

Harry had never heard of it.

'It's rare,' Gordy explained. 'Sounds ridiculous, but I've been told it might be linked to a cold sore she's had for a while, and that's even rarer. Rare things happen, don't they, but a cold sore? Really? How is that even possible? How could something like that have Anna end up here?'

'So, this encephalitis,' said Harry, 'it's why Anna collapsed?'

Gordy gave the shallowest of nods and Harry could see she was working hard to stop herself from crying again. She tapped the side of her head.

'It causes the brain to swell.'

'That would do it.'

'She's so lucky Geoff found her,' said Gordy. 'I don't want to think what would've happened if he hadn't popped round.'

'Then don't,' said Harry. 'He did, he called an ambulance, and Anna is now receiving the care she needs. Don't do the what-ifs.'

'They're hard to ignore.'

'True, but you have to.'

'I know.'

Gordy fell quiet for a moment. When she spoke again, Harry heard in her voice how hard she was fighting to not give in to despair.

'She's ... they've induced a coma.'

Harry said nothing, waiting for Gordy to say more.

'They've told me it's to shut the brain down so that it can recover from the swelling.' Tears came then, but Gordy made not a sound, and they streamed down her face freely. 'I've called her parents. They live in Northumberland. They're on their way. I've booked them into a hotel. It's nothing luxurious, but it's the best I could do on short notice. I've got myself a room as well, just in case. And I thought they'd want to be close, you know, rather than staying at the vicarage? And I don't know if the spare room is in a fit state anyway, because Anna's a terror for hoarding stuff, books especially so. She's got boxes of them all piled up. I'd need to sort the bedding out as well. I can do that, get things ready once I know what's what, can't I? Get some food in, make sure that—'

Harry rested a hand on Gordy's own. She was rambling, just talking and talking to stop herself from thinking, from being where she was, facing what had happened, dealing with the fear and the worry. He was about to say something when he noticed someone was standing next to him. He looked up to see a face he recognised staring down at him.

'Jim?'

'I sent a message to Matt about my dad. He'd sent me a message a few hours ago, asking how he was, so I thought I'd better reply. He told me you were here, that Anna had been rushed in.'

Jim sat down next to Gordy and put an arm around her, and Harry saw then the bond the team had. There were no senior officers here, no PCSOs, just friends looking out for each other regardless of age or rank. It wasn't conventional by any means, but it worked, and Harry knew he was lucky to be a part of it.

Gordy looked up at Jim.

'How is he?'

'Grumpy,' said Jim, 'but doing okay. He'll be home in a day or so. Won't be able to do much though, not for months.'

Harry caught a fleeting look from Jim and knew that he was already worried, wondering how to manage the farm, his job, to make sure his parents were okay. Now was not the time for that conversation.

Gordy then turned to Harry.

'I'll be okay,' she said. 'But you can't stay here, can you? Not with everything that's going on.'

'There's no rush,' Harry said.

'I think we both know that's not true,' Gordy replied. 'Look, Anna's not going anywhere, that's for sure. And who knows for how long? I'll let you know if and when things improve. But your place isn't here, Harry. You know that. Though I do appreciate you coming over, believe me.'

Harry pushed himself to his feet.

'Only if you're sure,' he said.

'When am I ever anything else?'

Harry smiled.

'Sometimes, I think we're a little too alike.'

'I'm much better looking though,' said Gordy, and for a moment, the glint in her eye that Harry had really only come to notice over the last few months, shone star bright with mischief.

With a nod, Harry turned and headed to the door. As he pushed through, Jim followed.

'Mum and me, we're taking it in turns visiting Dad,' he said. 'I'll make sure that whichever one of us is in pops down to see her and Anna, keep an eye on them as well.'

'That's very kind,' Harry said.

'It's just what we do, isn't it?' said Jim. 'Look after each other?'

And with that, he headed back into the waiting room, and Harry made his way back through the maze of corridors and out into the night.

TWENTY-SEVEN

Harry was wearing a thin, white overall covering his clothes, white rubber boots, and a facemask. Opposite him, Sowerby was wearing the same, though looked considerably more at ease in it and their surroundings. Between them, and so far thankfully hidden from view beneath a white sheet, was the body from the woods.

After a quick catch-up with everyone first thing, he had made his way over to the mortuary to see what Sowerby could tell him. He'd passed on what he could about Anna to the team, then sent them all off on various tasks. With Gordy now also unavailable, they were now down to five, but that would've been four if Harry himself hadn't been well enough to get properly involved finally.

Matt was checking out the house where he'd followed the owner of the truck seen at the fly-tipping site — the amusingly named Mr Bacon — the day before. Harry would join him once he was done at the Mortuary, and he'd instructed Matt not to do anything until he arrived. He was just there to keep an eye, and jot down anything unusual going on.

Dave was checking up on the couple who had found the body in the woods, and Jen and Jadyn were door-knocking to see if anyone in the area had seen anything suspicious. He doubted anything would come from it, but it needed to be done, just to be on the safe side. He doubted very much whoever had gone to the trouble of killing someone so elaborately would be clumsy enough to be seen doing it.

'Gordy's let you come back to join in the fun, then,' Sowerby said, and Harry saw a smile crease the corners of her eyes.

'Didn't have much choice, I'm afraid, and it had nothing to do with me being stubborn, either. Though I am well enough, before you ask.'

Harry then explained as much as he could about Anna.

'Bloody hell, that's awful.'

'It is that,' said Harry. 'I've been keeping up to date with everything, so I know where we are with it all. Not that it's much use so far. Seems like a proper mess, doesn't it?'

'Well, allow me to add to it,' said Sowerby, and she reached up to pinch the corners of the sheet and pulled it down to reveal the body.

Harry remembered all too vividly what he had seen through the camera on Gordy's phone. Somehow, seeing the body cleaned up and now on a stainless-steel slab only made it look worse. The wounds to the side of the victim's head were pale ribbons of ripped flesh. But the face was what drew Harry's attention, the swelling of the lips, the whole area around the mouth. Just what the hell had been done to the poor sod?

'What can you tell me, then?' he asked.

'I'll begin with the obvious,' said Sowerby. 'The ears; he doesn't have any.'

'I'm hoping I didn't travel all this way just for that.'

'They've both been cut off, along with quite a large amount of flesh, and he's lost a lot of blood.'

Harry said, 'But not enough to kill him, right?'

'Right,' said Sowerby.

'What was it, then? Shock?'

'Around one in five people in shock die from it, so there was a chance, but no, it wasn't that.'

Harry looked at the rest of the body. Other than the cuts that

Sowerby would have put there herself while investigating the body, he could see no other wounds. There was bruising, yes, and cuts and grazes, but nothing that looked life-threatening.

'Then what?'

'Catastrophic organ failure,' Sowerby said, pointing at the victim's chest. 'Full system shutdown. Messy affair, too.'

Harry scratched his head.

'How?'

'Poison,' said Sowerby. 'Rodenticide, to be exact.'

Now that was news to Harry.

'Rat poison?' he said, but said no more, and instead waited for the pathologist to explain further.

'Mouth was stuffed with pellets of the stuff,' Sowerby explained. 'Quite the variety of colours, too. Never knew there were so many. Not just his mouth, either; someone had really forced it in there. He died from the poison, but he also choked on the stuff, seeing as his throat was rammed full with it, too. Look ...' She leaned over the body a little and prised open the lips. 'See?'

'He's missing a few teeth,' said Harry. 'So? He's what, in his sixties, maybe his seventies; there's a good chance he would be missing a few.'

'We found them in his throat,' Sowerby said. 'As I said, someone really forced the poison into him. The chemicals used in rat poison are basically anticoagulants. They cause uncontrolled bleeding, which means the rats can't form blood clots and die. Same happened to our friend here, just in a more violent, horrifying, and explosive way.'

'Explosive?'

'Bit of an exaggeration, I suppose,' said Sowerby. 'But I've never seen anything quite like it.'

'That's saying something.'

'It really is.'

'What else?'

'A small plastic bag was found tied around his neck. That contained poison as well.'

'Whoever did this was trying to make a point, then,' said Harry. 'How long has he been dead?'

'Three, maybe four days,' said Sowerby. 'But that's just a rough guess. We're analysing insect larvae, that kind of thing, to get something a little more accurate.'

'He was killed after the body in the field, then?'

'He was,' said Sowerby. 'But there's no trace of salt or anything like that. He was killed where he was found, rather than killed first and transported later. He's been nibbled at a fair bit by wildlife. We didn't find his ears either. Probably provided a tasty snack for a passing fox or badger. There were a lot of buzzards flying around as well.'

'Or were taken as souvenirs,' said Harry. 'That first body had no eyes, this one no ears ...'

'Like the Predator, you mean?'

Harry laughed at that.

'That's quite the movie reference,' he said. 'And one I wouldn't pick to be on your list, either.'

'It's a classic,' said Sowerby. 'And there's something else.'

She handed Harry a thin, brown folder. He opened it and looked at the photograph it contained.

'What are they?'

'Scraps of material,' said Sowerby. 'That's really all I can tell you. We found a few caught in the trees near where the body was found.'

The scraps were various shades of green and brown, with ragged edges, like they'd been ripped from a larger sheet of cloth.

'A similar piece was found in the field,' he said.

'It was,' said Sowerby. 'So, there's another link.'

'That's five,' said Harry. 'The knots, the rope, these scraps of material, the way the bodies were strung up, and the mutilation.'

Sowerby took the sheet and covered the victim again, hiding him from sight.

'Anything else?' Harry asked.

'Sadly not,' said Sowerby, and led Harry back out of the

mortuary and into the small office to get out of the overall and boots. 'If the team or I come up with anything else, obviously I'll let you know.'

Outside, Harry walked over to his RAV, Sowerby still with him.

'How's the house-hunting going?' she asked.

'You heard, then?'

'Mother hears all,' Sowerby replied.

'There are no secrets in the Dales,' Harry said. 'I've learned that.'

'Why would house hunting be a secret?' Sowerby asked. 'I think it's great that you're so serious about you and Grace.'

'Well, of course I am,' said Harry. 'Though I've never liked that word, because it makes it all seem almost onerous, doesn't it?'

'You know what I mean,' said Sowerby. 'But yes, you're right, it does.'

Harry opened the driver's door.

'House hunting is a bit like that, though,' he said. 'I didn't enjoy it much when getting my place in Gayle; I was hoping this would be more enjoyable.'

'It isn't?'

'There's a lot riding on it, isn't there?' Harry said. 'What if we buy the place and move in and we end up hating it and each other?'

'Most folk move in together first, before buying somewhere,' said Sowerby.

'Not really an option,' said Harry. 'My place isn't large enough, and Grace's isn't much bigger.'

'Sounds very impulsive of you, you know?' Sowerby smiled, then winked and added, 'You know, I might even start thinking that you're actually in love.'

Harry laughed and climbed into the RAV. Then, with the door closed and the engine on, he lowered his window.

'If I wasn't,' he said, 'then why the hell else would I be buying a house with her?'

'Why, indeed?' said Sowerby, then waved as Harry pulled away to head back to Wensleydale and Matt.

TWENTY-EIGHT

Harry rolled up behind Matt, who was in the old police Land Rover, then walked over and rapped his knuckles on the window.

Matt opened it.

'Anything?' Harry asked.

'Nowt,' said Matt. 'I've not seen anyone go in or come out, and I've been here all morning.'

'Which is why I thought you might like this,' said Harry, and passed through the window a white paper bag spotted with grease.

Harry watched Matt's eyes widen. He also noticed that they were considerably redder than they'd looked at the team meeting earlier that morning.

'It's still warm,' Matt said, opening the bag.

Harry had stopped off in Leyburn and bought a couple of pies from the bakers. He'd already eaten his, though watching Matt tuck into his own made him wish he'd bought another to fill up the corners.

Still eating, Matt closed the window, then climbed out.

Harry pointed down the street.

'That one, is it?'

'You already knew it was a bungalow,' said Matt. 'You can't pretend that was a piece of amazing detective work.'

'Actually, I can,' said Harry. 'For a start, there's four other bungalows that I can see along here, yes? So, to get it with a first guess, that's impressive.'

Matt said nothing, kept on munching, then sneezed, sending a lot of what he was eating in a wide arc spray onto the road.

'Nice,' said Harry.

'Sorry.'

Harry focused them again on the bungalow.

'There's something different about that one, though, isn't there?' he said.

'Is there?' Matt asked, wiping his mouth, then his nose.

'It's still cold, isn't it?' said Harry. 'The sun's up, but there's still ice everywhere. Puddles are frozen over, roofs covered in frost.'

'What's your point?'

'Look at the bungalow again,' Harry said.

Matt did just that, finishing off what remained of his pie, and brushing crumbs off himself, careful to rescue any larger ones he could still devour.

'The roof,' he said. 'No frost.'

'No frost,' said Harry. 'Exactly.'

'Exactly what?'

'Why would that roof have no ice, when all the others around here do?'

'It's warmer in the loft?'

'Shouldn't be, though, should it?' said Harry. 'Not if it has decent insulation. Or, indeed, any insulation at all. So, you have to ask yourself why, don't you? Why is it, that specific roof is warm when all the others in the street aren't? What's up in that loft space that's hot enough to melt the frost?'

'Not a clue,' said Matt, and sneezed again.

'Well, that's what we're here to find out,' said Harry, and without waiting for Matt, was across the road and marching towards the bungalow. But halfway along, he stopped.

'You're ill,' he said.

'No, I'm not,' Matt replied. 'It's just a sniffle.'

'You covered the road in half a pie.'

'Don't remind me. Anyway, you need me, now that we're down one more.'

Harry frowned.

'Down one more what?'

'Jen,' said Matt. 'She's had to go home.'

'She seemed fine at the meeting.'

'She was working very hard to make sure you didn't notice.'

Harry sighed.

'So, it's now just you, me, Dave, and Jadyn?'

'It is,' said Matt.

'Except after this, it's going to be three,' said Harry. 'Because you'll be going home, too.'

Matt opened his mouth to argue, but all that fell out of it was another sneeze, this one so violent Harry was sure he heard the man's back crack.

'No arguing,' said Harry. 'We do this, then you're back home to bed. Understood?'

Matt grunted a yes.

HARRY WALKED the rest of the way down the street, then walked through a small, rusting gate, which separated the pavement from the narrow, winding path to the front door, and stopped.

The bungalow was well hidden from the road and passersby thanks to a messy conglomeration of overgrown bushes and weeds. But Harry could still see just enough to make him very suspicious of what they might discover.

'Look,' he said, and pointed through the bushes at the barely visible windows.

'They're boarded up,' said Matt.

'And it's not been done on the outside either, has it?'

'Why would they board everything up on the inside?'

'Why indeed?' said Harry and made his way to the front door.

'What about this?' he asked as Matt joined him, pointing at the door.

'That's a lot of Yale locks,' said Matt.

Harry counted six.

'Let's see who's at home, shall we?' he said, and hammered the heel of his fist on the door.

'Reckon they heard that,' said Matt. 'By which I mean, all the way over in Leyburn as well. But you don't think they'll answer, do you?'

'No,' Harry said. 'But sometimes, you just have to give these things a go, don't you? And if they don't, they'll only be adding to my suspicion.' He leaned in close to the door. 'And it's been too long since I last smashed a door in. I'm rather in the mood ... Oh, I think someone's coming ...'

From the other side of the door came the sound of various chains and locks being dealt with, and then the door swung warily into the darkness of the hallway beyond.

'Yes?'

Harry glanced down to find he was being stared up at by a man so grey and thin he looked as though he had recently been buried only to be then dug up again, much to his own very apparent dismay. He was wearing a threadbare dressing gown, which could've been any number of colours at some point in its life but was now a dirty shade of filthy. His bare, blue-veined calves were visible, and on his feet he wore boots with no laces.

A reek from inside the bungalow thrust its way into Harry's nostrils and he winced. A thick stench of unwashed dishes, mouldy food, out-of-control damp, and right at the back of it, a sweet floral smell of something that was definitely not your average house plant bought from the local garden centre.

Harry showed his ID and introduced himself and Matt.

'Oh, no,' the man said, his voice weak and distant and thin, as ghostly as he looked. 'You ... you can't come in. You can't. It's not allowed. I thought you were him, because he always knocks, you see. Doesn't ever have a key on him. That's my job, isn't it? Or I ... or I don't get fed.'

That's already a lot of information, Harry thought, but he needed to get inside the bungalow and have a proper look around before he decided what action to take next.

'Perhaps we should talk inside?' he said, and placed one foot inside the door, while also holding his empty hands out in an attempt to show the man that everything was fine, that they came in peace.

'No ... no, you can't come in, because he'll know, and then ... and then I won't have anywhere, will I? Or worse ... worse ...'

Harry had already stepped into the hallway, and Matt stepped in behind him and closed the door.

'Can I ask your name, Mr ...?' said Harry.

The man seemed to shrivel up in front of him, fear in his eyes. Then, before either Harry or Matt could do anything, the man shuffled as quickly as he could towards an open door to their right.

Harry and Matt followed and found themselves standing in what Harry guessed had once been the lounge. Now, though, it was little more than a bedsit, and calling it that was being overly generous.

A thin, single mattress was on the floor piled high with blankets and duvets, all of which he could smell from where he was standing in the door. To the side of the bed was a small fridge, a pile of empty food tins, and a microwave. The rest of the room was given over to storing boxes.

'What do you think, then?' Harry asked, looking at Matt.

'I think,' said Matt, dabbing something under his nose from a small pot he'd just pulled from a pocket, 'that I'm more than a little surprised he's conscious never mind alive, with that stench in the air.'

'You've noticed it, too, then?'

'How could I not?' Matt asked and handed Harry the pot.

Harry dabbed vapour rub under his nose and handed the pot back.

'I need to have a scout around the place, see what's what,' he said. 'You okay staying here with Mr...?' Harry looked at the man, hoping for an answer, but again, no name was given.

'Won't be long,' Harry said, and left Matt with the man.

TWENTY-NINE

The first two rooms yielded nothing of interest. The tiny kitchen was a shell, just empty cupboards, a cooker that Harry suspected hadn't worked in years, and a fridge with the door hanging off. However, a thin tube had been attached to a tap, and that led out of the kitchen and down the hall to a room at the far end.

The bathroom, also tiny, had the pungent tang of a gent's urinal, the kind found in a pub where, with ease, you could order a pint and have a fight thrown in for free. Harry was happy to close the door, but the smell stayed with him, managing to pierce through the unique aroma of the bungalow itself, and the vapour rub under his nose.

The final room was locked by a single Yale device, and Harry suspected that was mainly to keep out the spectral entity who had let them in. The smell coming from this room was enough to tell Harry that there was no point asking for a key because there wouldn't be one in the house. The tube from the kitchen led under the door, which had been chipped away a little to allow it to do so unimpeded.

Harry hoofed the door open with a deftly placed boot. Not exactly procedure, but this was an emergency. For all he knew, someone was trapped in that room and choking on what was in the air. Well, that would be his story if anyone asked.

A wall of hot, humid air barreled out of the room and into Harry, causing him to stumble back a step. It seemed to fall out into the hallway in great chunks, an invisible iceberg calving off great lumps of itself.

Harry shook his head clear and walked into the room.

'Well, then,' he said, stunned by what was in front of him.

The room, which was little more than a cave thanks to the thick boards screwed into the wall around the windows, was full to bursting with the healthiest cannabis plants he'd seen in years.

Lights were strung from wires screwed into the ceiling. A step ladder was resting against a wall. There was an irrigation system set up from the pipe leading back to the kitchen. The air was hot and dry, which gave Harry some inkling as to just how sophisticated the set-up actually was. He'd been into other operations where the air had been so thick with moisture that it was running freely down the walls, blackening the wallpaper and carpet with rot, stunting the growth of the plants, covering the leaves and buds with fungus. In those cases, such incompetence and glaring lack of understanding of hydroponics had had as much to do with the ease of arrests, as the work of the investigating officers. This wasn't that, though, not at all. What he was looking at now was all about profit.

Harry stepped out into the hallway, and gave himself a moment to get his thoughts into order about what they'd found at the bungalow. Then he spotted another tube, this one leaving the room he'd just come from, back down the hall, and up through a hole drilled into the ceiling to the side of a hatch.

Harry turned back into the room and grabbed the step ladder, opened it beneath the hatch, and climbed up to thrust it open.

Light burst from the opening in the ceiling and the same smell that had come at him from the bedroom now fell on him from above.

A few more steps and Harry's head and shoulders were in the

loft. Whichever way he turned, all he could see was cannabis. And the heat here was even more suffocating than the first room.

Harry dropped back down into the hallway and went back to see Matt and the man. Matt was sitting on top of the small fridge, and the man was huddled under the blankets on the mattress, hugging his knees.

'We have a name,' said Matt. 'Harry, this is Mr Wilson.'

Mr Wilson's eyes flickered up at Harry, but he said nothing, didn't move.

'What did you find?'

'A very healthy crop of some of the finest cannabis I've seen in a long time,' said Harry.

Matt said, 'The most we've ever found round here is someone growing a plant or two.'

'I don't think anyone expected us to find it,' said Harry. 'The security's okay, but it was hardly going to keep us out, was it?'

'You mean the locks or Mr Wilson?'

'Both. And I don't think Mr Wilson is security. They've cuckooed him, just moved in, probably with a lot of threatening to make sure he complied and had no choice but to, either. Then they've taken over the whole house, stuffed him in here out of the way and given him instructions to talk to no one. He's probably allowed to leave the house once a day, just to keep up the impression that everything is fine. My guess is that they keep him fed and watered, to give him zero reason to interact with another human being. He'll be too scared to do anything, too old, too vulnerable.'

'Poor bugger,' said Matt, looking over at Mr Wilson. 'So, what do you want to do, then?'

'First,' said Harry, 'we need someone over here sharpish. Mr Wilson needs looking after and sorting out because he can't stay here, that's for sure. We'll have to get the health services involved, social services, too.'

'We've not got anyone we can have over here sharpish,' said Matt. 'We're just you, me, Dave, and Jadyn. And as I recall, you're going to be sending me home, too, remember?'

'Then get them both over here,' Harry said. 'That way, once they've arrived and can look after Mr Wilson, you and I can get on with what's next. After which, yes, I will be sending you home. And there'll be no arguments about that, either.'

'And what exactly are we going to be getting on with next?' Matt asked.

Harry grinned and patted his stomach.

'I'm getting hungry,' he said. 'And I rather fancy me some Bacon ...'

THIRTY

Once Jadyn and Dave had arrived and were duly left in charge, not just of Mr Wilson, but also of yet another crime scene, Harry followed Matt over to Constable Burton and the house of Mr Bacon. Just before leaving, he'd confused Matt greatly by grabbing a bin bag he'd spotted on the floor, filling it with all the dirty cans of food he could find in the room where Mr Wilson had been surviving, and then carrying it back to the RAV.

'Not sure you really need to do that,' said Matt.

'Oh, I think I do,' Harry replied, just mysteriously enough to shut Matt up.

The journey was short, but with every second of it that passed, Harry could feel himself getting stronger. And not just because the illness was abating, either. Being out was helping, he was sure of it, and a part of him suspected that just being in the Dales, breathing the air streaming in through his open window, was as good as anything any doctor would be able to prescribe.

Arguably, he wouldn't have been able to do any of this even a day ago, but he still refused to discount the *healing properties of living in the Yorkshire Dales*. That last thought made Harry laugh, not least because the words had slipped across his mind in the voice of Matt.

Arriving in Constable Burton, Harry parked up just off the main road and climbed into the passenger seat of the old police Land Rover, next to Matt.

'Something's bothering me,' he said.

'Well, a lot of things are bothering me as well, like,' said Matt. 'Such as why I can't stop sneezing, and how is it that my nose can just keep on producing so much slime? It's endless, Harry; the more I wipe, the more it produces.'

'Not quite the discussion I want to be having,' said Harry, and if they weren't in the middle of something, then he would've sent Matt home already. But he knew Matt too well, and thought it was probably sensible to have him help up to a point, because then he would feel useful enough to leave without much argument. At least, that was what Harry hoped.

'Out with it, then,' said Matt. 'If it needs discussing, then best we do it now before we go and see our good friend Mr Bacon.'

'I don't know where to start.'

'The beginning is very popular.'

'I can't say that I know where that is. At all.'

Matt coughed, and it quickly turned into a crescendo of hacking.

'Well, best you hurry up,' he said, once it had subsided, 'or I might be too ill to care.'

Harry spent a moment trying to work out what it was that he wanted to say, then gave up and just sort of dived straight in.

'I know I've not been right in the middle of things, but maybe that's given me a chance to get a better overview,' he said. 'And right now, I can honestly say, nothing lines up.'

'Go on,' Matt encouraged, as he continued to wipe his nose with some tissues he'd managed to find in the Land Rover somewhere.

'Armitage was killed days ago,' Harry said, remembering what Gordy relayed to him from Sowerby and the postmortem. 'Stored in some way, covered in salt and plastic, buried, then dug up and staked out in a field. We can't say if he was killed by accident or on purpose. Between those two things happening, the as-yet-unidentified victim number two ends up in the woods. Armitage has his eyes taken, victim two, his ears. Souvenirs, maybe? Some weird scraps of material are found at each crime scene, also suggesting a link.'

'All good so far,' said Matt.

'So, what's any of that got to do with where we are now?' Harry asked. 'With a sodding cannabis farm? What, Matt? Because I'm not seeing it. Yes, there's a reason for Mr Bacon to deal with Armitage, because we know from what you and Dave found in the house that Armitage knew about the fly-tipping. But how? And to what end? Was it blackmail? If so, how did Armitage know where they'd dump all that shite? And if Bacon killed Armitage, and the crime scenes are linked, why did he kill victim number two? It doesn't add up, does it?'

'What about Helen and her boyfriend?' Matt asked.

'What about them?' Harry asked. 'They've an alibi for the night Armitage's body was found over by Kettlewell, and that all checks out. Like Bacon, they've got motive, I agree, but that's not enough, is it? If it was, I'd never be out of bloody prison with the number of folk I've met in my life I'd happily encourage off this mortal coil.'

'And by encourage you mean ...?'

'Push,' said Harry.

'Thought so.'

'So, where does that leave us, other than nowhere at all? We've got two bodies, and we think their deaths are linked. Except that the motive for Armitage's death seems to be either some kind of revenge due to his apparent love of drugging women to fulfil his own twisted sexual fantasies, or a need to get rid of him, because he was blackmailing a fly tipper who turned out to turned out to be a not-insignificant cannabis producer. And as for the second victim, we have no motive at all, but one hell of a lot of rat poison. Is that a message? Was he a rat? If so, in what way? And why take his bloody ears? What's that got to do with poison?'

Harry was very aware that he was now shouting, mainly because Matt had leaned away a little and was staring at him through wide, even puffier, eyes.

'Matt, you look bloody terrible.'

'I'm inclined to say that I think I may actually feel even worse. I know it didn't take us long to get here from the bungalow, but I feel like I've aged about thirty years.'

Harry looked down the lane to where Mr Bacon lived.

'You know what, I can handle this,' he said. 'I want you gone.'

Matt went to argue, but he sneezed, grabbing the sides of his head in the process.

'Ow,' he said. 'Bloody hell, Harry, that hurt.'

Harry opened the passenger door.

'Get yourself home,' he said. 'Now. And I don't want to see or hear from you until you're well. We clear?'

'We are,' said Matt. 'Sorry.'

Harry smiled.

'There's nowt to be sorry for,' he said. 'Of all the places to be ill, you could do far worse than Wensleydale. Now bugger off.'

Harry didn't wait for an answer, climbed out of the Land Rover and went to slam the door behind him, but Matt called him back.

'Here,' he said, holding out an evidence bag as Harry leaned in. 'Forgot I had this. Picked it up at Armitage's house.'

Harry took the bag.

'Dave thought it looked like a camel,' said Matt.

Harry looked at what was inside and saw a key attached to an odd-looking, brown plastic key fob.

'A camel with three humps and no legs?'

'That's exactly what I said,' Matt laughed.

Harry shut the passenger door, then watched Matt drive off, rolling the heavy vehicle back the way they had come.

Harry had another look at the contents of the evidence bag, turning it over and over, trying to work out what it was. *Definitely not a camel though*, he thought, but it did remind him of something. What, though, he couldn't put a finger on. Animal, perhaps even animals, but beyond that, he had nothing, so he dropped it in his pocket, clapped his hands together against the cold, and jumped back in the RAV to roll along the lane to Bacon's house. At the gate, he pressed the intercom button.

'What?'

The voice was thin and electronic.

'Detective Chief Inspector Grimm,' Harry said. 'And I'd rather like a word with Mr Bacon, if that's possible.'

'What? Why?' came the reply. 'I've already had a visit from the police about my truck. What could you possibly want to discuss?'

'Probably best we talk in private,' said Harry.

'I'm a busy man.'

'And yet you're wasting your time, and mine.'

A moment later, the gates opened.

Harry drove through and parked up in front of the house. A man was standing at the door. Harry eased himself out of his vehicle, grabbed the large black bin bag from the back seat, and walked over to meet him, his ID already visible.

'Shall we talk inside, Mr Bacon?' Harry asked.

He didn't wait for an answer and walked past the man and into the house.

'Hey, you can't just—' Bacon protested.

'Treat your house like it's mine?' Harry asked. 'Why not?'

'Pardon?'

'Why can't I treat your house like it's mine?' Harry repeated.

'Because you can't! Why is that a question? This is ridiculous. Why are you even here? And what's that you're carrying?'

Harry ignored the question and walked deeper into the house, the bag at his side, and clenched tightly in a very large fist.

'Live here alone, do you, sir?'

'What? Yes, but I can't see how that's any of your business.'

'And my guess is that you believe every man's house is his castle, or something to that effect.'

'Yes,' said Bacon, then added a little too smugly for Harry's liking, 'Especially as I'm in the process of buying a castle.'

Harry laughed at that, at the way Bacon had so quickly and easily dropped that little brag into the conversation.

'You're taking the piss.'

'And you're not behaving like any police officer I've ever met before,' said Bacon.

Harry narrowed his eyes at that.

'Met a few then, have you, sir?' he asked.

Bacon shook his head. A little too vigorously, Harry thought.

'Don't be ridiculous.'

Harry left Bacon in the middle of his muted rage and found himself in a kitchen that was both larger and more expensive than his own house.

'A castle, then,' he said, absolutely believing it. 'But this is home, yes?'

'One of them,' said Bacon.

'How can anyone need more than one?' Harry asked. 'Isn't that a bit greedy?'

'I've done well for myself,' Bacon replied.

'Some people, though, a good many actually, can't even afford one house,' Harry said. 'And some, not even a single room.'

Bacon stuffed his hands in his pockets, shrugged.

'Life's hard,' he said. 'There's always going to be winners and losers.'

'Ah, so you're a winner, are you, sir?' Harry asked.

'I like to think so.'

'But have you won by playing fair?'

Harry picked up the bag and dumped it on the white granite worktop.

'Hey, be careful!' Bacon said, rushing around to stop Harry from doing whatever it was he was about to do.

'You're proud of your house, aren't you?' Harry asked, a hard stare at Mr Bacon enough to have him skid to a halt far enough away to be just out of reach.

'Of course I am. I've worked hard for it.'

Harry gave no warning and tipped the bag upside down, emptying its contents all over the worktop.

'What the—'

Harry stepped back, leaned against the white stoneware sink, folded his arms across his chest.

'Not nice, is it?' he said. 'Someone comes into your house, just barges in, treats it like their own. No, not nice at all. Disrespectful.'

Bacon had his phone out.

'I know you're not calling the police,' Harry said. 'Not least because I'm already here, aren't I? So, who could it be, I wonder?'

'Whatever it is you think you're doing, you've made a big mistake,' Bacon said.

'No, I don't think I have, actually,' said Harry. 'You, on the other hand ...'

'Yes, right now,' Bacon said, speaking into his phone. 'In the kitchen.'

Harry pushed himself away from the sink and shuffled along to where a collection of pots and pans were hanging from hooks attached to the wall.

'Your first mistake was to think you could get away with it,' he said. 'And I'm guessing you have done for years, haven't you? It's allowed you to buy this place, for a start. And my guess is that what I found in a certain little bungalow, in a certain little village not too far away from here, is only one of many, many similar enterprises. Am I right?'

Bacon put his phone away.

'You're dead, you know that, don't you?' he said.

Harry reached for a large frying pan on the wall and unhooked it, flipped it in his hand.

'Your second mistake,' he continued, 'was to think you could just dump the waste from your little enterprise wherever you wanted to. Obviously, you couldn't just take it to the tip, could you? No. People would ask questions. But what if you paid off a dodgy environmental officer? That might work. Not to have him get rid of it for you, because that would be ridiculous. But he could help, turn a blind eye, that kind of thing. It would certainly make sure you were never caught, wouldn't it? And if you were reported, he could conveniently be unable to prosecute due to lack of evidence. Warranted, some of this is guesswork, but I'm close, aren't I?'

Bacon folded his arms, and grinned.

'Dead,' he said.

'But your third mistake,' said Harry, 'was somehow managing to find an environmental officer even more bent than you. Ironic really, but there we are. And he turned the tables on you, didn't he?'

Harry knew he was really riffing now, taking what he knew and trying to spin something from it, get a reaction, and it was working. Bacon's mean grin, which had a moment ago been all indignation and violence, had slipped a little.

'My guess is that he sent you footage of you dumping stuff. We can check that easily, of course, there's bound to be evidence of that up in the cloud or wherever emails and messages go to die. Not just any stuff either, is it? He had you over a barrel, probably enough to keep him sitting pretty every month without any worries at all. So, you paid him, but then, after a while, you got pissed off, didn't want to pay any more, tried to discuss it with him, but that didn't work, did it?'

Harry saw a change on Bacon's face. It had now moved into stark confusion.

'What are you talking about?' he asked.

'Don't play innocent with me,' Harry growled. 'I've seen the footage Armitage had of your truck, the one you seem to think was stolen.'

'Not that, the rest of it,' said Bacon. 'I paid him a retainer to keep him quiet, of course I did, but that's just all part of the business, isn't it?'

Harry was surprised at the confession, but sometimes, when pushed, people would end up saying more than they realised.

'And what business would that be?' he asked.

Bacon laughed as another figure appeared in the kitchen doorway.

'Well, it's been fun,' he said. 'But I think it's time for you to leave.'

The other figure stepped forward, and to Harry's eye, straight out of the catalogue of enormous, violent goons for hire.

'Why did you kill him?' Harry asked, his eyes on the new arrival. 'Armitage, I mean; why do it like that?'

'Like what?'

Harry was about to describe how Armitage had been displayed, when he realised that Bacon hadn't the faintest idea what he was talking about.

'You don't know, do you?' he said.

'Know what?'

'Armitage; he's dead.'

'What?'

'Oh, don't think that means I walk from here and we're good,' said Harry. 'You're under arrest for that lovely little cannabis farm I stumbled upon, and a whole host of other things I'm sure, but that'll do for starters.'

The goon ran at Harry, lifted a fist, threw it.

Harry lifted his hand, holding the frying pan as casually as he would to check the watch on his wrist.

At the sound of flesh and bone crunching into metal, Harry let out a long whistle.

'Sorry about that,' he said, spinning the frying pan in his hand. 'Self-defence, I'm afraid.'

The goon was on the floor, on his knees, holding his arm like it was made of glass and that at any moment Harry might smash it.

Bacon stared across the kitchen.

'You mean, you came here thinking I'd killed Armitage? Are you mad? Why the hell would I do that, when I could keep him at arm's length for the price of a few holidays a year in Lanzarote? And trust me, I never want to holiday in Lanzarote.'

Harry left the goon on the floor and walked over to Bacon, pulling his phone out of a pocket.

'You know, I actually believe you,' he said.

'Good,' smiled Bacon.

'You're still under arrest though,' said Harry, and lifted his phone to his ear.

THIRTY-ONE

By the time Jadyn arrived at the house, Harry had already dealt with the smashed-up hand of the gorilla who had tried to punch him. His combat medical training had kicked in, and he quickly ascertained that the man had a couple of broken fingers and a badly sprained wrist, quite a lot of bruising, too, but that was about it. His bruised ego he could do little about, nor did he want to. He made a make-shift sling from a thin, cotton tablecloth, gave him some painkillers he had in the glove box of the RAV, and then bundled him, and Mr Bacon, into the rear of Jadyn's vehicle.

'Here,' Jadyn said, handing him something from the back of his vehicle. 'I meant to file these earlier in the week.'

Harry had a quick look at what he was now holding.

'What are they?'

'Leaflets or posters, I think. I've not actually looked at them. Only just remembered they were there. I think that group I chased in Leyburn made them.'

Harry rolled open what Jadyn had handed him.

'"Fish Don't Belong In Farms"?' he read, and very much none the wiser for doing so, the words neatly penned on the paper in thick felt-tip pen, and illustrated artistically with little cartoons of fish in the same pen.

Jadyn laughed.

'Well, that clears that up, then, doesn't it?'

'Clears what up?' Harry asked.

'Dave's visit to that Mr Howes bloke. Someone's not happy about his aquaculture plans.'

'Aquaculture?'

'Fish farm,' said Jadyn. 'He wants to build one. And the group I chased obviously don't want him to.'

Harry rolled the leaflets back up, then filled Jadyn in on why the two men were being arrested. Once that was done, he sent the constable on his way.

'And then there were two,' he muttered to himself, as Jadyn drove off, and punched in a call to Dave.

'It's just you and me for now,' he said. 'Where are you?'

'At the office,' said Dave. 'And I was just about to call you.'

'Why?'

'Jen's been on the phone.'

'She's supposed to be at home because she's ill,' said Harry.

'Oh, she is. She tried to call you, but couldn't get through, so called here instead. She's ID'd that second body from the photos.'

Harry sat up.

'What? Who is it? And if she's off, she shouldn't be checking out photos or anything else, should she?'

'Probably not,' said Dave. 'But my guess is she's only doing what you'd do.'

'Fair point,' Harry muttered. 'Who is he then?'

'His name's Brian Haygarth,' said Dave. 'Farms over Agglethorpe way. Those woods he was found in? They're his.'

'How does Jen know him?'

'Popped out there a while ago, because he was complaining about people walking across his fields, blamed them for damaging his walls or something, I think. She mentioned that Jim's dad called him Bullshit Brian, though she couldn't remember exactly why. I sent a message to Jim, though, and it's because his dad, and most folk it seems, think Brian's always blaming others for things going wrong or not being right, something like that, anyway.'

'Not sure I understand,' said Harry.

'I checked up on Jen's visit to his farm,' said Dave. 'Didn't want to call her back, what with her being ill and all. Seems the problem was that he just doesn't like people using footpaths and had blocked some of the stiles. Someone had obviously taken issue with that and undone his work.'

'We have another location, then,' said Harry.

'I can send you the address,' said Dave.

'Do it,' Harry replied. 'I'll see you there.'

Twenty minutes later, Harry was standing in the yard of a small farm. Dave arrived soon after.

'Anyone home?' Dave asked, walking over to meet Harry.

'There's no answer at the door,' Harry replied. 'Do we know if he's married or living with anyone? Any family?'

'Jen didn't say,' said Dave.

Harry looked up at the house. No lights were on, the place looked dead. The yard was no different, just a collection of outbuildings in varying states of disrepair, patched up in places, ignored in others.

'I've seen neater farms,' said Dave.

Harry walked up to the front door of the farmhouse and gave another knock, just to make sure, then tried the handle. A twist and a shove, and it was open.

'Dave, you go have a nosy around outside, see if you can find anything. I'll see what's in here.'

'What am I looking for?' Dave asked.

'Not a clue,' Harry replied, and walked inside.

The house was cold—more so than it was outside—and dark. He wandered along the hall, ignoring the scattered piles of unopened post, and came to stand in what was the lounge. A single armchair sat close to a dead fire, and the room carried a stale tang of soot and ash. A television was perched on a small table against a wall, and against another was a writing bureau, open and spilling its contents onto the floor.

Harry had a shuffle through it all, found unopened bills, old newspapers, junk mail. A bin at the side was also piled high with scrunched-up rubbish. He dropped to the floor and had a rummage. Here he found more of the same, more bills, more junk mail, but amongst it all, a handful of A4 sheets, all of which were artistically illustrated with cutouts of birds of prey, probably from a wildlife magazine, Harry thought, and the cryptic message: *They're protected, are you?*

Harry remembered then what Jadyn had handed him back at Bacon's house and swore. Was this yet another line of enquiry? And if so, who the hell was this group that Jadyn had chased? There'd been no mention of them at all until now.

He took the sheets, left the lounge, and had a look around the rest of the house, finding nothing other than the sad echoes of a hard and lonely life.

Back outside, he saw Dave jogging across the yard towards him.

'You'll want to see this,' he said.

'What have you found?' Harry asked, noticing a dark look in Dave's eyes.

Dave said nothing, and quietly led Harry over to one of the buildings he'd been investigating.

The building, like the house, was cold and dark, and draught danced around them from cracked windows and holes in the roof.

'There,' said Dave, and pointed at something hanging from a beam at the far end of the building.

From where he was standing, and because of the gloom, Harry couldn't make out what it was he was looking at, but as he drew closer, it soon became all too clear.

'Are those buzzards?'

'Yes,' Dave said. 'They've been nailed to the beam.'

Harry edged closer until the birds were within arm's reach.

'What kind of person would do that?' Dave asked. 'These animals, they're beautiful, protected ...'

Harry showed Dave what he'd found in the bin in the lounge.

'Not a coincidence,' he said.

'They're a bit like—'

'The ones you were given by Mr Howes?' said Harry, finishing off what he guessed Dave was about to say. 'Jadyn gave me a load of others as well; something to do with what he was on with in Leyburn. Look ...'

Harry showed Dave the leaflets from Jadyn.

'They're different though, aren't they?' said Dave.

'How?' Harry asked, looking between the leaflets, unable to see what Dave was getting at.

'Well, the ones Jadyn gave you, they're actually nicely done, aren't they? Someone's put a bit of effort in, made them arty. But what you've just found, and the ones I got from Howes? Well ...'

'Well, what?'

'They're a bit shit, aren't they?'

'How do you mean?' Harry asked, and looked again at the leaflets, then saw exactly what Dave was getting at. The ones from Jadyn were, as Dave pointed out, artsy. But what he'd found just now in the house were rough, scrappy, done in a hurry perhaps, or at least with little care for how they looked.

Dave asked, 'Do you think all of this has something to do with him ending up in the woods?'

Harry didn't answer straight away. Though he was staring at the leaflets in his hand, and wondering why there would be such a marked difference between them, he was thinking back to a conversation he'd had with Gordy over at the field near Kettlewell, then something Sowerby had said in the mortuary as they'd looked at what he now knew to be the body of Mr Brian Haygarth.

'We need to go to the woods,' he said.

'You think we've missed something?' Dave asked.

'Possibly,' said Harry, and walked over to the RAV. 'I've not been there myself. All I've seen of it is what I could make out through the camera on Gordy's phone.'

'I'll follow you,' Dave said.

A quick drive later, and Harry was striding across the field to the woods where Brian Haygarth had been found. The day was getting brighter, the sun high, and with every step, Harry could feel his strength returning. At the edge of the woodland, he glanced back across the field, saw his and Dave's footprints drawn in the frost still clinging to the grass, and behind low hills bright with the light of day.

Turning into the woods, Harry realised then that he wasn't really sure where he was going and allowed Dave to take the lead.

'We're here,' said Dave, a few minutes later, and Harry saw the tree where Brian's body had been found, the area still showing all the signs of a thorough investigation by the SOC team. Cordon tape was still around the area as well. Harry would leave it there for now.

'What are we looking for?' Dave said, for the second time since they'd met up.

Harry turned his eyes skyward, saw the skeletal branches of the trees reaching up, twisting into each other, waving and tapping in the breeze.

Then he heard it.

'That,' he said, pointing a single finger into the trees.

The sound was faint, far off, but then another joined it and soon he heard others. *Closer, too*, he thought, and wondered if they were now being watched by keen, predatory eyes.

'Buzzards,' said Dave.

'Exactly,' said Harry. 'That's why he was here, because of the buzzards.'

Dave went to say something, but Harry held up a finger and stopped him.

'Give me a minute,' he said. 'I need to think ...'

Harry walked away from Dave, circling the tree where Brian had been found. He was even more aware now of the sound of the buzzards, their call beautiful and haunting. And they would've been the last thing the poor bastard would've heard, he thought, the last thing before the poison killed him, before his ears were ...

'Bloody hell ...'

'What is it?' Dave asked, as Harry pulled something from his pocket and held it up in front of them both. 'That's the key from Armitage's. Thought it might be for the back door. Don't think we ever checked. I still think looks like a camel.'

Harry looked closer.

'Three lumps,' he said. 'Definitely not a camel.'

'Then what?' asked Dave.

It was hard to make out, and Harry wondered if he was maybe seeing things where there was nothing to see in the first place. But what if ...

'Ears,' he said, looking at Dave. 'That's why they were cut off. That's the message here, isn't it?'

'It is? And what's that got to do with what you're holding?'

'Probably nothing,' Harry said, as a few pieces of the puzzle started to click into place, 'but it's got me thinking. What can we hear? Buzzards, right? And what did we find back at the farm? A buzzard nailed to an old beam. My guess is that with a bit more of a search, we'd find a healthy store of rat poison there, too.'

'You're saying that someone killed him because of what he was doing to the buzzards, aren't you?' said Dave.

'That's why it was done here,' said Harry. 'So, the buzzards would be the last thing he'd hear. Rather twisted, but it does make sense.'

'Does it?' said Dave. 'Actually, no, you're right, it does ... I think.'

'And before Brian was poisoned, he heard the birds he'd been killing, and then his killer took his ears,' continued Harry. 'That's the link, between what happened here and what happened to Armitage.'

'Armitage had his eyes taken, though.'

'Exactly,' said Harry, and held up the evidence bag, giving it a little shake. 'That's my point. This isn't a camel. But what if it was monkeys? Three of them? You know what I'm talking about, right? The three wise monkeys?'

Dave's eyes widened with realisation.

'See no evil ...' he said. 'Those monkeys?'

'See no evil, hear no evil,' said Harry. 'Armitage had his eyes taken, that's see no evil, isn't it? And Brian, he had his ears taken, which is hear no evil.'

'There's one left, then,' said Dave.

'Speak no evil,' said Harry, then asked, 'Do you have the phone number for Mr Howes?'

'I do,' said Dave. 'Why?'

'Because he's a politician, right? And what is it that politicians do better than anyone else on the planet?'

'Talk bollocks?' suggested Dave.

'Exactly,' said Harry. 'Call him. Now.'

THIRTY-TWO

Harry and Dave were sitting in the large house belonging to Mr Howes. He was staring at them across an oak dining table and somehow managing to look both smug and annoyed all at once.

'So, I was right, then,' he said, staring very pointedly at Dave. 'I need police protection.'

Harry had taken an instant dislike to the man, and not just because his handshake was as damp as it was weak. He carried himself around with such a supercilious air, that Harry half wondered if, in a past life, Howes had been a foppish seventeen-century lord with servants, a large house, and even less chin. Though how anyone could have even less chin than Howes was something Harry simply couldn't envisage.

Harry placed some of the leaflets Jadyn had given him on the table.

'Do you recognise these?'

Howes leaned over and looked down his beakish nose.

'No,' he said. 'They're very similar to some of the ridiculous rubbish that's been shoved through my letterbox and stapled to my trees, but they're not the same at all.'

'In what way?' Harry asked.

Howes held up one of the ones Harry had placed on the table.

'This shows talent,' he said. 'The one's I've been receiving decidedly don't. Why?'

'These were found at a property in Leyburn,' said Harry. 'We think there may be a small, local group of ...' He paused, trying to find the best way of describing what it was that Jadyn had stumbled on, and which was now possibly linked to everything else that had been going on. 'I think the best way to describe them is wildlife activists,' Harry eventually said. 'We're trying to establish if there's a connection between the two, or if it's simply coincidence.'

'There's no such thing,' said Howes.

'I'm inclined to agree,' said Harry.

'So, there's a group of hippy terrorists out to get me, is that what you're saying?'

Harry had to work hard not to laugh at the phrase *hippy terrorist.*

'Officer Calvert tells me you have footage from your security cameras, is that correct?'

'It is,' said Howes.

'And can I see it?'

'What, now? But I'm busy! I'm preparing a speech for a dinner this evening.'

'This shouldn't take too long,' said Harry.

'This is all very inconvenient.'

Harry stood up.

'Something that crime excels at, I'm afraid. Now, if you wouldn't mind?'

With a huff, Howes got to his feet and led Harry and Dave to a small room at the back of the house.

'Used to be a gun room, you know,' he said, almost proudly as he started to fiddle around with a computer.

Harry wasn't entirely convinced the room had ever seen a gun before in its whole life. A few cakes in tins, perhaps, and various other food supplies, but he was doubtful any kind of gun. He wondered if the estate agent who had sold Howes the property had been a little too creative with the house particulars.

'There,' Howes said, 'and what do you say to that, then?'

He then gestured at the computer screen with such drama and pride, it was as though he had just uncovered some vast criminal network and was now presenting it to the head of MI5.

Harry stared at the flickering black-and-white image of a blob-like thing with legs climbing over a fence.

Howes then clicked on another video. It played out much the same, this time with the blob-like biped running up to the front door to post something through his letterbox, before disappearing again.

'You have any more?' Harry asked.

'Yes,' Howes said. 'And it's always the same individual.'

'And why is it they look so, well, odd?' Harry asked.

'It's hair,' Howes said, and flicked a look up at Dave, who, Harry noticed, rolled his eyes.

'Hair ...,' said Harry. 'You've seen them then? And what do you mean by hair, exactly? They have long hair, or ...?'

Harry wasn't sure where to go after saying *or*, so decided to say nothing instead.

'I mean that yes, I've seen them, with my own two eyes, and that they're covered in hair! Like a ... like a ...'

Harry could tell that whatever Howes wanted to say, was strange enough to get stuck in his throat.

'Like a what?' Harry asked, trying to encourage Howes to get to the point.

'You promise you won't laugh?'

Harry pointed at his own face.

'Does this look like the face of someone who laughs?'

'Yes, about that,' said Howes. 'And I don't mean to be rude, but ...'—*Oh, I bet you do*, thought Harry—'how did that happen, exactly?'

'I had a run-in with a bear,' Harry said.

Howes' face fell off.

'What? Really? Good God, man!'

'No, of course not, really,' said Harry. 'IED, Afghanistan. Long story, very painful, lucky to be alive, the usual. Anyway, back to what we were talking about ...' He jabbed a finger at the computer screen.

'Well,' said Howes, 'and I know this is going to sound completely ridiculous, but ...'

'I'm not a patient man,' Harry said. 'Out with it. Now!'

'A yeti!' Howes said, the word coming out so suddenly that he seemed shocked to have heard it himself. He looked at Harry and Dave accusingly, as though it was one of them who had said it instead.

'A yeti ...' said Harry. 'As in—'

'As in the abominable snowman, sasquatch, a yeti, yes!' Howes said. 'I know it sounds ridiculous, but that's the only way I can describe it. Laugh all you want, but whoever they are, they gave me the fright of my life. Actually, that reminds me ...'

Without another word, Howes pushed past Harry and disappeared into the house, only to return a minute or so later with a brown paper bag.

'Here,' he said, handing the bag to Harry.

'What is it?' Harry asked.

'I found those caught in some of the bushes after whoever that is had been climbing over my fence.'

Harry opened the bag and pulled out some grubby scraps of material, each of them about six inches long, and all varying shades of green and brown.

'I think that the hair I saw is actually that,' Howes said, but offered no further explanation as to why.

Harry held the scraps up close.

'What do you think, Dave?'

Dave leaned in.

'Reminds me of something,' he said. 'Now that I've seen that footage again, and these. Didn't really occur to me before. I've only seen pictures, but now, up close ...'

'What?' Harry asked. 'You think you know what this is?'

'You do too, I should think,' said Dave. 'All that soldiering.'

'I'm going to need a bit more,' said Harry, still unable to grasp where Dave was going.

'Ghillie suit,' he said. 'I have one myself; I wear it sometimes when I'm out watching badgers or deer or whatever. You feel a bit ridiculous, but it's very effective. I could be just a few metres away, lying in some tall grass and brush, and you'd be hard-pressed to spot me. And I'm not exactly small, am I?'

Something clicked into place in Harry's mind, something so unexpected that it took him a moment to realise where Dave's revelation was about to take him.

He slipped the strips of fabric back into the paper bag, and stuffed the bag into a pocket.

'Dave,' he said, 'I need you to stay here for a while. I'll assume that's okay with you, Mr Howes?'

'Of course,' Howes said. 'But you're not staying as well, then? Why?'

'Between you and me,' Harry said, 'I think I'm beginning to smell a rat ...'

THIRTY-THREE

On the way over to the Dent's farm, something else had started to bug Harry, and he knew it had to do with both the field where Armitage had been found, and when Jen had arrived at the farm the day before and had him on-screen.

Arriving at the field, Harry drove past the large pile of rubbish in front of the gate. The waste from the cannabis farm had already been removed by Sowerby and her team, but the remaining detritus was still there, waiting for the Dents to accept that they would be the ones to clear it up.

He turned around in a wider section of the lane further along, then drove back and parked up directly in front of it, so that the rubbish was between him and the gate.

Stepping out of the RAV, Harry was angered once again by the sheer vandalism of it, the total indifference to the beauty of the Dales. He navigated his way around it, the smell of it tainting the air, opened the gate, and headed into the field. He soon found the hole in the ground where Armitage had been staked out, and turned around to stare back at the rubbish, the RAV's windows just visible. Then, with a sigh, he walked back across the field, sent a quick message to Gordy to check up on Anna, climbed back into the vehicle, and made his way to the Dent's farm.

Parking up in the farmyard, Harry walked calmly to the door. Gordy had sent a quick reply to say that Anna was still unconscious, but stable, so that was something.

He was about to knock when the door opened, and Debora Dent was standing in front of him.

'Oh,' she said, clearly not recognising him at first.

'DCI Grimm,' Harry said. 'I was sort of with DC Blades yesterday when we—'

'That's who you are!' Debs said, then added, 'You're a lot bigger in real life ...'

Harry asked, 'Is your husband around?'

'Sam?' Debs replied. 'No, not right now. Is there anything I can help with?'

'Possibly,' said Harry. 'Any chance we could have a drive down to that field again, have a look around?'

Debs gave a nod. 'Of course. Is there something you need to check up on?'

'Possibly,' said Harry. 'And would it be okay if we took your car? Mine seems to have overheated on the way over.'

'I'll just get my keys.'

As Debs disappeared back into the house, Harry strolled over to the only other car in the yard, the small, yellow hatchback he'd seen when Jen had arrived the day before and had him on screen.

'Here we go,' Debs said, jogging from the house over to the car.

She opened the door and Harry dropped down into the passenger seat.

A few minutes later, Harry was back at the field, this time with company.

'Mind if we take a stroll?' he asked.

In the field again, Harry led Debs over to the hole in the ground from the stake Armitage had been lashed to.

'Must've been quite a shock for your husband, finding Armitage's body the way he did,' said Harry.

'It was,' said Debs.

'Why was he here, though?' Harry asked. 'That's what's been

bothering me. It's out in the open, isn't it? Just the fields, the fells, and that pile of rubbish to look at.'

'Don't get me started,' said Debs.

'I remember you getting pretty angry about it when DC Blades and I had that chat with you and your husband,' said Harry. 'Understandable.'

'It's not just the people who dump it, is it?' Debs said. 'It's the council. Absolute bloody inertia.'

'Armitage would've been responsible for that kind of thing, wouldn't he?' said Harry. 'Environmental officer or something, I think.'

'Well, he never did a damned thing,' said Debs. 'People just don't care enough for the Dales, do they?'

Harry pointed over at the rubbish.

'Blocks the gate something terrible, doesn't it?' he said.

'We won't be able to get in here until we shift it,' said Debs.

'Really blocks the view,' added Harry.

'It's an absolute bloody eyesore is what it is,' agreed Debs.

Harry allowed a moment of silence between them, breathed in the air, then said, 'You saw someone in the field the night before Sam was in here and found the body.'

'I mentioned it to him when I got back. I'd been out dealing with—'

'Rats, yes,' said Harry, then scratched his chin, confused. 'Where did we park your car again?' he asked.

Debs pointed over to the gate.

'Just to the right of the rubbish,' she said.

'Oh yes, that's right,' Harry replied. 'Just can't see it, can we?' He pulled from his pocket the brown paper bag Howes had given him. He opened it and showed Debs the contents. 'Any idea what this is?'

Debs peered inside.

'More rubbish?' she said. 'You've not found another pile, have you?'

'No,' said Harry. 'These were found over at a property where the owner's been getting a bit of hassle from someone who we think doesn't want him building a fish farm.'

'That'll be the wildlife group my Sam follows on Facebook,' Debs said. 'No idea who they are, but they're putting leaflets here, there, and everywhere. Though what good it'll do, I've no idea. None whatsoever, probably.'

'You mean these?' Harry asked, and from another pocket took out what he and Dave found at the farm earlier that day.

Debs stared at what was in Harry's hand.

'Thought you said it was about a fish farm?'

'I did,' said Harry. 'I found these myself this morning at another farm. Owner was found in his own woodland, dead, his ears sliced off.'

'That's awful,' said Debs.

'It is,' said Harry. 'I think whoever did it wanted the last thing he heard before he died to be buzzards.'

'Then he shouldn't have been killing them, should he?' said Debs.

Harry tucked the leaflets back in his pocket.

'Do you have a ghillie suit?' he asked.

'I have,' said Debs.

'I've not seen one in years,' said Harry. 'Not since the days when my work colleagues were soldiers, and the uniform was designed to help you hide rather than stand out. Snipers use them.' He reached into the paper bag. 'One of my officers has one as well. Not for shooting or anything like that. He's into wildlife photography and can get very excited about expensive binoculars. Likes to hide in fields and watch badgers, that kind of thing.' He then held up the scraps of material in front of him and Debs. 'He told me that he thinks that's what these are from, ripped off a ghillie suit.'

Debs said nothing, just stared at Harry.

'The reason I'm asking you all of this, the reason we're here in the first place,' said Harry, 'is because of a key ring. It was found at Armitage's house—where he was killed, by the way—and it got me thinking. Do you know of the three wise monkeys?'

'I do,' said Debs, her eyes narrowing a little.

'Well, this key ring, then; one of my team thought it was a camel, but there was no way it was that. Camels don't have three humps, do they? I realised then that it was the three wise monkeys, or it had been at some point; it was fairly worn, hard to tell exactly. But anyway, the monkeys ... see no evil, hear no evil, speak no evil.'

'I'm not sure what you're getting at,' said Debs.

Harry tapped his foot on the ground near the hole that had held the stake to which Armitage's body had been lashed.

'I couldn't work out why Armitage was here,' he said. 'Couldn't work out why his eyes had been taken. Then this other body was found with no ears. And in the meantime, there's that pile of rubbish, and a cannabis farm. That proved to be quite the distraction, I can tell you. Very unexpected.'

Debs was quiet now, so Harry kept talking.

'That key ring, the rubbish, Armitage, with his eyes gone ... see no evil ... That's what this was about, wasn't it? He was staked out here to prove a point. You see, I don't think the killing was something that was planned, but after it, all of this, and what happened then, well, that was definitely planned.' Harry looked at Debs, held her gaze just long enough. 'Wasn't it, Debs?'

Debs' eyes went wide.

'What?'

'For a start,' said Harry, 'from where we're standing right now, we can't see your car, can we? So, there's no way you drove along that lane the other night and saw Armitage where we are now. The only reason you knew he was here at all was because you put him here, didn't you?'

'No,' said Debs. 'I didn't ...'

Harry slipped the paper bag back into his pocket.

'Here's what I think happened,' he said. 'You'd had enough of that rubbish. Fair enough, too. I completely understand why. Sam wasn't rushing to clear it away. I think you'd spoken to Armitage about it, and about other piles being dumped on your land, and finally, for some reason, you decided you'd had enough. So, you went round to his house to have it out with him. Maybe you were doing some pest control out that way, I don't know. Anyway, you turn up at his house, knock, there's no answer, you try the door, find that it's open, and you let yourself in. But what you find there isn't Armitage on his own ready for a good ear bashing. You find something so unexpected and so disturbing that you react.'

Harry paused, gave Debs a moment to speak, but she was quiet now, just listening, her face growing pale.

'There's a lot of details to be ironed out,' Harry continued, 'but you helped a young woman escape from Armitage and, in the process of doing so, Armitage was killed. Perhaps you spotted the keyring yourself, perhaps it's just coincidence, but I'm not a big believer in those. You had a body to deal with, and with what you'd just seen of the darker side of Armitage's life, something flipped inside you, and you decided to kick things up a gear.'

'You've no proof,' Debs said.

'The scraps of material, they can be matched to your ghillie suit,' said Harry. 'The leaflets are easily checked against your handwriting. We'll undoubtedly find DNA, not just on those, but at Armitage's house, the other crime scene, especially now we know what we're looking for. Also, there's the salt.'

'What?'

'Armitage,' Harry said. 'You buried him while you worked out what the hell you were going to do with him, what you were going to do next. And you used rock salt, the kind used on roads. I noticed when DC Blades was in your yard how there was no ice, which was odd considering the weather. So, I'm going to guess that you have a good pile of the stuff on the farm in a shed or something, and that's what you used. Again, easy for us to check.

'Once you decided what you were going to do, you staked him out, took his eyes. Good job on those knots as well, by the way; useful as a farmer, but also for putting hides together when you're shooting, right? Shall I go on?'

Debs shook her head.

'Well, I'm going to, anyway,' said Harry. 'Because of something you said a few minutes ago.'

'What did I say?'

'Armitage, he was see no evil,' Harry said. 'Brian Haygarth? He was hear no evil. I said to you how I think his killer dealt with him in the woods so he would hear the buzzards, didn't I? And you replied with, *then he shouldn't have been killing them, should he* ... I didn't tell you that, Debs. I just showed you those leaflets or posters or whatever they are, the ones I found at his house, that was all. And that leads nicely onto speak no evil, doesn't it? I think you got a taste for what you were doing, which was taking your little pest control business to a whole new level, in your eyes, anyway. Howes was next. I've had a look into aquaculture. I can see why people have problems with it. Not sure killing someone to stop them doing it is the answer, though.'

Debs screamed, and the sound cracked the bright day in half.

'Then what is?' she yelled, turning her rage against Harry. 'People don't listen, nothing's ever done, and we all just have to put up with it while the world burns?'

'Murder's never right,' Harry said.

'Armitage was an accident! I was looking for him, went upstairs, saw him standing there, buck-naked in the doorway, staring at whatever was on the other side. Then this girl, she just ran out, knocked him out onto the landing. She was naked, too, but terrified; I'd never seen anything like that.

'Armitage, he turned to chase her, saw me, lunged, and I just grabbed him and threw him, I guess. Not like he weighed much, the skinny little shit. He fell against the banister, dropped like a sack of spuds. I just stood there, staring at him lying there on the floor, like a dead bird.

'I went to check on the girl. She was in shock, just staring at me. I helped her get dressed, found her phone, told her to call for help. While she was doing that, I went back upstairs, tried to work out what to do, but what I found in that room, and in the other one, those photos ... I ... I just saw red. It came down like a mist, I suppose.

'I know that's a cliché, but that's what it felt like. I heard a car outside, the front door slam. That was the last I saw of the girl. Next thing I know, I'm dragging that skinny little bastard down the stairs. He didn't weigh anything, you know? It was like lifting a child when I dumped him in the boot of my car and drove home.'

Harry said, 'I think we need to take this discussion to the station.'

He reached out to gently take Debs' elbow, to guide her back across the field, but she snatched it away.

'No, not yet,' she said. 'You can't make me go anywhere.'

'I can,' Harry said. 'Detective, remember? Police?'

'Sam knows none of this,' Debs said. 'It'll break his heart.'

'Please,' said Harry, 'just walk with me, back to your car.'

Debs hesitated, then started to walk.

'I just grew tired of it,' she said. 'Armitage, what happened, it kind of just flipped a switch. The wildlife group was an easy target to shift the blame to, not least because no one knows who they are. And I thought, if I can stop Armitage, what about others? I knew about Brian because everyone knows about Brian. He was a seeping boil of a man, always blaming other things for his own inadequacies, blaming other people, blaming nature and wildlife and the weather. I knew he was killing buzzards; I'd seen the evidence myself, had spoken to him about it so many times I grew tired. He had to go, and people needed to know why.'

At the gate, Harry led Debs back to her car, then held out his hand.

'If it's all the same with you, I think I'll drive,' he said.

Debs looked at him a second.

'Your car hadn't overheated at all, had it?' she said, a sad smile playing around her lips.

'No,' replied Harry. 'I just needed to see if the rubbish blocked your view of the field from your car, that's all.'

Debs handed him her keys.

'I'm not sorry for it,' she said. 'For what I've done. But I don't think I'll ever forgive myself for what this will do to Sam.'

Harry opened the car and waited for Debs to get in before he slipped in behind the steering wheel.

'It's always the ones we love we hurt the most, isn't it?' he said, keyed the ignition, then drove them back to the farm.

THIRTY-FOUR

Harry was in the office, his only company Smudge. The rest of the team were out and about, and he was forcing himself to do the one thing he hated above all others (and it was a long list): paperwork. The last few days had been a blur and the resulting admin associated with it was already building up. Avoiding it wasn't an option, so he'd arrived early and set to it with if not enthusiasm, certainly a level of determination few could match.

The arrest of Deborah Dent and all that had entailed, including dealing with a confused and now very broken husband, had taken up a lot of time and involved officers brought in from further afield.

The same had been necessary for the cannabis farm and the arrest of Bacon and his bodyguard. The missing truck was found at the bodyguard's house, inside a garage, covered in a large tarpaulin. Mr Wilson was in the hands of social services, and the appropriate support was now being given to Helen Nevill. They'd also returned her keyring, the one found at Armitage's, which Dave had thought looked like a camel. And she'd held it like some lost heirloom.

Further officers had also been brought in to investigate everything else Armitage had been involved with, and they were now actively involved in tracing the girls in the photos, the footage on the computer, and everything they had on the various blackmailing rackets he had going. It was a big operation, and one Harry knew would be ongoing.

Busy times ahead, he thought, and got up to make a fresh mug of tea, when Matt walked into the office.

'Well, that's peace brokered in the short-lived and now infamous Swaledale Ukulele War,' he said, slumping down into a chair. 'Who would've thought that such an annoying little instrument could cause so much bother?'

'What happened?' Harry asked, now over at the kettle.

'Well,' said Matt, 'let's just say things escalated.'

'You're going to have to give me more than that.'

'The neighbour who took issue with the ukulele being played in the garden next door decided to fight fire with fire.'

'How do you mean?'

'He bought a ukulele.'

Harry laughed.

'What, so they both ended up playing them in their gardens?'

'Exactly that,' said Matt. 'He'd wait until the other was outside, then rush out and just start playing any old nonsense to try and put him off.'

'Did it work?'

'No,' said Matt. 'I've confiscated the ukuleles and given both parties a damned good talking to. Anyway, how's things here, then?'

'Don't ask,' said Harry, the kettle now boiled. 'Want one?'

'Of course,' replied Matt. 'Anyway, onto more important things; how's everything with going with finding a house for yourself and Grace?'

'We've put in an offer,' Harry replied. 'And it's been accepted.'

Matt clapped his hands and beamed.

'That's amazing news!'

'It's a relief, is what it is,' said Harry, walking over to Matt to hand him a steaming mug of tea. 'Not sure I could listen to the estate agent telling me how much potential even just one more house had.'

'Grace must be happy.'

'Bouncing is the word I'd use.'

Matt sipped his tea.

'Nice to have everyone fit and well and back to work, isn't it?' he said.

'Ben's ill now, though, would you believe?' said Harry. 'And according to Liz, he's even worse than me.'

'I find that hard to believe.'

Harry laughed at that.

'So do I.'

'Anything from Jim?' Matt asked. 'That's going to be a tough one to manage, isn't it? He's going to be pulled in two directions now.'

'And the family and the farm will pull the strongest, no doubt,' said Harry.

'What will you do?' Matt asked.

'Just take it as it comes; not much else I can do, really, is there? He's good at his job, but family's family, isn't it? It'll all be fine, whatever happens.'

The office phone rang, and Harry was tempted to ignore it, but he was already reaching for the handset.

'Grimm,' he said.

'Harry ...'

Harry recognised Gordy's voice.

'Look, if you're calling to check I'm on with the paperwork,' he said, then stopped talking. Something was wrong. Gordy's tone was off, and she'd sounded distant, as though she was somehow detached from her own voice.

'Gordy?'

Down the line, all Harry could hear was breathing.

He tried again.

'Gordy ...'

Harry heard a long, slow exhale, then at last, Gordy spoke.

'It's Anna,' she said. 'She's ...'

'What's happened?' Harry asked, and saw Matt was now staring at him, mug hovering halfway to his mouth. Smudge's eyes were on him, too. 'Is Anna okay? Do you need me there? Gordy?'

'She's gone, Harry,' Gordy then said, her words breaking on her sobs as she said them. 'She's gone ...'

THIRTY-FIVE

Harry had no memory of the journey from the office to the hospital. One minute he had been staring at Matt as Gordy had broken down at the other end of the line, the next he'd crashed through the main entrance of the hospital, eyes working like searchlights to find Gordy. He'd left Smudge with Matt and instructed him to say nothing to the team until he knew more.

Racing through the hospital corridors, Harry quickly found the ward Anna was on and there in the waiting room, he found Gordy. She was sitting alone, one arm crossed in front of her, the other holding a clenched fist in front of her face. And her eyes ... Harry had seen that look before, in warzones as a Para, and back home, dealing with the aftermath of crime: the thousand-yard stare.

Harry approached the DI as quietly as he could, careful to avoid spooking her. Gordy turned bloodshot eyes towards him. He saw her face break as she did so, then he was over to her in a beat, she was on her feet, and Harry wrapped his arms around her without a second thought.

The next few minutes were a thousand years long, as time slowed, and Gordy sobbed into Harry's shoulder. He said nothing, just held her so firm that had her legs given way, she would have stayed where she was, and not budged an inch.

Medical staff walked by, other visitors, but they were left alone, a silent understanding among strangers that interfering was not an option.

After a while, Gordy's sobbing eased, and Harry felt her slump a little in his arms, so he guided her gently back to the seat she had been sitting in and sat down beside her.

'There's nothing I can say that will make any of this better,' he said. 'But whatever you want, whatever you need ...'

'I know,' said Gordy, and she reached out and gave Harry's hand a gentle squeeze. 'You didn't need to rush here. There's nothing you can do. Nothing anyone can, really.'

'I can go,' Harry said. 'You do need someone here with you, though. Is there anyone you can call?'

'Stay,' said Gordy. 'Please.'

Harry gave a gentle nod, then leaned forward, resting his elbows on his knees, his hands together.

'She loved you,' he said at last. 'I don't know if that's the right thing to say or not, or if you even want to hear it right now, but she did, Gordy; everyone could see it. And you made her very happy.'

'She was moon bright,' Gordy said, 'and I flew to her like a moth. I couldn't do anything else. From the first moment I saw her, I knew, I just knew.'

Harry could tell Gordy wanted to say more, so kept quiet, and allowed her time to find the words, whatever they were.

'This doesn't feel real,' she said at last. 'How can she be gone? I can still hear her voice, smell her on my clothes, my skin. It doesn't make sense! Why leave me now? After everything we've been planning; why now, Harry? Why?'

Harry shook his head, said nothing.

'I can't make any sense of it,' Gordy continued, her voice desperate and broken. 'I know it's too soon to, but I don't see how I ever will. How can I get used to this, to her absence? Christ, it's so loud!' She grabbed her head with both hands, almost as though she was afraid that at any point it would suddenly explode from the pressure inside. 'It's like it's screaming in my head, this sudden emptiness, this hole ... I don't know what to do!'

'Small steps,' said Harry. 'That's the only way.'

'But where the hell are those steps leading me to? We're supposed to be taking them together, Harry; together! That's the whole point of all of this, of every damned thing! It's what we were planning!'

Gordy stood up. Harry watched her walk away from him, pace around the room, hold her head with both hands, pull at her hair, then turn round and head back to him. She sat down again, pulling something from a pocket as she did so, then holding it out for Harry to see. It was a small, black box. Harry knew what it was before Gordy had even opened it.

'I've been carrying this around for weeks,' she said, as the hospital lights glinted off the diamond ring Harry was now staring at. 'Trying to work out the best time to ask, to pop the question.'

'I didn't even know you were considering it,' said Harry.

'No one did,' said Gordy. 'And if anyone asked, I'd always deflect. Just ask Jen! But I was just scared, terrified about what the answer would be, how Anna would react.'

'She'd have said yes,' said Harry. 'No doubt in my mind about that at all.'

Gordy shut the box, stowed it away again.

'Don't know what I'm going to do with it now,' she said. 'I can't keep it, and I can't just sell it. God, Harry, this is ... it's too much.'

Harry saw fresh tears spill down Gordy's face.

'Lean on your friends, your family,' he said. 'It's what we're here for.'

'But what am I here for, now?' Gordy asked, turning her eyes on Harry. 'What? We're supposed to be moving in a few weeks, starting new jobs, a new life together! That's what that ring was about, that's what this has always been about, sharing my every-thing with Anna, and now she's gone, Harry! She's dead! I wanted to give her all my tomorrows, and now, they're gone, aren't they? Every single damned one of them. The life we'd been dreaming of, building together, it's been smashed to pieces, and there's nothing I can do to ever put it back together again.'

'The shock, it's seismic,' said Harry. 'Your world has been shattered. You were preparing for something else, and now this. Don't punish yourself for how you're feeling; it's normal, natural, and you only feel like it because you loved Anna as much as you did, and her you.'

'But she's gone, Harry!' Gordy snapped back. 'She's dead! Every day from now till the day I die myself, she won't be there. How can I ever understand that? How?'

'You can't.'

'She was my everything! And now what have I got other than this godawful void inside me and ahead of me and all around me? She was my heart, my forever, and now all I'll ever have is a grave and a box of memories too bloody painful to ever open again!'

Harry reached out for Gordy, but at that moment a shadow rested on them both and he looked up to see a nurse staring at them.

'Sorry,' she said, 'it's just that ...'

Harry saw then that the nurse was holding an envelope.

'What is it?' he asked.

'She wrote this, Anna, I mean,' the nurse said. 'Just before she was put into the induced coma.'

Harry saw Gordy's eyes grow wide.

'What are you saying?' she asked.

'She was unconscious when she came in but regained consciousness just long enough to know what was happening,' the nurse explained. 'I was with her and she asked for a pen and some paper. She gave it to me and told me to keep it in case something happened. I've only just found out what ... I'm ... I'm so sorry.'

'But what is it?' Gordy asked, then pointed at the envelope. 'What is that?'

The nurse held it out for Gordy to take.

'She just said for me to give it to you if she ... well ...'

The nurse's voice faded and with a final look of genuine concern and grief, she turned and left.

Harry stared at the envelope in Gordy's hands, waited.

Gordy looked over at Harry, then held the envelope out for him to take.

'That's for you,' he said.

'I know,' said Gordy. 'But I can't read it. I'll hear her, it'll be Anna speaking to me. And I know it'll still be her, but if you read it to me, it might be a little easier.'

Harry hesitated.

'Only if you're sure.'

'When am I ever not?'

Harry took the envelope and opened it. Inside, was a single sheet of notepaper. Anna's handwriting stared back at him, the words spidery and faint.

'Please ...' said Gordy.

Harry started to read.

'Gordy, I can't believe I'm writing this, but just in case things don't go to plan, and I wake up at the pearly gates with a hell of a lot of questions, I wanted you to know something ...'

Harry paused, looked at Gordy.

'You sure about this?' he asked.

'I am,' Gordy replied, and for the first time since he had arrived at the hospital, he saw a faint smile dare to show itself.

'You were, are, and always will be my everything,' Harry read, hearing now Anna's voice in his own head. 'Whether you know it or not, you rescued me. I wasn't looking for someone; quite the opposite. But you shone so brightly I couldn't look away. And from that moment, I knew I wanted to share the rest of my days with you. It was the simplest and easiest of things falling in love with you, and I can never thank you enough for taking me as I am, accepting me, and loving me back. I know what you're facing now is terrifying and I'm sorry. But please don't waste your life grieving about something that never was. Instead, think of what we had, how happy we were, how we turned to face the world together with a love I honestly never realised could even exist, and keep on living, because the way you live, and with such brightness, is why I love you, Gordy. Why I always will. You were the marrow of my bones, my day and my night. Thank you. All my love, forever, Anna.'

Harry folded the letter, slipped it back inside the envelope, and handed it back to Gordy.

'Well, that's me crying,' he said, wiping a tear away with a knuckle. 'Bloody hell, Anna ...'

Gordy took the envelope, slipped it into a pocket.

For a moment, neither Harry nor Gordy spoke.

Eventually, Harry pushed himself to his feet.

'Probably best I leave you to yourself for a while,' he said. 'But you know where I am, so if you need me, just call, understood?'

Gordy stood up.

'Got a way with words, hasn't she?' she said.

'Just a bit,' Harry replied. 'You going to be okay?'

'Not right away, no,' Gordy said. 'But it's like Anna said, isn't it; I have to keep on living.'

'As hard as it is, yes, you do,' said Harry.

With nothing left to say, Harry turned from Gordy and made his way to the door. As he was about to leave, Gordy called him, and he turned around.

'Thank you,' she said.

And with a final nod, Harry smiled, and pushed on into the rest of the day.

WANT to find out how Harry deals with the seismic changes in his team while facing the next fiendish case in the Dales? Scan the following QR code to grab your copy of the next book in the DCI Harry Grimm Series and to start a brand new adventure with Gordy as she heads down south. You'll also be able to download an exclusive free short story and sign up for my VIP Club and newsletter.

ABOUT DAVID J. GATWARD

David had his first book published when he was 18 and has written extensively for children and young adults. *See No Evil* is his seventeenth DCI Harry Grimm crime thriller.

Visit David's website at www.davidjgatward.com to find out more about him and the DCI Harry Grimm books.

 facebook.com/davidjgatwardauthor

Milton Keynes UK
Ingram Content Group UK Ltd.
UKHW040625190824
447134UK00001B/11